⊖⊖⊖

"**P**rincess Beatrice," he said with a nod. How could it have taken him so long to recognize her?

She was as tall as George, long and lean and muscular, with a regal neck and calloused tapering fingers. Her skin was badly freckled, but it complemented her flame red hair perfectly, and her hazel eyes shone up at him.

She spoke baldly. "You are not what I expected."

The Princess and the Hound

METTE
IVIE
HARRISON

An Imprint of HarperCollins*Publishers*

Eos is an imprint of HarperCollins Publishers.

The Princess and the Hound
Copyright © 2007 by Mette Ivie Harrison
www.harperteen.com

Library of Congress Cataloging-in-Publication Data
Harrison, Mette Ivie, 1970–
    The princess and the hound / Mette Ivie Harrison. — 1st ed.
        p.   cm.
    Summary: George has always felt burdened by his princely duties, and
even more by the need to hide the magic through which he speaks with
animals, but when he is betrothed to the strange princess of a neighboring kingdom, his secret, and the persecution of people like himself, must
come to an end.
    ISBN 978-0-06-113189-9
[1. Princes—Fiction. 2. Human-animal communication—Fiction.
3. Magic—Fiction. 4. Kings, queens, rulers, etc.—Fiction. 5. Self-actual-
ization (Psychology)—Fiction. 6. Fairy tales.] I. Title.
PZ8.H248Pri 2007   2007009306
[Fic]—dc22   CIP
                                                                AC

Typography by Larissa Lawrynenko
❖
First paperback edition, 2008

For my father

The Tale of King Richon and the Wild Man

A HUNDRED YEARS AGO and more, before our current line of kings was founded, long before King Davit or his grandfather or his, the animal magic was thought of as no more or less than a gift of growing corn higher than others or having a way with a needle to make a fine dress. Those who had animal magic spoke to animals and learned from them where water was polluted or which caves were filled with blood-sucking worms. They were good at training horses in particular. And they were prized for their use in a hunt, for they knew how to kill animals swiftly and kindly.

But there was one hunter who would have none of those with the animal magic. He was proud, young King Richon, who hunted on horseback or on foot, in the great forest in the south or in the smaller, quieter woods around the castle and to the north, by Sarrey. Best of all,

1

he loved to hunt on the plains, where a wild animal could be set loose to the sounds of horns and chased to exhaustion in plain view, with no place to hide or find respite. The terror of the animal's screams was part of King Richon's pleasure, and for all his skill with a spear, ax, or knife, he would let a beast go free if the chase had not been sporting or long enough.

Yet when the beast was dead, King Richon did not even bring the meat back to the cook, for flesh from wild animals was always tougher and less flavorful than that from the animals kept soft and quiet in the castle yards. Now and again, if the head was large and impressive enough, he would cut it off and have it stuffed and mounted, to impress visitors to his hall. But that was all the use he made of his hunts.

Those with animal magic kept away from King Richon naturally, and so in time King Richon was surrounded only by those who encouraged his penchant for cruelty. They had discovered that the king was generous at the end of a particularly long and exciting hunt. To those who had hunted with him, King Richon offered fewer taxes and other favors, such as a gentler sentence on judgment day or the promise of an advantageous marriage.

Even those who had no animal magic, but who disliked the king's hunting, found themselves cut off from his attention. Some complained loudly of this. Others kept their dissatisfaction quiet. Still others began to save a certain amount each month and pool it together, in search of a hero to offer it to, someone who might have the power to change the king.

But they did not use their money, after all. Their hero came of his own will, though he was not at all what they had expected. He was small and thin, with a long, dirty beard, and he smelled of animals and forest and walked as if he had learned natural grace from the animals themselves. Yet even those with their own animal magic stepped back when they saw him, for his power was far beyond anything they had ever wielded themselves. It was boundless, uncontrolled, wild, a raging river in comparison to a trickling mountain stream.

As he made his way north through the kingdom, the wild man did not ask for assistance but accepted the food or drink that was offered and listened to the tales of King Richon as if he could recite them from memory himself. He had heard them all, it seemed, and more. Then he was on his way, and those who watched him shivered as he passed and felt a little sorry for their king, despite all.

When the wild man reached the castle gates at last, he called out in a loud voice and demanded an audience with King Richon. The king was busy preparing for a hunt. He told his guards to take the man to the kitchen for a good meal of fresh bread and soup and send him on his way.

But the wild man would not take the soup, nor

would he leave the castle willingly. The guards set him out at sword point.

By evening he was back with his own guard, a hawk whose claws were closed about the bare arm of the wild man, who showed no signs of pain. And this time when the wild man was stopped, the hawk flew from his arm and attacked. Four of King Richon's guards were blinded by the time one of them made it to the throne and begged for assistance.

"It is a trick of the animal magic, no more," said King Richon. But he did agree to see the wild man—if the hawk remained in the open air, where it belonged.

The wild man sent the hawk away and went into the palace. He did not bow before the king. Instead, he spoke as if he commanded an army at his back. And he demanded from King Richon the promise that he would cease hunting forever.

King Richon laughed at the boldness of the wild man. Why should he make such a promise? Why should he not hunt? The animals belonged to him after all, as did the woods they lived in, the grass they fed on, even the air they breathed.

At that, the wild man walked out of the gates without a backward glance. King Richon thought that would be the last of him, but he was wrong.

Soon there was a royal parade through the town of Wilbey, which surrounded the castle. King Richon was dressed spectacularly in the green and black of the kingdom and mounted on his favorite horse, a gelding named Crown, who was large and strong, and well trained.

Suddenly Crown took off on a wild canter through the streets, and nothing King Richon did could stop his course. He galloped past the familiar woods, toward the dark southern forest. There he stopped short and threw King Richon overhead. Then he galloped away, back to the castle stables.

King Richon wandered in that strange forest a week before he was found at last by his fearful guards. They brought back a much thinner and quieter king. Those with the animal magic thought the king must have learned his lesson. But when the wild man returned that evening, a wolf striding at his side, King Richon still would not promise to abandon the hunt.

Instead, he offered a bag full of ten thousand golden talers. "If you leave here today and never return, it is yours."

The wild man spat on the ground and told the king, "Your third lesson will not be so painless." Then he strode out of the court.

For a few weeks King Richon was cautious and remained inside the castle, in case the wild man dared appear again. But then it was summer, and so fair that a hunt had to be made, and besides, what could such a small man do against a king and all his court? So he sent out his call, and his greedy nobles came to him for the hunt, fearing the result as little as he did.

This time King Richon went in search of a bear he had caught a glimpse of in the dark southern forest itself. It was larger than any he had seen before. He intended to make a rug of it and to keep the head as a trophy above his throne, in case the wild man dared come again. His confidence great, he slew the bear in one motion, with a spear through the head. Jubilant over the kill, he returned to the castle to celebrate.

A bear dance was presented for his amusement, and minstrels sang new songs of his hunting prowess. But the celebration was cut short by the cries of sentries stationed atop the castle walls. In the dawn light they saw in the distance signs of a great army approaching. King Richon came out with his men, drunken and swaying, and saw the army for what it was, an army of animals.

Bears, wolves, stags, bobcats, foxes, wild horses and hounds, eagles, hawks, and smaller creatures of every kind: raccoons, possums, mice, sparrows and robins, deer, and bees. Together they stood at the top of the hill overlooking the castle. And slowly, out of their midst, came the wild man himself.

King Richon felt a chill in his heart, yet he was still too stubborn to offer the promise he knew the wild man wanted. After all, what could animals do to his well-trained men?

"Attack!" he shouted.

They did their best. Footmen loped forward with swords and spears. Archers loosed their arrows. There were dead animals everywhere in a few minutes' time, but it seemed there was an unending supply to take their place. Meanwhile the king's soldiers lost ears, eyes, and limbs. They stumbled or became confused. They threw spears at their own kind or ran away in terror.

By the end of the day the battle had been lost. King Richon, defeated, stepped forward in the dying light and held up his hands in surrender to the wild man. Then he knelt and bowed his head.

"I will make the promise now if you will take it," he said.

But it was no use. The wild man laid his hands on the king's shoulders, and a few of the wounded then saw the plain and terrible workings of the most powerful animal magic of all. They saw King Richon transformed from a man to a beast, a huge, towering black bear like the one he had killed that very morning.

"You will live as a bear until you understand what it is to be hunted," the wild man proclaimed. "But there is hope. I promise that much. If only you will ask."

And so it was. King Richon was never seen again as a man, but there are those who claim to have seen a certain bear on the outskirts of the dark southern forest, taller than others, with very black fur and a human look to his eyes. A bear that will stand if you speak to it and cock its head to one side, as if it were asking a question and listening for an answer.

As for the wild man, he has never been seen again.

His army disappeared that day, melting back into the uncanny forest from which it came.

Some say his magic was an evil perversion, that it has nothing to do with the other, smaller animal magic. But there are few who believe this. And so now all those with animal magic are burned when they are discovered, no matter what their age. It is a kindness perhaps. For what man or woman would choose to live stretched between those two worlds?

CHAPTER ONE

RINCE GEORGE COULD not remember seeing his father without the crown on his
head, except perhaps in bed, and even then
the imprint on his temples was clear enough. But the
crown could have been melted down or stolen away, and
it would not have mattered. George could see kingship
in every movement his father made.

When King Davit spoke to Cook Elin, he always
complimented her on how well suited her cheese was to
her tart, how her salad reflected the colors of the
autumn mountains in the distance. George had no idea
if his father liked the flavor of the salad or the tart. He
did not know if his father knew either. He knew only
that the king had a duty to offer approval to his subjects
who strove to please him. And the king always did his
duty.

When speaking to the scarred and muscular lord

general of the mounted army, King Davit nodded and talked wisely of the best way to deal with the effects of the war. George had no sense of what the war had been like for his father, whether he had been afraid of the sound of the enemy's war cry, as had the guardsman at the gate. The war was the kingdom's war, and so it had been fought.

Even when George was alone with his father, it seemed there was no difference. The king told George the story of the baker who had made too many loaves but at the end of the day would give none of them to the poor and then found in the morning they had been eaten by mice instead.

The king told George of the seamstress who left an unfinished seam in a fancy ball gown, thinking it would never be noticed, then went to the ball herself—only to watch the gown gradually spin away from the wearer until she stood in nothing but her undergarments and wrath at her betrayal.

In the stories there was always a message for George to remember. For the prince of Kendel, from the king. Never a story for fun, with magic and wildness, with adventures and threatenings and the promise of more to come. Never a story that made George want to cry, or to laugh, or to dance. Only a story to make him think.

And though George had seen the king's servants take off their uniforms and play like children outside in throwing or wrestling games, he never saw his father play. His father smiled when it was right for the king to smile. He frowned to show the king's displeasure. He was always right and good, but he never felt like a father.

Yet George's mother, for all she wore long gowns with glittering jewels and even the fragile, ruby-encrusted crown on her head when she had to, seemed to be his mother no matter what else she was. For when she looked at George, whether she had come to his own chamber to play with him or held out her hand for him to meet her in the throne room, she had a way of making him feel complete in himself. And as though there were nothing he could do that would make her turn away.

That look was the most wonderful thing in the world.

She started taking George to the stables before he was old enough to speak his own name. That was where he learned to recognize the smell on her hands and sometimes even the dirt beneath her nails. She seemed most alive there, and the smell of the stables fit her as the crown fit his father's head.

The horses perked up when she came close to them, before they could possibly have heard or even seen her. They began to stamp their feet, and their heads came up, all turned in the right direction. George used to think this was a delightful trick and would clap his little hands in delight.

"This is Sugar," his mother said, introducing George to the new foal that stood shakily in a stall with his mother, Honey.

George held out his hand. The little foal came and licked at it, and George laughed at the delicious, gentle sensation.

His mother then bent over and gave Sugar the full attention that she often reserved for George.

He might have been jealous, but she kept her hand warm in his the whole time.

Then she brushed Honey until she shone, and Sugar too, talking with every stroke. Nonsense words, it seemed at first to George, but gradually he began to understand them. They weren't human words at all; they were horse words.

Words for things that had no names in his human language, except the words that George made up for them.

Sweet-green, for the smell of his mother's hands.

Warm-red, for the touch of her brush.

Purple-light, for the sunrise in spring.

Summer-burn, for the hot light that made them blink.

They were private words, George learned quickly. For if there were others in the stables who might cross their paths or if the stablemaster had come with her, she wouldn't speak the horse words at all.

She would sing or let out a stream of syllables that

had the cadence of the horse words, but left their meaning up to George to fill in. He had grown very good at it by the time he was four years old, and now and again he tried to say a word aloud himself.

His mother smiled at him if they were alone, but if someone else was present, she put a hand on his shoulder and shook her head very gravely. Never with fear in her eyes, but with enough darkness that he stopped instantly.

It was only three or four times before he learned that lesson, and likely those who heard him speak to horses in the animals' own language thought simply that they did not understand his babyish pronunciation or that he was speaking nonsense words as babies sometimes will, even when they are too old to be babies anymore.

George and his mother knew better.

The horses were dear to his mother's heart, but now and again she took George to the kennels as well. George liked how the hounds danced and barked at him, and he was sure that if only he listened long and hard enough, he would begin to understand them. But it did not happen.

Stranger still, he never heard his mother talk to the hounds as she did to the horses. She let them lick her hand, and she patted their heads or scratched behind their ears when they seemed to want it. She knew words to speak to a passing sparrow, but not to the hounds.

Yet she nonetheless seemed to understand them, for

when the great white hound that was one of the king's favorites had a tick burrowing behind his left leg that not even the houndmaster had seen, she knew it was there. And she understood when Solomon, the old, drooping hound that had ruled over the kennels for as long as George could remember, was entering the long illness that led to his death. She knew he could not be saved, that the best the houndmaster could manage was to offer comfort.

George could see that his mother did not love the hounds as she loved the horses, but he did not understand why. He thought it was no more than a matter of taste. George knew that his favorite sweet, made light and fluffy with egg and then colored brightly, made his mother shake her head and hold a hand to her mouth, while her favorite, a dark, hard licorice, was no more than passable to him. So it must be with hounds and horses and his mother.

Then, on the day of George's fifth birthday, his mother took him to the houndmaster, a great big man with a red face and a broken nose who laughed too loud. He stood up when George and his mother entered, and at his feet George saw one of the bitch hounds and a litter of newborn pups. They were slick and wet yet, and the houndmaster shook his head at the queen's ability to know that the bitch had been delivered of them just this minute.

The houndmaster turned to George. "Happy birthday,

Your Highness. I had planned to bring news of these to the castle tonight as a gift. But as long as you're here, you may choose which one you like the best right now. You can't take it with you, but you can come back and visit until it's ready to be weaned. Then it will be your very own hound."

George had never before felt so excited. He knelt down and watched the pups for a long while, unmoving. The bitch had a shaggy red coat and long ears that flopped around her face. Two of the pups looked just like her. The other two were more golden colored, and their ears were not as long. They had sharp noses, though, and seemed perfect to George.

He pointed to the smaller of the two, the one that whined less for its mother's milk. "That one."

"If you're sure?" asked the houndmaster, his eyes turning to the queen.

"The choice is my son's entirely," she said in a grave tone that made George look at her, but only for a moment. Then his attention went back to the pup.

"You'll want to think of a name for it," said the houndmaster.

A name? The horses always named themselves.

George moved closer and put his hands to the tiny pup. It nudged at him, then tried to suck at his fingers but was soon disgusted at the lack of milk and pushed him away.

"I'll think about it," George said.

He thought about nothing else during his party or in the days that followed. He dragged his mother with him to the hounds every day, hurrying her through the stables, and then he sat and watched, intent on every sound of the pups. He waited for a name. He knew there must be a name.

But not yet.

Three weeks later the houndmaster said it was time for George's pup to be weaned. He lifted it away from its mother and its littermates in a small blanket, then wrapped it up in it and handed it to George.

George went to his bedchamber with the squirming, wiggling package, his mother at his side. There was something she wanted to say to him. George could tell that, and he waited for her to say it when they were alone again.

But as he teased the pup, she did not speak. And when a bit of meat was brought from the kitchen, George put it in front of his pup and watched him tear at it.

"This pup is a pet," his mother said at last. "Do you understand that, George?"

Of course George understood that. His mother went away for the night, and George waited until it was too late for anyone to check on him again, then got out of bed and curled up with the pup by the fire. There they slept together until morning.

George was sure then that he knew the pup's name.

Teeth, he called it, because that was the word the pup used most when they were playing together.

The pup spoke a simple and incomplete language, but George didn't think about that or about the fact that the older hounds did not speak words at all. He accepted it as easily as he accepted the wounded war veterans in his father's guard and the girl in the kitchen who had been born without an arm.

If he did not speak to Teeth as his mother spoke to the horses, well, he was pleased that he had learned to communicate with his pup in his own way. That seemed to be more than his mother had ever done with the hounds. And George was proud of himself for that.

Of course for the next few weeks George took Teeth with him wherever he went. He showed him to any of the castle servants who were willing to take a moment to admire the prince's pup. There was no detail of his pup's life that George would not share, if one was willing to listen long enough.

George's mother came as she always did and asked if George wanted to visit the stables with her. But now George said no more often than not, and she would sigh and go alone. Now and again she would stay with George and his pup. Yet there was a sadness about her. A look in her eye when she watched Teeth, something like the look that she had given Solomon, the old, dying hound.

Then came the day that George used a word he had learned from Teeth, the pup's own sound for water. But

Teeth would not respond. The pup stared up at George as if he had never heard the word in his short life.

George shrugged it off, thinking that the pup was tired or that he himself was tired.

But the next day it happened again. With the word for jump.

And it kept happening, over and over, every day.

Until Teeth knew none of the words that George knew, the words that Teeth himself had taught George. But when George would say a short human word, Teeth knew it.

Teeth had forgotten his own language and learned the language of humans.

George had never seen it happen before, not with any animal. And yet why should that be so bad? Why should George mourn over it? He told himself that it was the pup's way of showing love for him.

But George could not bear it.

Day after day he watched as his pup began to sound like no more than any of the other hounds that George had heard in the stables, barks meaningless and empty. There was no more communication between them. George spoke. Teeth understood. But he could not speak back. He could only obey.

George remembered then what his mother had said.

"This pup is a pet."

George had not understood then what she meant. Now he did.

And it seemed to him that there was only one thing left for him to do.

He wrapped Teeth once more in the small blanket the houndmaster had given him and, tears streaming down his face, he took the much larger package back where it had come from.

"What's wrong?" asked the houndmaster, utterly bewildered at the prince's return of the birthday gift and of the stubborn and hurt expression on the prince's face.

"I don't want it anymore," said George.

"Why not? What's wrong with it?" the houndmaster asked. "Is it sick? Did it bite you? Young pups will do that sometimes. It doesn't mean anything. A little nip like that doesn't really hurt, anyway, does it? Take it back; take care of it and train it. It will be a fine hound, you'll see."

George shook his head. "No, I don't want it," he said. And he turned his back on the whining pup and did not look back, though nothing he had ever done before was so difficult.

The houndmaster took the pup back to his litter-mates, and though the pup moped about for a time, eventually he seemed to forget that he had ever been chosen by the prince and became quite a good hunter.

The houndmaster did not think well of George, however. The queen went to him later and told him that he should not mind a young prince's whimsy, but it was not whimsy that bothered him. It was the way the prince had given up on the hound. Without a second chance, without mercy. What kind of prince does that? What kind of prince can feel nothing for a pup that has lived with him for weeks?

The queen did not answer the houndmaster, but she went to George, took his hand in hers once more, and led him not to the stables this time but out to the forest that lay beyond the castle. It was a long walk for a five-year-old's short legs, but she did not offer to carry him, and she did not coax him to hurry. They went at his pace, and he walked faster when he smelled the forest and had the first taste of its sounds.

The animals of the forest were even louder than the horses in their anticipation, and each group had a language of its own that George could learn easily. His mother went from one to the next, teaching George a few words at a time. It was so exhilarating that he did not think of anything else until she said it was time for them to go home.

She promised him that they would come back many times and speak with these animals. She also promised him that there was a deeper, darker forest with animals in it he could not imagine, of such great power and beauty that he would weep when he saw them. She would take him there someday soon, when he was ready.

But by then it was cold and almost dark, and George shivered against her as they headed away from the forest.

"Can I come back here alone?" George asked. He did not know of this forest his mother spoke of, and the way she looked when she thought of it made him unsure he wanted to go at all.

"When you are older," said his mother.

George began to grow tired and stumbled over his feet. Finally, his mother picked him up in her arms and carried him flung over her shoulder as if he were much, much younger. He did not wake until he was snug in his own bed once more and his mother was kissing him good night.

"Wait," he said sleepily.

She put her hand to his cheek. "Yes?"

"Why do the hounds stop speaking?" he asked.

"Because they are with us so much, I suppose," said his mother. "They lose themselves."

"But not the horses," said George, struggling to make sense of it. After all, the horses were with humans just as much as hounds, weren't they?

But his mother shook her head and sighed. "I don't know." Then her eyes twinkled. "Perhaps it is because horses are simply more obstinate than any other creature."

George could believe that. He had never met a horse that could be made into a pet. But—

"What if I brought home a rabbit?" he asked, thinking back to the feel of the little creatures against his chest, the way they nibbled at each other and chided

21

him without restraint. They did not know he was a prince, and they did not care.

He could love them for that alone.

His mother shook her head, and George had the sense that there were a great many stories she could tell on the subject. But for now all she said was: "You would not want to do that."

George thought of poor Teeth, who had become only what he had thought his master wanted. Then he shook his head in fervent agreement.

"No," he said. "I wouldn't want that." And after a long while, his mother standing by the door to watch him, he went to sleep.

He dreamed of pup words and woke crying, to find he was alone.

CHAPTER TWO

ONE NIGHT, WHEN his mother came to tuck him into bed, as she often did, George demanded a story. She often told him stories about the kingdom of Kendel, such as the tale of King Richon and the wild man. Or stories from even farther back in time, about the founding of Kendel, how it had been torn from Sarrey by the great hero Alan, King Richon's great-great-great-grandfather. Other fiefdoms or principalities had come and gone with good or bad leaders. But Sarrey had remained because of the ruthlessness of Sarrey's kings. And Kendel had its kind ones.

For this night the queen told about George's father's father, King Taran, who had been known as such a great warrior that no one had dared challenge him. Even when he was seventy years old and near blind, he had struck a man through the heart when on judgment day the man's case had gone against him.

"Was my father there?" asked George, remembering how his father had told him that when he was older, he would come to judgment day as well.

"He was indeed," said his mother.

George could only imagine his father's watching with no expression on his face, as stalwart as he was now. "Was he afraid?" he asked, knowing that he himself would have been.

"He was afraid of being afraid," said his mother.

When George's face twisted in confusion, she laughed gently. "With a warrior for a father, he knew that he had much to live up to. He thought he must be like his father."

George nodded.

"But your father has had to find his own way, and it has been a difficult path for him."

George saw his mother's face soften, as it always did when she talked about his father. He never understood it. How could she feel like that about a man George found as terrifying as any soldier he had ever seen?

"I think that I admire him most for his fairness. At the beginning of his reign some saw him as weak, but he has never been that." Her voice was fierce. "He is so deep I sometimes wonder if I will ever come to the end of him."

But George did not like to hear about how much his mother loved his father. He wanted her to love only him. And perhaps horses and other animals, as he did, but no more than that.

So he said, "Tell me a story about animals. Please!"

His mother thought for a few moments. "Once there was a young girl," she said, winking at George so he understood it was a story about her.

"And she loved animals. Her father was a traveling man, who did odd jobs here and there. He never stayed in any place more than a week or two, and he never spoke a word about her mother. She knew she must have had one once. All children had mothers, living or dead. Even the animals had mothers. But where hers was, what she had looked like, and what had happened to her, the girl could only guess at."

Thinking of the little girl his mother had been, George felt sorry for her. To have no mother, to have only a father? That would be the worst life he could imagine.

"Sometimes her father was asked to shoe a horse or to see to an ailing dog. He was so good at everything else he did, seeming to find as much ease in cutting wood for a new table as he did in making a dinner of stone soup or opening the neck of a dammed stream, that the girl believed he could do anything. Yet he would always refuse.

"'Why?' the girl asked when she had been given the pick of the litter among a sow's piglets by a boy she had befriended, a boy with a wild eye whom others shunned.

"Her father would not let her take it, nor would he give her any reason for his response.

"She wept. She pouted. She begged and pleaded. All

to no avail. He would have nothing to do with animals.

"After that, the girl watched her father carefully. She noticed that whenever there was a horse nearby, he held his shoulders straighter and kept his head turned to the side. Yet he did this before the girl had any knowledge of the horse. Before it could be seen or heard.

"And once, when the girl came across a dying otter by the bank of a deep, cold stream, she saw her father weeping. His hands twitched, and he made a strange sound in his throat, one that seemed to match the sound the otter made in return.

"'Come away from there,' he said then.

"But when the girl was poking at the fire that night, her father told her the story of a male otter that had died saving the lives of his mate and children from a wolf. There was no question in the girl's mind that her father was telling the story of the otter they had seen, that he knew the story just from the sight of him or perhaps from the one word that had gone between them.

"She had always thought that her father hated animals, but now she began to see the ways in which he made sure that any ailing animal he had been asked to cure got the treatment it needed. He would talk in a roundabout way to the owner or to another, or he would sneak off himself at darkest night, when he thought the girl was asleep.

"The girl followed him when she could, and she began to learn to speak to animals as he did. Never when he could hear her. Never when she could be seen by others, but always in secret."

As she had taught him to speak to animals, George thought.

"The girl had never thought that there were any others like her or her father. Until the day came that they found a man in the woods who was speaking to his horse. They had come upon him so quietly that he had not heard them. But he started at the first sight of the girl and went very pale at seeing her father.

"The girl watched as her father put a hand on the horse and spoke a single word of peace to him. Then he nodded and went on.

"The girl asked her father if he had met any others like them. Her father, as always, would say nothing to her on the subject.

"Or he tried to. But she bothered him so much that at last he told the tale of King Richon and the wild man."

George knew that tale. His mother had told it to him long before.

"'Can you do that too?' she asked, in surprise and with a little fear.

"Her father shuddered and said only, 'That is the great gift that very few have. And certainly not I.'

"'And me?' she asked.

"He looked at her and only shook his head. 'I do not know. I do not believe so.' After that he was silent on the matter.

"The next day, when she came back from picking berries, her father was gone. She hurried to the village and found him tied to a stake. His body had been burned badly, but she recognized the clothing he had been wearing.

"Weeping with horror, she turned around and saw the man her father and she had seen, the one talking to his horse. With his eyes the man seemed to beg forgiveness. His tongue had been cut out, but he could speak with something like the words of an owl by moving his lips like a beak. She made out at last: 'My life if I gave up another of my kind. That is always the trade. But your father would not give you up. Not even for his life.'

"The girl went away and made her own life. She knew the danger of loving animals, but her only compromise was caution, especially of those who might hear her and betray her, as her father had been betrayed.

"As she grew, she discovered other dangers. There were people who came into villages and promised they would find those with animal magic. And the promise always came true, whether the girl had heard animal language spoken by the accused or not. When the promise maker left, it was always with the stench of a great bonfire following behind.

"She told herself to look away, and to go on. But she grew in her ability with horses, her favorite of all the tame animals, for they were as stubborn as she was in her heart.

"One day she was asked to come to the king's stables,

to take care of his fine horses. And there she stayed."
She looked at George.

He thought how strange it was that she had told her
life history without ever speaking of herself. Always
"the girl."

"But what of the magic?" he asked in a whisper. He
wanted to know more about it, and wasn't his mother
the one to tell him?

Her eyes went a little distant, more like his father's
than he liked. Was she angry with him?

Then she said, "Now and again I have heard bits and
pieces. But I have never known for certain if it came
from those who knew the truth."

"Knew the truth" instead of "had the magic." She
had said his father was deep, but it was true of her too.
Did his father even know she had the magic?

"There is the tale of the turtle and the snake," she
said. "It begins with the turtle challenging the snake to
a race in the water. And ends with the turtle snapping
the snake into his jaws and holding tight even as the
snake thrashes about and transforms from fish to shark
to human."

George swallowed hard.

"There is the tale of the worm's egg, in which an
eagle discovers in her nest a large and unround egg,
speckled and throbbing. She sits on it with the others,
but when it hatches, she discovers a wormlike creature,
without any feathers and with little fur, with eyes large
and blinking. She thinks to feed it to her children for

lunch, for the creature seems little good for anything else. But then the strange pale thing speaks in the eagle's language. She still cannot bear to see it in her nest, but instead of feeding it to her younglings, she pushes it out of the nest, then watches to see it fall to the ground. It falls indeed, but just near the ground it is transformed into the shape of a hawk and sails away."

"But—" said George. He could not finish. He had never seen his mother transform herself. Could she become a horse herself? Could he? It made him feel heady with excitement.

"There is also the tale of the man who could not be made happy," his mother said. "This man was fed well as a babe. He was rocked to sleep and sung songs. He was shown how to make a living raising and shearing sheep. But he was not happy. And so he began to try to understand the language of his sheep, to hear how to make them fatter and more woolly. He was soon wealthier than all the other sheep farmers in his village. But he was not happy.

"He next wished to speak the language of his sheep, to command them to become fatter and make more wool. Soon they did, and he was the richest man in the entire district. But he was not happy.

"So he began to learn to become a sheep, so that he could make his own wool, as much as he wanted, and his own meat. He learned the secret of becoming a sheep, but he had not first learned the secret of becoming a man once again. He roamed his own hills, baaing for help, but no one else understood the language of the sheep, so people did not know what he was saying.

"And soon, because there was no one to shepherd the sheep, his neighbors began to take them one by one into their own flocks. Then he was taken into a flock, sheared as a sheep is sheared, and sent to the slaughter. And still he was not happy." His mother made a grim face. "Not much of a story for a little boy for bedtime. I am sorry."

"But what does it mean?" asked George.

"It means that there are times when one should be happy with what one has and not ask for more." His mother sighed.

"I am happy, Mother," George said. He reached for her hand.

She brushed his hair back from his forehead. "I am happy too, George," she said.

"There is another story," she added. "About a bear in the great dark forest who can speak in a way that only those with the animal magic can understand."

George yawned. "And what does he say?" he asked.

"He asks for hope and for the fulfillment of a promise."

"Promise," echoed George, trying to stay awake.

His mother smoothed his hair behind his ear. "Someday, perhaps . . ." she said softly.

But George did not hear the rest of it, for he fell asleep.

CHAPTER THREE

EORGE WAS SEVEN years old when his mother died. He was not told when she was found missing from the castle. He was too young to know that the searchers had gone south to the great forest on command of the king, who feared she had been stolen by King Helm of Sarrey in some plot of vengeance following the war.

All day he kept busy playing with his "friends," tiny creatures he had made, to whom he spoke in their own languages, quietly and privately so that no one could hear. And yet he must have a chance to practice, or the animals would laugh at him when he went back to the woods with his mother. When would he go back? He didn't know.

His mother had been spending more time with the new woman in her court, Lady Fittle, whom George had disliked on first meeting. The other women who were part of his mother's court had always given her distance and time to spend on her own. But Lady Fittle was everywhere, at the queen's side at every dinner, bringing breakfast to her bedchamber, helping her dress, meeting her for lunch in the gardens.

George remembered Lady Fittle's staring pointedly at him when he raced by after a stray mouse Cook Elin had screeched at. George had cornered the mouse, tucked her into the pocket of his vest, and smiled broadly at his mother. He knew her name was Cheep and that she liked bread better than cheese. He had known he could not speak to his mother aloud of what he had done, but he had thought she would see the bulge and be proud.

Not only was she not proud, but her eyes were bright with terror that George could not understand. She was queen. How could she be afraid in her own castle?

Then George saw Lady Fittle, and he knew that he must not give the mouse any reason to show herself. He held himself very still.

"And this is Prince George?" said Lady Fittle in a tart tone.

"Yes. This is my son," said his mother. In her voice was a trace of herself, but only that much.

"He is very . . . active, is he not?"

"He is a dear boy," said George's mother.

"So much like you there is hardly a breath of his

33

father in him. Do you not agree?" asked Lady Fittle.

"Oh, there is enough of each of us in him. Neither the king nor I would wish for more."

"Come, let me touch his fine hair," said Lady Fittle, reaching.

"No!" the queen stepped in her way.

Lady Fittle answered in a pinched voice. "So protective of him. If he is to be king one day, you must let him go a bit more, my queen."

I never want to be king, thought George. *Never.*

"I only meant that you would get yourself dirty, Lady Fittle," said George's mother, apparently calm, but George could see how her lips twitched at the edges.

"Ah. Well, then, I must thank you for your concern, must I not?" asked Lady Fittle with false gratitude and a slight inclination of the head.

George thought the encounter was over and waited for Lady Fittle to leave.

But Lady Fittle had one more comment, as much a threat as any George had ever heard. "Another time, my prince," she said, then nodded and went on her way.

George breathed deeply and looked to his mother to offer him comfort, but she sighed and moved a step away without another word.

"Mother." George called her back.

"Not now, George," she said.

"I only wanted to know—what is that lady's name?" said George.

His mother told him as she walked away. "Lady Fittle of the south."

George had to hear the rest of it later, from the gossip that was passed in the kitchens and by the hearth fire among the guards. Lady Fittle was from the southernmost reaches of the kingdom, and she had been sent as a spy. But no one said a spy for whom. Sarrey? The war was over now.

Nonetheless George was careful to watch his mother as often as he could, to make sure that Lady Fittle did not poison her or stab her in the heart with a dagger, as he had heard in stories that spies sometimes did.

Lady Fittle never so much as grazed his mother's arm. The queen was very careful about that, George noticed. Though they were often together, the queen held herself apart. George was puzzled. If Lady Fittle was a dangerous woman, then why would his mother allow her in the castle at all?

George began to think that it was his father's fault, in part because the king seemed utterly oblivious of Lady Fittle's role in his mother's discomfort. Could the king not see the way the queen hated to be with Lady Fittle? Could he not see that she needed to be alone? And why did he not allow her time anymore to visit the stables, to be with the animals . . . and her son?

The very next morning George arrived in his mother's bedchamber to save her. He had decided to throw a fit and demand that she go with him to the stables again.

35

Then they could go off together and laugh at how clever he had been to get her free to spend time with the horses.

But it did not work that way.

The king was in the bedchamber already, as was Lady Fittle. They were discussing the case of a man in the northern part of the country whose eyes had been burned out because he had been judged to have the power of transforming himself into an eagle.

"But why?" asked George, his curiosity overcoming his distaste for Lady Fittle.

"Because no man should have an advantage like that over another. And because it is unclean for a man to become what he is not," said Lady Fittle. And then she said, beckoning with both hands, "Come here, dear boy."

The king pushed George forward to Lady Fittle.

His mother stepped between them, nearly colliding with Lady Fittle as she did so. "George, this is no place for a little boy," she said roughly.

George struggled not to let his eyes fill with tears. His mother had never spoken to him so before.

He stared at her once, to give her a chance to take back what she had said or to explain it. But she only pointed to the door.

George ran out, all the way down the stairs, past the kennels, and into the stables. He wrapped his arms around Honey, who asked after the queen, but George would say nothing. He would not speak a word of the horse's language. That belonged to his mother, and he wanted nothing to do with her then.

That night, still hiding in the stables, George heard two of the king's messengers speaking as they brushed down their horses and readied them for the night.

"There are some who are known to have a gift of touching those with the animal magic, of knowing with that touch if they have it or not," said one man. "They say Lady Fittle is one of them, that she has been sent to make sure the king's court is free of such evil. Of course the king welcomed her. What else could he do? He cannot allow anyone to see that he is easy on the magic."

The other man shivered. "Well, I hate the sight of her. And I'm no lover of the animal magic myself."

They went by, and George was left to puzzle out their meanings. How much longer could his mother keep herself from Lady Fittle's touch? How much longer until the queen was known to have animal magic—and her son as well?

George went numb at the thought. It was too terrible to dwell on, so he pressed it out of his mind. He kept away from both his mother and Lady Fittle, and he kept away from all animals as well. He played with his hand-made creatures and kept to himself until that night, when the king entered without the customary knock, his face utterly changed.

Stricken. Panicked. Unsure.

Whose face was this? Not the king George had always known before. Another time it might have frightened him. But at the moment George was too afraid of his own guilt in speaking to animal friends, even pretend ones, to feel anything but fear.

The king must never know. His mother would never forgive George.

So as quickly as he could, George hid his creatures behind his back, the tiny bear made of a fluffy bit of dark lamb's wool, the fish made of a polished black rock, the robin made of maple wood, and the vole made of an old sock.

His father nodded to him, then held out his hands.

George was unsure for a moment what that meant. Was he to clasp his father's hand? He saw that his father's eyes were red. Was he ill? That was when George began to think of death, but not of his mother's. Never his mother's.

"We get along well enough, do we not, you and I?" asked the king.

George sat gingerly on his father's lap and craned his head away from him. His smell was so strongly . . . human.

"I was once a boy, and you will be a man one day. The king, as I am." The king went on.

George shrugged.

The king took in a breath, then seemed to choke on it. George did not understand until later that this

38

was his way of weeping.

"I have come — I have come to tell you — "

George waited.

At last the king's mouth stopped opening and closing and got the words out. They were strange and formal. "The queen is dead." It sounded as though he had practiced the words, as if he were saying them before some crowd of citizens, a solemn proclamation to the kingdom of Kendel.

It was a long moment until George recalled that the queen was also his mother. Even then he could hardly take it in.

He stared at his father, hoping that this must be some joke, though his father never joked, or some misunderstanding, though father always spoke too clearly to be misunderstood.

"She died in the forest where she had gone to . . . meditate. Attacked by a bear," said the king, each word added reluctantly, as if he wanted to keep the details to himself.

"She had a fever. She was ill." He continued. "I do not know why the queen would go so far in such a state. And yet she went. Not one of her women stopped her."

She wasn't the queen, thought George. *She was my mother. Mine. I know things of her that you will never know,* he wanted to say.

"You will be a brave boy, won't you?" asked the king. "And come stand with me while I light her fire?"

He smiled a false smile.

And George could think only of his mother's father, who had also been burned, for his animal magic. "Not burning," he said.

But the king seemed to think he was simply refusing the reality of his mother's death. "It is a hard truth," he said. "But she is gone." He thought for a moment, then added, "She will be cleaned for the burning. You may see her then if you wish."

If that was the only way he would see his mother again, George realized he could not refuse it. So he nodded, and said, "Yes, Father." That, and no more.

The king stood, but he remained a moment longer, his hands twisting in each other.

If George had said something then, the right thing, perhaps things might have been different between them ever afterward. But he only wanted his father to be gone, so that he could grieve in his own way. After all, a boy could not cry in front of his king. Even if the man was also his father.

CHAPTER FOUR

A T THE LIGHTING ceremony, George felt a great resentment that he had to share this most private moment with all of the kingdom. That he had to hold his head steady and keep his eyes dry and speak clearly when it was his chance to offer the leaf of his mother's favorite tree.

In the end George chose the maple leaf simply because the true gift for his mother's pyre that he had tucked into his sleeve, unbeknownst to anyone, was the maple wood robin from his own collection. He liked to think that his mother was flying above the ruined body that was atop the wood, that would soon be lit and burned to ashes.

It was easier too if he looked up as much as he could, and not down, at what was left of the hands, the hair, the gentleness, and all of her that he had known.

King Davit came and held his hand as he put the leaf

up on the pyre. Then the king himself lit the fire with a word of benediction, standing back afterward and watching it burn down. For hours and hours he stood. And so George too had to stand, even when the king asked if he would not rather go in with the others when it began to rain lightly or when it grew dark.

How could George go inside if the king remained?

How could George allow the king to prove that he had loved her more than George had?

Later, George went back to his chamber, stumbling in the new light of dawn, alone. A brave servant woman named Shay, who had lost all four of her sons in the war, came in eventually and took pity on him.

"Now, come along. Time for you to rest," Shay said in a thick accent from the south. But when she touched George's arm, she jerked back.

"Great animals above," she whispered, then reached for his forehead. "Like a pyre, it is."

George could feel how cold her hands were.

Of course. He was sick.

That must be why everything was wrong.

He clutched his remaining animals, but the servant woman tried to pull them away from him and push him into his bed.

He didn't want bed. He wanted his mother.

His mother.

A flash of memory.

"She had a fever." His father's voice. His mother had

gone into the forest alone and had been attacked by a bear.

Why hadn't she been able to speak to it? Because she had a fever?

But George soon stopped thinking at all logically. He was sure that the only thing that could possibly make him feel better was the cool quiet of the forest, the sound of animal voices, real animal voices, in his ears, and the smell of animals all around the ground. In the dirt, in the water, in the air above.

He needed animals.

"I must—" he said, struggling against Shay.

At last she gave up the fight, telling George that she was going to fetch the physician.

George knew the physician would make him drink something strong and foul tasting, something that would make him sleep. It would not help him at all. George had to get to the little woods outside the castle, where his mother had taken him.

He waited until Shay was out of sight, then ran headlong down the stairs.

Who followed him, if anyone did, George did not know. He did not care.

The woods, the woods, was all he thought.

The fever grew worse with every passing moment.

As he ran past the moat, out onto the cleared field that lay before the wood, George fought flashes of burning heat combined with shudders of chill. His throat hurt. His chest ached. His head whirled, and he could hardly think.

His mother must have felt the same. Not ill as his father thought. But ill with the magic of animals calling to him.

Even when George thought of his mother's death, of the bear, of the dangers of the woods alone, he could not stop. Fear was no antidote to this need. It pressed him and pressed him, and there was no relief from it until he could at last smell the sharp scent of the pines, could feel the tempting cool shadows, could hear the crackle of branches beneath his feet.

Then the fever abated, and George breathed deeply. How free he felt here, not the king's son at all. Only George.

He sat with his arms wrapped around his knees and his eyes wide open. He let the peace and quiet of the woods sink into him. This was how he had always felt with his mother, a contentment that seemed to run as deep as his bones and his blood.

His mother. Who was dead.

George thought of Lady Fittle. She had suspected the truth about the queen's animal magic, and the prince's. She was the reason his mother had not taken him to the woods for so long, why she had not dared go herself. Until the fever was terrible upon her, and there was no choice.

She had died for her magic. Or died trying to deny her magic. Which was it?

George had felt only the magic's wonder before.

Now he realized that there was a danger in the magic itself. The fever was the demand of the magic that it be used. It could not be locked away, not completely. Even his mother's father had not been able to do that, however much he had tried.

George could run away from the castle, but he could not run away from his magic.

The magic that had seemed so wonderful when he had first discovered it was different now. It had killed his mother. The magic, and the animals she had loved. The anger so consumed George that he did not notice the passing of the smaller beasts or their signals of fear. All he noticed was the sudden sound at his left.

He turned to see running toward him a boar with tusks so long they might have been made into curved swords.

What could he do? He had come without a weapon, without anything at all to protect himself. Frozen in terror, George just stared.

For a moment he was sure that he would die as his mother had. The beast lumbered headlong toward George.

No, he thought. And then he shouted it. "No!" Somehow, the word came out in the language of the boar.

Nonetheless the boar kept coming.

"No! I command you!" George tried again, adding to what his mother had taught him by guesses of his own, gathered from the boar's heaves and snorts.

This time it seemed to have some effect, for in the end the boar rushed by him, the left tusk so close it ripped his leggings. A line of blood welled out and dripped to the forest floor.

George was not dead.

Not yet.

He breathed again, a quick, shallow, grateful breath.

The boar turned and came back to George, but slowly this time. It snorted around George in a circle, once, twice. Then it tested its tusks once more against his leg, pressing, digging.

"Hello." George tried more calmly, again in the language of the boar. It was a cross between a snuffle and a grunt.

Now the boar stared, eyes narrowed in confusion, to hear its own language in the mouth of this human creature.

"It is hot." George babbled anxiously. "Too hot to kill. Better to find cool water or a stream."

Would the boar listen to him? His mother had taught him that being able to speak to animals did not mean they would obey.

But this boar snuffled and seemed inquisitive rather than angry. Perhaps it was not really hungry. Or perhaps it was a young boar and, like George himself, curious about the world.

Trying to control his trembling, George tried again.

"I know stream. I show you."

"You . . . who are?" demanded the boar.

"One to help," said George.

"Don't need your help, I don't," said the boar.

But it turned away. And sauntered away from George, in the direction of the stream.

George would not have followed, would have been glad to sit against an old tree trunk and rest, but then he saw that the ridge the boar had gone toward was very close to his favorite rabbit hole. He told himself the rabbits would surely smell the boar and know to stay hidden.

But still he got up and tried to lead the boar away from the hole. It was no use. The boar was stubborn and, now that it had been set on a new course, persistent. It knew the fastest way to the stream, and George could think of no way to divert it.

He tried to call out to the rabbits in their language, but rabbit words were very hard to shout. Rabbits nibbled and sniffed and twitched their noses. Their language was a quiet one.

George saw the small gray rabbit born with a short hind leg, the one George had played with more than any of the others the last time he had come to the forest with his mother.

Perhaps the rabbit could not move fast enough or was distracted by the smell of some sweet flower. All George saw was the brief change in direction by the boar, a widening of its nostrils as it took up pursuit. And then the lame gray rabbit was in the boar's mouth, never to be seen again.

George now let out the tears that he had held in at his mother's funeral pyre, in the shadow of his father's silence. He sobbed, fell to the ground, and rolled in the dirt in paroxysms of grief.

Why could he not save those he loved? Why was he so powerless? He might have magic, but it was of no use.

The boar was long gone when George was worn out by his weeping. He wiped at his face with dirty hands, then brushed his hands on his filthy tunic. He tried to be brave again.

He went to the stream to quench his fiery thirst and then to cool his feet. And perhaps simply to forget himself.

Though the boar was long gone, the streambed showed signs of its clumsy passing, and the water was a little dark from raised mud. George wanted his mother back with a rage as loud as the boar's. He wanted the magic's burden gone as well. He did not know how she had survived it, how she had found happiness.

He was by turns angry with her and desperate for her to come back. Guilty for not having been with her to save her from the bear and bitter that she had not loved him enough to take him with her.

Some time later he looked up, trying to tell how long

he had been gone from the castle. The trees were so thick that he could see only patches of sky here and there. He squinted and tried to find the sun. Well, did it matter? Here in the forest there seemed no time. It was only in the castle that people worried about such things, and he was glad, very glad, to be away from the castle right now.

He dozed off, curled under a huge fallen oak, and when he woke, he was quiet enough that he could hear the tiny movements of the grubs and beetles. Their language was not one to be spoken aloud. His mother had taught him to read it, however, in the paths their bodies left across the crumbling wood. They spoke to one another, showed where the best places for digging were, and warned against the open places, where birds might come and peck them out.

In his concentration, he did not notice the shadow of the beast moving toward him or hear the low, rumbling growl that came with it.

It was suddenly at his side, looming over him, its smell blotting out all else. An enormous black bear, one that surely did not belong in a small woods so close to human villages as this one. It stared at George as if waiting for him to speak. As if it had been called.

George unwrapped his arms from around his legs and pulled his head away from the ball he had made of himself. Then he looked up into the bear's face, towering above him as it stood on its hind legs. A great black bear with a face that seemed very old and very patient.

George's voice was hoarse, but he forced out a few words in the language of the bears. He had learned them from his mother, though she had not explained why, when it was unlikely they would ever meet a bear here in these woods.

"Hungry? Honey?" George sputtered. But his mother had taught him more than that. Something about hope and a promise. It made no sense.

The bear's mouth opened, then closed. A paw lifted, swiped to one side, then the other.

George realized the bear was trying to speak to him. But not in the language of the bears.

Why did it not speak in the language of the bears? What was it trying to say?

The bear made the same motion a second time, and George realized it was pointing to him and then to itself. Insistently.

The bear was so pitiful. So towering and huge . . . and so helpless.

He put his hand out to the bear.

The bear leaned forward eagerly.

With a shock, George smelled the bear's foul stench. He felt the pulse of blood under his fingertips. He felt matted fur and life and—more.

His head whirled, and he felt as though something inside himself, something vital and dangerous, were being pulled out. He pushed it back, gasping.

When he at last recovered himself, sweat drenched and exhausted, he turned back to the bear. "I'm sorry," he whispered, in his own human tongue.

The bear made the gesture again, from George to itself. But jerkily, as if it had given up already.

George shook his head. He would not look into that part of himself again. He did not dare.

Slowly the bear fell onto four paws and lumbered away, not looking back.

He had failed something here, George thought. His mother had spoken of a bear and a promise. But what had she wanted George to do?

No. He had done the right thing. He had protected himself.

It was dark by the time George made his way out of the forest.

But the fever was gone now. He wanted only to be away from the bear and the feeling of wrongness that dogged him. He would return to the castle and be the prince his father asked him to be. He would not fail, for he knew how to be silent, never to speak of his mother or the magic they had shared, and to keep himself from animals. To be safe from whatever it was the bear had touched inside him.

CHAPTER FIVE

*Y*ET HE COULD NOT escape so easily. Dreams of the bear haunted George for many years after their strange and terrifying encounter in the woods. He would become the bear, hunting for honey or berries or watching for a lame animal or an old, slow one to take down. The bear seemed as sickened as George was by the mess that it made of eating, and it never ate much. George could feel the pangs in its stomach. Large as it was, the creature grew thinner day by day. And in the winter, when most bears were asleep, this one moved restlessly through the snow, still searching for a rabbit or a squirrel.

George could not doubt that the dreams were real, for they were too vivid. Yet this shared dreaming had never happened with any of the other animals George had met. It was surely part of the animal magic, and George dared not speak of it to anyone. Though Lady

Fittle had been turned out of his father's court after his mother's death, George had to remain careful.

George was often afraid to go to sleep. Some nights he sat upright all night in a chair by the fire, pinching himself to stay awake. Or he stood by the door to his bedchamber, pacing back and forth. Yet the magic of the bear, whatever it was, was always waiting for the moment when he would drop to the floor, in a dead faint.

Then the dreams came again.

George wondered if there was some way for the bear to stop the dreams. He went back to the woods now and again, half fearing he would actually find the creature. But he never did. And the bear, in its dreams, did not seem to think of George at all or even remember him.

In time the dreams changed. George still had dreams of the bear, but there were bits and pieces of a man's world mixed in with them. A wealthy man, well dressed, who rode the best horses.

Sometimes George thought the horse rides were hunts, but he never caught a glimpse of any creature being hunted or of the end of the hunt either. The man he dreamed of loved the feel of his bare feet on wet grass, and had tried and tried to juggle.

George saw him meeting young ladies at this ball or another, and how they tittered and made eyes at him. The man was embarrassed and determined never to marry, not one of them. But then he was so lonely and had to pretend that he was not. He watched his friends with their children and envied them that pleasure that could not be his.

This part of the man George understood. All around him were those who made friends so easily, perhaps not the same friends George wanted, but still, they had something. He had nothing.

When George woke in the morning after such a dream, he always ran to the kitchen, starved. Cook Elin had a place in her heart for the little prince. She did not think him nearly plump enough by her own standards. But she never referred to him by name. He was always "boy," no more than that, and she would not watch him while he ate. She simply gave him what he asked for and went back to work.

George was as close to Cook Elin as he was to anyone in the castle, and he stayed by her for as long as he could in the mornings. Then it was back to being prince again, going to this event or that one, fulfilling expectations, and being told he was the image of his father. No mention of his mother at all.

Then night came, and more dreams, and George could not fight them, no matter how he tried.

The man in the dreams was often rude. He seemed not to know another way to speak, and those around him either learned to grow hard skins or left him. The man was abandoned many times by his own servants, without a word.

Yet he was not intentionally unkind. He came to see that there were those around him who were, and he hated them. And yet if they were the only ones who would not leave him, he felt he must not deserve any better.

It was difficult for George, on some mornings, to distinguish himself from the man in the dreams. But who was this dream man? Did he have something to do with the bear?

George could think of no other explanation. He remembered the way the bear had gestured so desperately at their first meeting, how he had wanted . . . something. But it was impossible. The legend of King Richon was no more than that. And a story could have nothing to do with this bear or the man, or the dreams George had about them both. Besides, George could do no transformations with his magic. He could only speak to animals, and no more.

Yet he did not speak to animals in any place where he might be seen. Certainly not in the castle and often not even in the fields around the castle or in the stables or the kennels. He had once mewed at the old cat Cook Elin kept as a mouser and looked up to see Cook Elin staring at him with a look on her face that frightened him. He did not speak to the old cat again, but sometime later he woke up in the middle of the night, before even Cook Elin was in the kitchen, and found the cat dead. He took the body to bury it in the soft dirt by the moat.

It was Cook Elin who noticed Prince George's aversion to rare meat and teased him about it, a "great, strapping lad like you," she said. "Afraid of a little blood?"

But the meat reminded him of the bear's meals, animals caught midflight and then dismembered, their messy entrails steaming on the ground. With his oversize knife and fork he felt as clumsy as the bear, and though he knew that these were not wild animals that had been slaughtered, it made little difference to him. His mother had always eaten sparingly of meat, though she had disdained those who claimed not to eat meat at all, saying that the law of the animals was that it was right to kill but only in necessity.

At last the dreams of both the bear and the man became less frequent. It was a relief, yet George missed his nightly companions. He even missed the temptation of thinking that his magic was something great and important and that only he could do what was meant to be done with it. Because he was great and important too.

But he was not. He was only Prince George, quiet and obedient and pitied by all who knew him, because of his mother's death and his father's neglect. Prince George could hardly be trusted to put his shirt on the right way around, let alone change the world with his magic.

CHAPTER SIX

TALL, STERN SIR Stephen became George's tutor when he was eight years old. He had the king to advise, as was his official position, but when other tutors complained the prince was too stupid to learn properly, the king appointed Sir Stephen to take over the task.

It was not that George did not wish to learn or even that he could not. It was only Sir Stephen who seemed to realize that George was best prodded by reminders of his mother. Sir Stephen was the one who would say, "Would your mother be happy if she saw you today?" and so George reluctantly kept at his lessons, for her memory's sake.

Sir Stephen might have given the hint to another tutor. Some claimed that he was looking to his future, that he wanted to assure he had the next king's ear. But George felt real sympathy from Sir Stephen, as if he understood what it was to be a boy of whom too much was expected. Also, only Sir Stephen had known his mother well enough that now and again he could surprise George with a new story or two about her life.

He told of her first state dinner, when she had used the wrong fork and all the other ladies at the table had been forced to use the wrong fork with her. George went red with embarrassment for his mother's mistake, but Sir Stephen shook his head and laughed.

"She did it every dinner after, for a year," he said, "just to tease them."

George smiled at this and went right back to work at his letter writing, though he did purposely misspell a word here and there: "I shall always fail my responsibilities" instead of "I shall always fill my responsibilities."

He watched as Sir Stephen tried to keep his temper. And waited for him to see how he had only followed his mother's example from the story.

Then Sir Stephen shook his finger and threatened George direly, but with a twinkle in his eyes.

Even with Sir Stephen's sympathy, George knew how different his life might have been had his mother lived. She would not have insisted on so many lessons. She would not have allowed George to be forced into the duties of a prince every hour of every day. And when the king said, "A prince must think of the kingdom first, its citizens second, and himself last of all," she might have said that there were times a prince could think of himself first, or there would be nothing left of him to give to others.

George wished he knew when those times might be,

but Sir Stephen could not help him there. He told stories to gain George's compliance, but he did not let George forget who he was. Not even for a moment. And he never, ever gave George the slightest hint that there might be reason to trust him enough to tell him the deepest secret of all, of animal magic.

There George needed no reminder of his mother, for the last weeks of her life and the manner of her death made it clear to him that he had to make sure there was not even a suspicion of his having animal magic.

Yet for all his secrecy, George could not make his magic go away, for he had learned that from his mother's death. So he did his best to find out what he needed to know. He found himself thirsty for any scrap of information or rumor. And he heard much, as he stood at his father's side, from adults and even from the servants' children, who ran freely in the castle as George could not.

He could do no more than listen, however. The moment he tried to ask a question directly or gave any sign that he was watching, the voices ceased. He received bows aplenty, as was suited to the prince of the kingdom, but nothing more.

Once he ordered a group of children playing in the field outside the castle to let him play with them. But they would only do exactly as he commanded them. They would stand here or there, run this way or that, but they would not play. How could they when he had power over their very lives?

Still, he could not stop himself from seeking more

information and more company. He was allowed little time indeed with animals, almost as if Sir Stephen had suspected George's animal magic and were trying to keep him away from them. And yet he did not watch so closely that George was in danger of another magical fever. George simply waited until he was thought asleep and went on his own, in the dark.

When George was nine years old, the king decided that it was time for him to begin making friends among the children who would be his peers when he was king. The sons and daughters of dukes and lords were invited to the castle, and George was commanded to play with them. This was hardly more successful than his own attempts at commanding friendship.

These noble children always let him win whatever game they played, but George supposed that was better than not playing at all. And there was Peter, the son of a minor noble, who George thought might actually forget now and again that he was supposed to be losing. Perhaps Peter even forgot that George was the king's son. Or so George allowed himself to believe.

Peter was several years older than George and taller too, but they often raced together. One day, as they both were lying on the grass after a race that George had narrowly won when Peter pretended to fall and sprain his ankle, Peter recovered his breath first. Unexpectedly he began to talk of animal magic.

"Don't touch that toad," he told George as it crossed their path on the way to the moat.

"Why not?" asked George, startled.

"A toad that has danced under a full moon will bring animal magic to any who touch him and to all their children forever after," Peter said in an ominous tone.

George jerked his hand away from the toad and stared at Peter. "Everyone who has the animal magic got it from a toad?" he asked. He knew that his mother and her father had had it. He thought it was simply passed along blood to blood. But what if it was not?

"Not everyone," said Peter. "There are other ways."

"What other ways?" demanded George.

"Well, I've heard that kissing behind a haystack after midnight on the third week of a month in summer will bring it too."

"Kissing?" George was dubious about that. At least the toad was an animal. Kissing behind a haystack didn't have anything to do with animal magic that he could see. Besides, kissing was far more disgusting than touching a toad. Very few people must get the animal magic that way.

"Or . . ." Peter's eyes shone. "Some say it comes from swimming in a castle moat, without clothes, at dawn."

"Really?" said George.

Peter shrugged. "It comes from any evil done or thought of. That's why it's part of them, the very smell of them. That's why even when they're dead, animals will come and tear into their graves and drag their bones into the forest to gnaw on."

"Evil?" whispered George.

"Evil," Peter hold him. Then he went on to describe other ways to get animal magic and to get rid of it.

George wondered whether he would choose to give up his animal magic, if he could. Not having anything to conceal would make his life easier. But it might also make him lonelier, and that seemed worse by far than the trouble he took to conceal it now.

Abruptly Peter said, "Meet me here an hour before dawn."

George's eyes widened. "What? Why?"

"To swim naked in the moat, of course. I challenge you to it. You aren't afraid, are you? Of getting the animal magic?"

How could George be afraid of getting magic he already had? The only problem he saw was on Peter's part if he got the animal magic. Then he would have to live as secretly as George did.

No. That was the marvelous thing, George realized. Once Peter had the magic too, they could always speak of it with each other. It would be almost as if his mother were alive again. They could sneak off together to the forest. They could speak together in animal languages.

George had not felt so hopeful in years. He knew it was selfish to want to make his friend like he was, especially when he knew the difficulties of keeping the animal magic secret. But surely Peter wouldn't mind, once he'd gotten used to it. Once he saw that he and George could use it together.

"I'll meet you," George said solemnly. A weight of

guilt tugged at him all day.

That night he woke to the sound of a rock being thrown at his window. He looked down and saw Peter and hurried out of his chamber without bothering to dress. After all, they were only going in the moat naked.

"Are you afraid?" asked Peter.

"No," said George truthfully, though he swallowed hard at the thought of his friend's daring. Was he a true friend to Peter if he let him do this? He thought of what his father would say about duty. Then George shook his head angrily.

"What's wrong?" asked Peter.

"Nothing," said George. He clenched his teeth and told himself that he wasn't king yet and didn't want to be king. Or prince either, for that matter. Besides, he had been a prince every minute of his life for so long now. He deserved a few moments to be himself. To make a selfish choice once, just a small one.

George walked toward the moat, feeling the weight of Peter's steps behind him.

They reached the edge of the moat. George opened his mouth, then closed it. He should at least warn Peter what it was like to have the animal magic. He didn't seem to have any idea at all. In fact he seemed—as excited as George was.

In the end that was what kept George silent. If Peter wanted the magic too, then who was George to stop him?

"You first," said Peter, waving a hand.

The water in the moat looked cold and the surface

was not even. There were things that lived inside there that George did not have the names of. The stench was none too pleasant either. But George stepped forward. Going first was the least he could do.

"I'll come in right after you," said Peter. "I swear it on my father's name."

George didn't doubt him for a moment.

He closed his eyes, took a step, and fell into the water. He went down for a long time. He opened his eyes, but he could see nothing. He could feel things bump against him, and he tried to get away from them, but he seemed caught in something that would not let go.

He thought he should try to speak the language of the fish, but he couldn't get any sounds out. He couldn't hear what the fish were saying either.

He struggled and thrashed, his lungs filling with water, until—

One of the castle guards dragged him out of the water and laid him out on his stomach by the moat. He whacked George several times across the back to get his breathing going again.

"What in the world did you think you were doing, you idiot?" he asked. Then he looked more closely at George through narrowed eyes. "Uh, Your Highness," he added belatedly.

"Swimming in the moat," said George in a low, hoarse tone. He looked around, but there was no sign of Peter.

The guard carried the naked, shivering George back

to his bed. He called for the physician, who insisted that George could not leave his chamber for ten days and forced down him the worst medicine George had ever had to swallow.

During every waking moment of those ten days, George thought of Peter's face as he had said, "You first." A tight face. A narrow, unfriendly face.

But Peter was his friend, wasn't he?

So why had he not gone into the moat too?

At first George told himself that Peter must have become frightened at the last, at the thought of getting the animal magic. After all, Peter had gone for the guard to save George, hadn't he?

But the more George thought about Peter, the more uncertain he became.

Then, as he was struggling with his thoughts, Sir Stephen came in to ask if there was anything he'd like to tell him about going into the moat.

That was when it came pouring out. He begged Sir Stephen not to do anything against Peter, but Sir Stephen would have nothing of it. He went away and came back with Peter and his father, and George was forced to relate the story Peter had told him about the moat and about the other ways of getting animal magic.

"Does he believe he has it now?" asked the nobleman, turning to Sir Stephen as though George could not be trusted to give an intelligent answer for himself.

"I have explained to him that it can't possibly happen that way," said Sir Stephen firmly, and he glanced

sidewise at George, as if to make sure he was not con-
tradicted.

"Good. Well, I'll make sure this one gets the punishment he deserves for telling stories." He took Peter off
roughly, and George saw him only one more time, at the
castle gate the next day.

Peter sneered at him and held up his hands. "Won't
touch you. Don't want your dirty animal magic," he
said, and laughed cruelly.

It took George several years to realize that Peter had
not believed even then that George had animal magic,
that it had only been a boy's mean joke. In those years
George became even more closed than before. He continued to meet with those his father insisted he should
make friends with, but he never again made the mistake
of believing their friendships to be real.

George had learned his mother's father's lesson all
over again. Betrayal was too easy against those who had
animal magic. George hadn't paid for his trust with his
life this time. But the pain in his heart had left a scar.

So George made a choice. He would never feel that
pain again. If that meant also never having a friend
again, he could live with that. Better no friends at all
than a friend who had the power to do that.

CHAPTER SEVEN

GEORGE WAS SMALL for twelve years of age and very conscious of how much he still had to grow before he was his father's height. But on his twelfth birthday, after the tedious and formal celebration, George was called to the king's chamber.

"How are your lessons with Sir Stephen?" the king asked.

George wondered if his father intended to take Sir Stephen away and replace him. Would George like that? He thought not. Though Sir Stephen was stiff and old, at least he was familiar. There were also advantages to a tutor who asked no more than he gave.

"Good, Father," said George.

The king nodded, tapping his fingers on his legs. Then he turned to look out the window. After a moment he spoke again. "We do not spend much time together, do we?" he asked.

"You have your duties," said George. He did not want his father to feel that he would like to spend more time with him. The time he spent with his father already was so nerve-racking that George chewed his fingernails to the quick in dreadful anticipation during the hours leading up to any event.

"Yes, I do indeed. Yet I think that if your mother were alive—" He stopped there.

George had caught his breath. His father rarely spoke of his mother, and usually when he did, he referred to her as the queen.

But the king said no more on the subject. He shook his head and turned back to face George directly.

"You have learned many of the duties of a prince."

"Yes, Father," said George.

"But I believe it is time for you to learn some of the duties of the king."

George's mouth gaped. What did his father mean?

The king stepped toward George and put both hands on George's shoulders. "It is time for you to make a judgment of your own."

"No!" came out of George's mouth before he could stop himself.

Since his mother's death, George had been accustomed to sitting at his father's feet in the long hall every second day of the week. His father sat not on a throne then but on a plain wooden chair, and he sat there from early morning until long past dark, if that was what it took to see all the people who had come to ask his rulings.

On judgment day, King Davit ate only the same small portion of coarse bread and cheese that he gave George, the same portion that was offered to all those who kept wait on the king that day.

But George had never said a word at any judgment. How could his father always be sure who was lying and who was not? How did he know which woman truly loved her children and had hurt them only in punishment and which woman abused them out of foolishness or anger? George could not possibly do such a thing.

"You are afraid," said the king.

"No!" George blurted out again. How could he admit to that?

"You do not want to learn then?" It was the same tone the king used when he had dismissed one of the lord general's soldiers from the army at judgment day last week. The man had been accused of drunkenness and would not admit to it. The lord general, whose temper was so hot he was rumored to have killed his wife for bringing him gray tea instead of green, would have sent the man packing himself—with a beating—but the king had insisted on hearing both sides.

George had seen it all. The soldier's stubbornness, the lord general's anger, and the king's frustration, which eventually led to a stern punishment. The soldier not only had ended up without his pay for the last month but had been forced to take off his uniform piece by piece while standing in the public square for all to see. His fellows had stood at attention surrounding him, to make sure he was not physically harmed.

As if that mattered, thought George. Far better to have taken the beating the lord general had suggested than the one his father had devised. Yet George could not think it quite cruel. His father was always just, and this punishment would at least have the chance to change someone.

"I will learn then," said George softly, accepting the inevitable. Of course he would do what his father expected. He always had.

"Good," said the king. "Shall I tell you of my first judgment?" he asked after a moment.

"Yes, Father," said George.

"My father had it planned. It was designed to test me, the players all given their parts, even the words that they would say to me. When I got it wrong, he told me, before all gathered there, what I had missed. I did not judge for many years after that, not even in the first year of my kingship." The king's voice wavered. "In my place I sent another, whom I thought the people must trust better than they did me."

George was unsure how to react. His conversations with his father were usually brief and formal. He had never heard his father talk about his youth and certainly not about any failure.

"I promise you this. I shall make sure that the case you are given is a true one, with no players. And whatever judgment you give, I shall not gainsay it. Yours will be the last word on the matter. And so you will learn to trust yourself, as I never did."

"B-but—" George stuttered.

The king stopped him with a raised hand. "A king cannot show his doubts before others, however much he feels them. If he does wrong, he must live with it. Do you understand?"

"Yes, Father," said George miserably.

The king dismissed him, and George left in a whirl of emotions. A real judgment. His judgment. Tomorrow.

All night George writhed in an agony of fear and anticipation. He had hardly fallen asleep when Sir Stephen came to wake him, and then he sleepily pulled on his best leggings and tunic and the silver circlet that proclaimed him prince.

It was spring, still cool in the morning, though it might become unbearably hot later in the day with so many people in one room. George settled himself in the chair that was his father's and felt his father's large hand on his shoulder with pride. Then the doors were open, and the people streamed in.

There were murmurs when George was seen in his father's place, but King Davit gave a short speech to explain what this was about. Then a man, struggling in ropes that bound his hands behind his back, was pushed forward by a half-dozen men. They all were farmers by the look of their clothing and the pattern of calluses on their hands. The man in bonds had greasy blond hair that fell into his face as he moved, but he could not push it away. He spat at George's feet when forced to kneel before him.

George wanted to look up at his father, but he kept his eyes straight ahead. He would do this alone.

"Speak your piece," George said. They were his father's words and had become the traditional opening of each hearing on judgment day.

One of the men, with several missing teeth, came forward. "All year long we work our fields, feed our beasts. Two years ago there was a terrible plague of locusts that ate everything they could. But his"—a nod to the bound man—"his fields were left alone, and he had a full crop come harvesttime.

"Last year half our animals died from some disease. But his did not. This year we watched him. He walks the fields at night, protecting his plants. He goes to his animals at night, speaks to them. They speak back to him. He has it: the animal magic."

The hall went still.

George felt cold sweat drip down his back. He did not look up at his father.

"And you: speak your piece," George spoke to the bound man through numb lips.

The man spat again, at George's feet. "That's all the

72

witness you'll get me to speak against my own self," he said.

George stared at the man. Did he not realize that this was his one chance to deny he had the animal magic? He could give some excuse for what he did with his animals, say that he was only lucky in the way his crops and animals had survived the last few years. He could say there was some other reason for his success, the seeds he planted, or the way he fertilized them — anything.

"They'll rally the animals against us all," said one of the other men, cowering with his head behind his hands, as if afraid that even in the presence of the king and the prince, the man with animal magic was the most danger-ous to offend. His body shook with fear.

George tried to think of a solution. He turned his eyes to the man with animal magic. He looked to the angry accusers. How could he make a proper judgment? He was, on the one hand, admiring of the man who refused to deny his magic and, on the other hand, angry and resentful of him. Why would he not live in silence and not make trouble for others of his kind, including George?

I am prince, thought George. *I must do something here. Something right.*

Everyone was waiting for him to say something. His father expected George somehow to make both parties leave here satisfied. It was what his father was known for. It was why he was such a beloved king.

"I don't care what you say," said the man with animal magic, his eyes turning from the king to George. "You're no king of mine, nor prince either. Not if you've no magic to your name."

George knew then that this was impossible. There was no right judgment. And yet he must do something.

Finally, it was the man with the broken teeth who spoke. "Burn him. That's the only way to deal with animal magic, the only way to make sure it does not spread."

George gasped, remembering his mother's pyre, then looked down, to gather control of himself once more.

George looked to his father at last, silently begging for help. And he saw cold terror on his father's face, the same pale, stricken, stiff expression that he had shown the night George's mother had died. The king saw the danger here. He had known of it all along and had never spoken of it.

George, terrified, trembled violently. Then his father, wiping all expression from his face so that he looked like the king once more, stepped forward. He turned to those who stood before him, waiting for judgment, and gave them something else instead.

"Go your way, all of you," he said. "Make your own peace with one another. As king of Kendel, I claim authority over land and animals, water, and even family.

But I claim no authority over magic."

What?

George jerked forward in astonishment. His father refused to make any judgment at all? George could not think of any judgment that would not have been wrong. Not to judge, though, that was more wrong. Surely it was.

"Unbind him," commanded King Davit, waving to his guards.

The man with animal magic cursed at the guards as they undid the ropes. Then he made a terrible sound, like a charging ram, and ran out of the long hall.

The other farmers ran after him.

George sat the rest of the day at his father's feet in that same hall, curled up with his arms wrapped around his legs. He had never felt so small in all his life, or so wrong. He was wrong because he had not made a judgment. He was wrong because he had made his father look weak. He was wrong because he too had the animal magic. And he had not even had the courage to admit it.

That night, long after the line of judgment seekers had departed and George had gone at last to his own chamber, he stood at his window and stared out. Despite the lack of sleep the night before, he was not at all tired.

The dark sky was lit with a terrible red column of flames. It came not from the forest or from the grounds around the castle but from the village. And from that direction came the sounds of shrieking.

A man was dying. A man with animal magic whom George should have saved.

The man was calling out in every tongue he knew. He called to doves, to owls, to sparrows and robins, to jays and hawks. He called to foxes and deer, to wolves and hounds and foxes, to moles and rabbits and bears.

He called for vengeance. Bring down this village. Bring down this castle. Bring down this kingdom, he demanded.

George could see animals here and there stop and listen. But they did not move to respond. They did not go to the man to save him or do what he wished. Because he had only the same animal magic that George did, the magic of speaking. And it would not save his life.

He was alone at the end, as alone as George was, part of two worlds yet part of neither.

At last the man's shrieking stopped. Even then George could not look away from his window. He stood watch until the last sign of the flames had disappeared in the pink rise of the dawn. Then he lay down on top of his bed, his hands folded across his chest.

He realized for the first time that his father had not done what the king should do. Only what perhaps his father should have done.

George wrapped that thought around himself and fell asleep at last.

His father came to see him sometime later that

morning. He lifted George into his arms and whispered to him, "I did not mean it to happen like that. I did not mean to hurt you."

It was a new beginning for both of them, fragile at first but growing stronger. In the years that followed, there were still many times when George spoke to King Davit rather than his father. And many times when the king spoke to the prince. But there were also times when George spoke to his father. And his father told a story now and again about his childhood or his queen.

The one topic they did not touch upon, however, was the animal magic. They spoke around it and past it, as the kingdom seemed to flare up in hunting those with animal magic and punishing them in brutal ways, for it was clear the king would not interfere.

Strangely, as he grew older, George found it far easier for him to forgive his father than to forgive himself for that judgment day. His father had not been the coward then. George had.

CHAPTER EIGHT

A T SEVENTEEN YEARS old, Prince George was still not as tall as his father. In fact he looked more like his dark-eyed, delicate-featured mother than his father in almost every way, yet he was known to lack the love of animals that had defined her. He rode a horse passably well, but not with his mother's passion. He was known to refuse point-blank the gift of any pet, from the grand offer of a green-collared rolluff brought all the way from the southern province of Jolla to the black tom kitten handed him by a grubby peasant girl at the Autumn Moon Festival.

Those who served the prince had never a bad word for him. They spoke easily of his kindness and generosity. Yet if asked, not one of them would have been able to say what color tunic the prince preferred of all those in his wardrobe or what his favorite feast food was.

Since the king had become ill a few months earlier, George had begun to do much to keep the kingdom running smoothly. He worked well with Sir Stephen, who had returned to his post as the king's right-hand man now that George no longer needed a tutor.

George could also manage a well-mannered conversation with the lord general, though the man made no attempt to keep back his disdain for a prince who could not hold his seat on a horse as well as a cavalryman. No one who heard the two speaking together would have any reason to believe that the prince returned the lord general's dislike.

That was the duty of the prince. And the prince always did his duty.

So when King Helm of Sarrey offered a betrothal to his daughter, Beatrice, there was no question what George's answer would be. For nearly all of his seventeen years, there had been an uneasy truce between the two kingdoms following the great war, and now was the chance to resolve that. Though George would not rule as king in Sarrey, for the king's nephew had long been groomed as his heir, still it was an alliance that could not be refused.

In but three days Prince George was to spend a whole week in Sarrey, meeting his betrothed and discussing their marriage with King Helm. He woke up that morning with a vague memory of a dream he had not had for many years, of a bear and a man. Why had it come back now, of all times? His body ached, and he felt entirely unrested. Now was not a good time to worry about animal magic. He had learned to deal with the threat of fevers before they struck, but he did not think he was as happy with his animal magic as his mother had been.

A knock on his door, and George heard a messenger announce that King Davit requested an audience with his son.

"Thank you," said George. "I shall be with him immediately." George sighed. He had hoped that his father was done talking to him about the dangers of dealing with Sarrey and the possibilities of a marriage to a young woman within the kingdom of Kendel.

Apparently not.

George had tried to tell his father again and again that he was perfectly willing to serve Kendel in this and that he had no attachments to other ladies he had already met. There were times when speaking changed nothing and only made duty more difficult.

Gritting his teeth, George put on his best tunic and went to face his king.

At the door at the top of the stairs George was met by four-fingered Jack, one of his father's servants. Years before, Jack had lost the fifth finger of his right hand at the king's command, as a thief. Out of mercy afterward King Davit had offered the man a position in the castle. Sir Stephen had been appalled.

"He will not steal from me again." King Davit had been certain.

When Sir Stephen had asked how he could be sure, King Davit answered simply, "I shall give him whatever he asks me for."

Four-fingered Jack tested the king's resolve once, asking for a golden goblet that had been passed on to the king from his father's father.

"Take it, and gladly," King Davit had said. "What else?"

Four-fingered Jack had been ashamed and tried to give the goblet back, but the king would have none of it.

"It's yours now. As is whatever else you wish for. Is that understood?"

Jack had nodded his head like a boy caught in a fight, and the king never spoke of that time again.

After that, George had watched Jack become the most trustworthy and devoted of King Davit's servants, even through the recent illness. Seeing him now made George feel small again, for he knew he could never fill his father's throne in Jack's eyes.

Four-fingered Jack opened the thickly carved door. When George had stepped inside, Jack closed the door behind him.

"Good morning, Father," George said.

In his bed the king started, then opened his eyes. His face was pale with spots of color high on his cheeks. He was not any better this morning than he had been yesterday, when George had seen him last. Apparently the treatments of the new castle physician, Dr. Gharn, were not helping the king much at all.

"George," said his father, then put out a shaking hand.

George met it with his own.

"You are sure of this?" his father asked.

George stifled his impatience. "Father, I am as sure as I have been from the first. And there is no time left now to change my mind."

The king was silent for a time. When he spoke, it was sudden enough to catch George by surprise. "My son, do you never think about love?"

George stiffened. Love was irrelevant. It was far better that he marry someone he did not love. Then emotion would not cloud his judgment, nor would he have to live through the pain of losing a loved one as he, and his father, already had.

But then the king spoke on in a rather unexpected way. "Do you not think you deserve to be loved as you are?"

George stared at his father. Since the judgment day debacle George had dealt with his animal magic his way and let the king ignore it. George intended that it would never interfere with the running of the kingdom again. It was his own private problem.

"Father—" said George, unsure.

But he felt his wrist encircled by his father's large

hand. "George, listen to me. Will you?"

"Of course, Father." That was his duty, always. And far easier than speaking himself.

"No, listen to me truly. With your heart, not your head." King Davit pointed to George's chest.

George took a deep breath and closed his eyes. "I shall try."

King Davit nodded, coughed, then began. "The day before we were to be married, your mother came to me. She told me that she had changed her mind, that she had decided not to marry me. She gave me back the ring that I had given her, the huge diamond and ruby. She said she should have known when she had seen the ring that it was not for her, a mere stablewoman. She was not worthy of it. And more important, she could not be happy wearing it."

His mother? George had always thought of her as serenely happy and self-assured, despite her animal magic. All the things that he was not.

"I took back the ring, but I told her that she should at least tell me the truth when she said she could not marry me. I deserved that much."

"Yes?" said George. Just thinking about his mother pained him. He had loved her so much and lost her. And it had been at least partly his fault. If only he had been able to do more with his animal magic . . .

But his father could not understand any of that.

"That was when she told me of her gift, of the animal

magic she held within her. I had always known that she had a special touch with the horses in the stables, that hounds were calmer around her, that birds would fly to her arm with a single call from her mouth. There were plenty of signs. Anyone could have seen them. Anyone but a man in love."

"You didn't know until then?" George was too astonished to keep silent. He had never been absolutely sure that his father knew his mother had animal magic.

The king waved a hand negligently, his eyes thickening with tears unshed. "I knew that she was a woman who embodied all I admired. She was kind. She listened to those who spoke to her. She tried to ease pain when she saw it. She did not pay attention to jewels or clothing or titles. She saw clearly to the spirit within. I did not know that it was because she always saw the animal beneath the skin, and so she had come to see humans the same way."

George had not thought of animal magic this way. He had always thought that it set him apart, made him different, dangerous. But perhaps it was not all burden. There could be good that came from it. If he could have been more like his mother, that is.

Still, he could not help turning his head around to be sure that there was no one listening, hidden in the curtains, at the window, or even in his father's wardrobe. If the truth were known, what would happen to him? What would happen to the kingdom? His father had no other sons to pass it to, and George did not even have any first cousins. His father had been an only child. And King Helm of Sarrey was far more likely to take control in a swift war than either of the second cousins George knew of.

Yes, King Helm. That was what he must think of.

"Father, I am no romantic," George said. He did not intend to take any risk in his marriage with Princess Beatrice. If that meant there was no chance that he would find a love like his parents', he could live with that. Better, easier.

"Do you remember nothing of your mother?" the king asked quietly. "Did she not leave any part of herself in you?"

"I remember her," said George, stung.

"Then tell me what she was like. Tell me how you remember her." King Davit lay back on the bed, so that George instantly regretted his angry tone.

Still, it took some time for him to find a memory of his mother. The truth was, he did not think about her often. It was too painful. Finally, he began: "She came to me one night when I was supposed to be asleep. I couldn't, because there was an owl outside my window, hooting his sad life story to all the world. He had lost all his young ones and his mate, and he had decided that he would not eat again, so that he might join them in death."

"She heard the owl too," said King Davit.

George nodded. "She held me in her arms and told me that she was sorry for the owl but that she thought he was very wrong. She said that all living things have an obligation to live as best they can, no matter what pain comes to them. She told me that I had that same obligation and that my gift, the animal magic, made it stronger in me than in others."

George took a breath, then continued. "She said that the animal magic was more than being a prince because any boy might become a prince. Only special boys, she told me, were given the gift of animal magic. Only special boys could speak to both animals and humans and find a way to bridge the gap that lay between the two worlds."

Did he still believe that? That the animal magic was special? His mother seemed naive to him, now. And yet the Kendel she had lived in had been just as prejudiced against those with the magic, just as likely to show violence to them. How could she have been as she was, despite it all?

George continued. "She told me she did not know what it was I was meant to do, but she promised me that I would find it. And that it would be a task only I could succeed at. She said that no matter what happened, I could never turn away from that task."

The bear, George thought suddenly, thinking of the dream from the night before. The bear that had wanted so much from him, more than he could give. But his mother—what would she have said? A promise . . . And someday . . . George was ashamed to think of it.

A long cough shook King Davit's frame. George stood and helped his father to a sitting position. When it was done, the king said, "Thank you." After a moment he added, "I had never heard that story of her."

Her. His mother.

His father and mother had lived such different lives, even as king and queen. Yet they had loved each other so much. It was one of the reasons his father had never married again, despite the urging of his advisers.

"She loved you very much, you know. Perhaps more than she loved me." The king's voice had gone to a whisper.

"No," said George. Never that.

"Well, then—" But before he could finish his sentence, the king began to cough, gently at first, then violently enough that his face turned purplish red.

Panicked, George grabbed the four boxes of medicine on the bedside table and held them closer to his father. They were from Dr. Gharn, whom George had disliked since he arrived several months ago. All his medicine had done nothing to prevent the king from sliding into a worse and worse illness, but at least he had tried. The other castle physicians had left when the king began to feel ill, saying they could see nothing to be done.

After a moment the king chose the elixir in the black

bottle and drank down a sip, then another, until gradually his breathing grew normal once more.

George had no special love for Dr. Gharn. The man
was proud, unwilling to speak, and dressed in the
stiffest, most formal attire—worse than the most
pompous noble of his father's court. He also gave off a
strange scent—no doubt from all his medicine making—
that made everyone keep away from him as much as
they could. And his voice was high and false sounding.

Yet he was the only hope the king had.

"You will think about what I have said?" the king
asked at last. He was lying back on the bed, his hands
outstretched, utterly motionless except for the movement of his lips.

"Yes, Father," said George. In fact, as George took
his leave, he found that he could not stop thinking about
it. About his mother and how much she had loved his
father. And George. George could never hope to be as
she had been. Not as good, or as brave, or as loving.

Dr. Gharn was forgotten entirely. The heart had
never been something that could be healed with an
elixir.

Chapter Nine

"Your Highness, have you found a betrothal gift for Princess Beatrice yet?"

Sir Stephen, his face as long and thin as always, caught George on the way downstairs.

Once years ago George had asked his father why Sir Stephen never laughed. The king had gone very still, then said simply, "If he is sober, he has good reason for it, George." And no more than that.

"No," George said. The truth was, he had no idea what to choose.

"There is a merchant in town who has a wide variety of pretty things. I have arranged for her to come to the meeting chamber if you'd like to see a sampling."

"Thank you, Sir Stephen," said George, with relief. This was why Sir Stephen had been one of his father's most valued advisers for so many years. How had the king ever managed to do without him for all those years he served as George's tutor? Or had Sir Stephen simply done double duty?

When they got to the meeting chamber, however, the merchant had not yet arrived. As they waited, Sir Stephen asked George, "Are you nervous about the marriage? It would be quite understandable if you were."

George's chin went up, and suddenly he found himself blurting out, "And what do you know about marriage?"

Sir Stephen's hand dropped, and his body went stiff. "I was to marry a woman once," he said. His eyes stared at some place far beyond George's head, just past his ears.

"Oh?" George breathed. This was a day for revelations, it seemed. He had never suspected such a thing in all the years he had known Sir Stephen.

"Her name was Elsbeth. She was small and lovely, like a pink shell from the seashore. She was killed quite accidentally by a group of soldiers from Sarrey. It was not meant to be the beginnings of a battle, I don't believe, though it became one afterward. One of the last battles of the great war, in fact. There were cannon . . . and—" Sir Stephen's voice had gone hollow.

George's hand lifted and fell away again. It seemed an insult to imply that anything so small as a touch could stop the raw feeling in Sir Stephen's suddenly dark and haunted eyes.

"Her father was a great healer. If only he were here

for King Davit, I am sure he would have found a cure by now. He was known far and wide for his knowledge and his kindness. He would always set his price at well below what could be paid. But he was never seen after Elsbeth died. I think he could not stand the grief."

Sir Stephen was staring into the distance.

"I am sorry," George said. He was surprised to find his voice hoarse.

Sir Stephen shook his head. "I should not have spoken of such a personal topic, my prince."

The merchant woman came in now and began by taking out of her cart an astonishing array of scarves, skirts, and gowns all in purest silk. George's eye was caught by the red, but he did not know if such a gift was too personal. He had never met Princess Beatrice. How was he to guess what color she would prefer? Or if she liked silk gowns or scarves at all?

He shook his head, and the merchant went out to get more.

George looked at Sir Stephen, thinking he might offer some assistance. But Sir Stephen said nothing.

The merchant woman brought in jewelry next, gaudy baubles and true gems simply set. George looked at each one, tiring more quickly than he had imagined. Couldn't he send the woman directly to Princess Beatrice, tell her to pick out what she liked, and have the woman send him the bill? Then he would be sure to get something that Beatrice liked.

George knew the betrothal gift was not meant merely to please the receiver but also to tell something about the giver. He looked through the jewelry again. He liked a set of blue beads, small and luminescent like pearls. They were not costly, and he was afraid Princess Beatrice might think he was cheap.

"Is there anything else?" he asked.

The merchant woman shrugged and took out a small bag. She had a wizened face, but she did not move like an old woman. Her fingers were spotted with sun, and her mouth was puckered, but George had not heard her speak a word since she began.

"My husband makes these himself," said the merchant woman slowly. She looked at George, as if daring him to laugh at her or tell her to be quiet and remember her place.

George only stared, intrigued by the small leather bag and what it might hold.

"He lost his legs in the war and can't see too good, but he has a feel for these." She laid out a series of small blown-glass figures in startlingly fine workmanship and color. There was a small, fierce-looking bear that made George's heart skip a beat, a hummingbird just the size of a real one, and a miniature hound that seemed to be running, its head up, its teeth showing in a wild grin, its eyes wide and blazing.

The hound was not at all like George's childhood pet. But there was something, not so much in the shape of its body as in the fierce expression of its face, that reminded George of what Teeth had been, at the very beginning. This was a true wild hound. And it was perfect.

George reached out a hand. "May I?" he asked. His hand trembled in fear of revealing too much of himself by his interest. But he could not resist. He was used to denying himself the kennels and the stables and the creatures all over the castle. But this he had not been prepared for.

The merchant woman gave it over. "My husband used to have a hound, but he sent it out to the woods after the war. Said the hound couldn't be expected to stay home with him all day, that it deserved to live its own life. This is the only glass he's made of it, though. Never have found anyone to show an interest in it. Mostly they shiver and say it looks too fierce and real."

"It is fierce and real," said George. It weighed almost nothing in his hand, but when he held it up to the light, some trick of the color in the glass made it seem as though it were suddenly moving.

"Cost you too much, it will. But I can't sell anything of his for the bit of the glass. He puts too much of himself into them. He'd feel it an insult, he would."

"Of course," murmured George. How could any price be enough for this perfect thing? He looked at it again, astonished at the detail. The long, sharp jaws, the sleek skin on the back, the shortened tail.

The merchant woman named a sum that made Sir Stephen let out an audible breath.

Would Sir Stephen try to tell George it would not be prudent?

"I'll take it," said George swiftly. "And . . . the blue beads." The hound was for himself, for he could not imagine giving such a personal gift to a woman he did not know. Nor would he risk the chance of it revealing his true weakness to her.

But after Sir Stephen had paid the merchant woman and she took her things away with her, he turned to George. "Princess Beatrice is rumored to have a wild hound, black and short-haired, with sharp jaws and a sleek coat. Did you know that?"

George shook his head and was surprised to find himself suddenly warm at the thought of the woman he was to marry. A hound? A woman who loved animals? Might there be something between them after all?

"They say she will not go anywhere without it. That she even sleeps with it in her own bed." Sir Stephen went on.

Suddenly all hope dropped from George. If she slept with the hound, it was surely nothing more than a trained pet. And he already knew what he felt about pets and those who made them. That was nothing akin to animal magic.

"I think you have tried to know as little of her as possible," said Sir Stephen after a moment.

George answered sharply. "What difference would knowing her make? I must marry her no matter what she is like."

Sir Stephen nodded slowly. "And so you fear to hate her, to begin with. As much as you fear to love her, I think."

Love her? But George knew now that was impossible. Not a woman who kept a wild hound as a pet.

Suddenly he wished that Sir Stephen had not told him that, had kept him in ignorance for just a little longer. And he wished most of all that he had never seen that tiny glass hound that looked so much like the wild creature that had so quickly died in a young pup's face.

Teeth had died just last year. The houndmaster had come to George to tell him of it, to ask if George wished anything in particular to be done with the body.

At first George had refused and sent the man away. But afterward he had gone back and begged for the body, then taken it to the moat and buried it with the other creatures he had lost over the years. And he wept for his hound, lost so many years ago, never to be regained.

CHAPTER TEN

TWO DAYS LATER George was ready to leave for Sarrey. In uniforms of crisp silver and blue the eight Sarrey guards who were to escort him had arrived on perfectly matched gray horses. They were to ride ahead of the carriage, leading the way. George's smaller group of four Kendel guards, in black and green, was stationed behind.

The lord general had just walked away, after a long lecture to the guards on the care of the horses. To George, the lord general had said nothing, though he had acknowledged him with a small nod of the head, the very least he could have done to the prince of the kingdom.

The four guards themselves were much less austere. One of them, with sandy hair and blue eyes, came forward as George stepped into the carriage. His young face looked uneasy. "Your Highness? I do not trust these guards. What if they mean you harm? They outnumber us two to one."

The man was overly cautious, but George appreciated it. Though the war with Sarrey had officially been over for years, border skirmishes occurred far too often, and the general sentiment among the people was that the whole kingdom was a danger to Kendel. In fact Sarrey merchants and travelers were treated with such suspicion that they complained frequently, both to their own king and to King Davit.

They were not subjected to the violence reserved for those with animal magic, George noted. But being spat at in the street, cursed at by old women, and refused even the most innocuous of flirtatious encounters with the women of Kendel was surely bothersome. As for the uniform of Sarrey, it was used in plays and other representations of the war, and its colors signaled danger and death.

But this guard was just doing his duty, reporting danger when he felt it. He was not the only one who would have to change his attitude about Sarrey. Could George simply make laws that demanded such a change? Or was it a matter of waiting for a second generation to rise, one that had not seen the horrors of war?

Well, George would have to start here and now. With this guard.

"Your name?" George asked him directly. He had probably seen the man a dozen times before yet did not know anything about him. King Davit would no doubt have known half the man's life history already.

"Henry."

George took Henry's hand firmly in his own and looked into his eyes. This had to be done delicately, making sure this Henry knew George did not think him a fool. He tried to think how his father would do it.

"Thank you, Henry, for your concern. It is a comfort to know I am so well guarded. I will make sure to praise you when next I speak to the lord general. But for now I think there is no need to worry."

Henry looked back to the Sarrey guards once more, then nodded and moved away.

With a quick hand out the window George signaled that he was ready to leave, and the carriage lurched forward and began its long journey on the best (but still very bumpy) road in the kingdom. The inside was so stifling that over the next several hours George wished more than once he were outside. At least then he could feel the wind in his hair, the smell of the spring.

But of course he could not. He was a prince, and why take a risk?

Truly, he should let himself enjoy this small piece of time to himself. It would not last long. He let his head lull forward on his chest and tried to nap, but he found he could not stop thinking about Sir Stephen's description of Princess Beatrice and her hound. He took the glass hound out of the pouch around his neck and stared at it again.

Why had he been so drawn to this piece? And why had he brought it on this journey? He could have left it at home if he truly did not intend to give it to Princess Beatrice. It would be madness to let her have any reason to be suspicious of him. And yet here it was.

Strange.

He almost dropped and shattered the tiny hound when there was a shout and the carriage lurched abruptly to a halt.

George tried to put his head out the window but was met immediately by Henry. "Stay here, Your Highness. Please, for your own safety."

"What is going on?" George demanded. He could hear more than one voice, and Henry's horse danced nervously.

"I don't know, Your Highness. My responsibility is to keep you safe. The lord general told me he'd have my sword arm if anything happened to you."

There were angry voices shouting and someone weeping, George was sure of it. A man.

"Go find out what is happening," George ordered Henry.

"Your Highness, I can't —" There was a flicker of fear in Henry's eyes, quickly suppressed.

"Then I'll go myself," said George. He reached for the door of the carriage.

"Your Highness, please!" Suddenly white-faced, Henry gestured the prince back into the carriage. "I will go if you promise to stay here," he said.

But once Henry was gone, George could not bear to remain in the carriage alone. He opened the door and climbed down the steps, then moved toward the noise and the tightly knit circle of men.

It was when George heard the language of horses from what had to be a human tongue that he stopped.

His neck went cold with sweat, and his legs trembled. He felt as if he were twelve again, in that judgment hall with a thousand eyes staring at him. And then it was as if he could smell that same fire of human flesh—

It will not happen again, George told himself firmly.

"Your Highness." Henry appeared. "Please, there is danger here. You should go back."

"Step aside," George said, poking his finger into the back of the guard ahead of him, one of Sarrey's, in silver and blue.

The guard turned, a snarl on his face, then realized who George was. "Your Highness," he said stiffly, "this does not concern you."

In fact George realized, as he looked over the countryside, that he was no longer in Kendel. He no longer had the authority to make his wishes law here.

"It has stopped my journey," George said, taking a different tack. "So what is this about? Who is this man you have caught here?" His words were calm; his voice was unshaking. He was not twelve years old anymore, no matter how he felt inside. And he had the right as a guest of the king of Sarrey to ask a question.

"He had been brought here to be punished but nearly escaped. He has the animal magic—" A long pause, and then the guard added the obligatory "Your Highness."

"May I see him?" George asked. And then, though he hated it, he said, "I am curious about them. My father has always kept me so protected in the castle, away from any danger. I have never seen one with the animal magic before. It would be . . . instructive, I think."

The guard shrugged, then called out to the others. They pulled back from their quarry, and George saw a man who looked to be his own age, though emaciated and terribly scarred.

"Help me, help me," the man begged of the horses closest to him.

The horses shied, but they did not move toward him. They did not know him and had little reason to risk themselves to help him.

"Who is the leader here?" George asked loudly.

"I am," said the burliest of the men.

"And how is it that you know this man has animal magic?" asked George, thinking fast. He had an idea of how to save this man, and though they had never met before, it seemed of vital importance to him. A chance, perhaps, to make amends for what had happened on that judgment day long ago. "Perhaps you have the animal magic yourself?"

"Me?" The man spat on the ground. "Of course I don't." He looked at the men who were with him. "They know I don't have it. Ask them, ask them," he said.

George did nothing of the sort. He sought out one of the other men, the tallest one, with boils on his face. "And you? You understand animal language too?"

The man with boils stepped back, unsure. "You hear him babbling? What else is he doing, then, if not speaking to the animals?"

"Perhaps he's mad," said George. "Or perhaps he's speaking some language you don't understand. A human language. There is more than one, you know." Why should George make this man look like a fool? Because he was a fool.

"But the animals move when he talks to them," said the man with boils.

A younger man behind him nodded. "They do," he said.

George turned to the younger man, heart pounding as he realized what he must do. "And do I have the magic too?" he asked boldly. "If the horse moves when I babble, will that be proof against me as well?"

Before he received an answer, George turned to the nearest horse and took hold of its bridle. Then he said loudly in the language of the horses, "Move to the right, in a circle. Do it now, or there's a whip on your side!"

The horse moved as he had said.

There was a gasp somewhere behind George, but he

did not dare pay it any attention.

Bland faced still, playing the game, he turned back to the burly man. "You see?" he asked. "Now, will you be telling me that I have the animal magic too? The prince of Kendel and the man betrothed to your own princess Beatrice?"

George saw several eyes turn away from him, and more than one man took a step backward.

The burly man licked his lips, and his expression turned sour. "Well, we might have been wrong then," he said. He let his head drop.

A couple of the men around him stepped back.

George had done it. He'd saved the man. This time. He wanted to fall to the ground and enjoy his moment of redemption. But he had no chance.

One of the guards from Sarrey came forward and shoved the burly man so that he stumbled and fell. "Get up and get out of the way, all of you!" roared the guard. When the other men had fled, he turned toward the man with animal magic.

"You too. Get out of here, and don't let us see or hear of you ever again, do you understand?"

The man gibbered a moment, then loped away, limping hard on his left side, not turning back to question the sudden reprieve.

George went back to the carriage and let himself triumph silently. But afterward, as the carriage began moving again, and he watched the man accused of animal magic stumble slowly away, George realized he had done very little. He had saved the man's life for a time, but he would still be an outcast to any village or town he entered. He could hide his true nature and live as George did, without friends or intimacy of any kind. Or he could let himself live his own way and face death once more in a few more weeks, a few months, or even years. But peace and happiness would always be denied him.

As they were to George.

George had used his animal magic to prove he had no animal magic. Such hypocrisy. How could he be respected? Most of all, how could he rule over both those with animal magic and those without it if he did not admit the truth?

His father's war was over, but that day George sensed that a new war was beginning. This one would be his own.

CHAPTER ELEVEN

A BAD HEADACHE BEGAN to tug at George that evening in the carriage. He thought it might be the aftereffect of the stressful situation or the lack of fresh air and the closeness of the carriage.

To combat the discomfort, George ordered the windows open and the curtains closed. He put his hands to his ears to keep all noise out, and he laid out a very large pillow to cushion the jolting stops in the road.

But the headache was relentless, and it was not long before George admitted to himself that this was no ordinary headache, to be cured with tea and sleep. This was a magical headache, one that would lead to a raging fever if it was not treated soon.

George had been willfully neglecting his magic and had known he was pressing his time limit. He kept thinking that he would have time to go into the woods to relieve it or at least spend some time in the stables. But he had been so busy. There had been so much to do, and his father's poor health always worrying at him added to his duties. Perhaps there had even been some of the stubbornness that his mother must have shared with her horses. He had not wanted to admit that he needed animals or their magic.

Idiocy.

As if he had not proved this to himself time and time again. There was no escaping the demands of the animal magic. Why would he try such a thing at a time like this?

The headache would only get worse the longer he spent indoors. After that the fever. Perhaps then convulsions. At least there were stories that said such things happened to those with animal magic.

What could he do now? Could he find a way to sneak out to a forest near the castle here in Sarrey? It was the best he could hope for.

He rubbed at his head for the remainder of the miserable journey, and then the carriage stopped at last. Warily he stared at the lights of the castle courtyard all around them. It was hours past dark now, and he sincerely hoped that Princess Beatrice was long in bed. He did not trust himself to speak to her for the first time tonight, for fear he would growl at her—and not necessarily in any human language.

Stumbling out of the carriage, George was caught by an arm that wrapped around his chest, holding him upright.

"I'll make sure you get inside to your chambers, Your Highness," said Henry's calm voice.

Shaking with the effects of the headache, George let him.

They made their way upstairs, through a corridor, and up another set of stairs, to a large and drafty chamber with a bed twice as soft as George thought he could possibly sleep in. This was what King Helm thought of the prince of Kendel, George thought. If he had not been so ill, perhaps it would have made him angry.

George looked at Henry, wondering why the guard had not yet left him on his own. Was he trying to find favor with the prince, perhaps even hoping to be appointed some kind of valet? It would not happen, for George had always hated keeping servants too close to him. He feared what they would learn about him and so had always managed alone.

"You may go, Henry," he said, knowing that he must sound supercilious and ungrateful.

Henry went.

George stared around the huge chamber, decorated in light shades of blue and purple—not quite feminine but not very masculine either. No doubt it was King Helm's idea of a little joke. George would try not to give any idea he had noticed it.

His chests had been brought in already, somehow even before he himself had arrived. He considered briefly the thought of changing into his bedclothes, then gave it up. He pushed the voluminous blankets aside as best he could and fell asleep.

His rest was far from peaceful. He dreamed of a new animal, a huge wolflike creature that came to his room and watched him while he slept. When he opened his eyes, his headache was suddenly so loud that it felt as if it would take his head off. He did not know if he could stave it off another minute, let alone another day. And once the fever struck, he would be that much more vulnerable.

There was a roaring fire in the hearth, despite the warmth of the spring morning. Another dig from King Helm at the strength of Kendel's prince?

He got out of his bed and, breathing shallowly, careened toward the window. He opened it, took several deep breaths, and began to feel a little better. A very little.

He stared at his unopened trunks, and knew he could not face anything so human right now. He needed to be outside, with the animals. It was so early he might be able to escape unnoticed. At least he hoped so.

He did not think that King Helm would have planned any important meetings for this first day, certainly not at this hour. If he thought George was so weak as to need a fire, then he would surely give him time to recover from his journey. No one would miss him if he went out for a long walk.

When George reached the bottom of the stairs, he

saw a maidservant laden with towels. Turning his head, he tried to look inconspicuous. Why should she imagine that a prince would appear in rumpled clothes at this hour of the morning? In any case, she did not look at him twice.

George had little trouble finding his way to the kitchen and out to the yard beyond. He walked for several yards, to make sure that no one would think he was running away. Then he let himself go. He felt his blood pumping freely, the ground pounding against his bare feet, and the stretch of muscles that had been too long kept tightly fettered.

He stopped short at the sight of a woman with streaming red hair coming toward the castle with a wild hound at her side. If George was not mistaken, it was the same wild hound he had dreamed about the night before.

But who was the woman? Her face wore a strangely distant expression. There was some old hurt in her, but from the way she held her head, she seemed used to pride. Her clothing was as rumpled as George's. The dress was cut with feminine frills that seemed entirely out of place on her. Yet she was beautiful, in a sharp and startling way.

He stared at her as she came closer.

She stopped when she came to him, then stared back unabashedly. "Prince George," she said. There was no warmth in her voice.

How had she guessed who he was?

Then it came to him, and he flushed with embarrassment.

"Princess Beatrice," he said with a nod. How could it have taken him so long to recognize her? The hound should have been a giveaway from the first moment. But the dream had confused him. The wolfish hound in his dream had been no pet.

The woman looked down at her hound, as if to see herself in those deep brown eyes. Then she nodded and said, "Yes. I am Princess Beatrice."

She was as tall as George, long and lean and muscular, with a regal neck and calloused tapering fingers. Her skin was badly freckled, but it complemented her flame red hair perfectly, and her hazel eyes shone up at him.

She spoke baldly. "You are not what I expected."

What had she been told of him? Not likely flattering, considering the accommodations in his bedchamber.

But then again, had the descriptions he had heard of her been any better?

They stared at each other some more. The hound came forward and sniffed at George's leg, then circled it gently, testing.

George bent down and offered his hand. The hound rubbed her nose over it, then licked at the places between George's fingers. When she was done, she stepped back to her place at her mistress's side.

George could not help staring at the hound for a moment, as long as he had looked at Beatrice — or longer. She had a look of wildness that was unmistakable. Her eyes were dark and deep. Her nose was long and sharp; her jaw was sharply cut underneath. Her hair was short and so black it seemed to glow in the snatches of sunlight that hit her. Her legs were long and lean, agile and steady. George wished right then that he could go running a race with her.

The headache that had been with him since the night before dulled a bit just at the sight of her, and he itched to try out the language he had learned from his pup. But of course he could not.

How was it possible for Princess Beatrice to keep a hound so close to her yet never tame it?

Or was he wrong? Was the hound no more than any other hound?

He turned his eyes back to the princess, suddenly realizing she would likely be offended by his long perusal of her hound instead of herself. But he could see no sign of disapproval or envy in her eyes. Another surprise in her, that lack of vanity. She was as captivated by her hound's beauty as George was, it seemed.

Yet she did not have the animal magic. For some reason, George was instantly sure of that. She was too open about her bond to her hound. No one who truly feared discovery could be like that, in either Kendel or Sarrey. And there was something else, something in the air that

111

George was sure he would have felt had she had the animal magic. He had felt it when his mother had been with him. And the man on the journey here: George had felt it then too. A similarity. A shared appreciation. A joined sensory experience.

She did not have it.

"Shall I walk you back to the palace?" he asked, pushing away the strangely decreasing headache and the demands it implied. He held out his arm.

Again, the princess looked down at the hound. Then she nodded. "If you wish it," she said.

George felt her hand rest on his. It was warm and slightly moist with her exertions in the woods, whatever they were. She did not appear to have gone out hunting. And if she did not speak with animals, then why was she here at this hour of the day—alone?

"Do you take walks often outside the castle?" asked George.

"Every day," said the princess coolly. "It is good exercise," she added after a moment.

"Yes." George was annoyed to think that he was reduced to these inanities. Yet what else could he say? This princess was not at all as he had expected her to be.

"Is that why you came out as well?"

"Yes, yes, of course," said George. Did he sound as much like an idiot as he felt? *Focus on the hound,* he told himself.

"Will you tell me your hound's name?" he tried. "She

112

is a wonderful creature."

"Her name is Marit," said Beatrice.

"Marit." George nodded. "And how long have you had her?"

"Had her?" echoed Beatrice distastefully. "We met five years ago, in the woods. We have been together ever since."

That would be a story worth hearing, thought George. But they had reached the outer courtyard that led to the kitchen. George moved toward the kitchen. When he reached the archway that led inside, he turned back and found Beatrice and the hound gone without a trace.

They had met in the woods, he thought, turning the words over in his mind as he wondered at the nearly dissipated headache. As if she were speaking of another person and not an animal at all.

Chapter Twelve

GEORGE NURSED HIS headache the rest of the day, but it did not go away. It tugged at George as if in waves. Always before it had grown worse and worse, until he could not bear it any longer. But now it was conquerable, and George took some pride in his own strength that he could do that. Perhaps as he grew older, the magic could be tamed. George hoped for that, though to do it, he had to push his mother's death out of his mind.

He spent the afternoon listening to the wealthy merchants at court complain about the taxes imposed on goods traded from Sarrey to Kendel's merchants. Sir Stephen would be better at this, he knew. In the end George agreed to take down some names and accept further communication on the subject. It seemed no more was required. Later, he had a moment to himself in his chamber, opening the window to breathe fresh air and wincing as he did so because the headache had come back full force.

George had not seen a glimpse of King Helm himself, nor had he been officially introduced to his bride-to-be. He puzzled over this, wondering if he should come to any conclusion on the long-term effects of this marriage. Surely King Helm would not marry his daughter away for nothing.

A knock at his door.

George rubbed his temples, put on a pleasant expression, and went down to dinner.

He saw Beatrice first, standing as he entered the dining hall and greeting him with a few formal words, her hound close by her side. She wore a blue gown that should have made her face come alive but instead emphasized her distant expression. Her movements seemed uncomfortable, and it was impossible to guess at what lay beneath the obvious expression of love for her hound, which anyone could see.

King Helm was a hulking man, with hair and a beard streaked with gray and a hint of what might once have been red, like Beatrice's. He wore a heavy gold crown and seemed too large for the table. George had the impression that he would have been happier to eat with his soldiers in the woods than here.

How would it have been for Beatrice to grow up with such a man for a father? George knew her mother had been dead since her birth, and King Helm had remarried twice in an attempt to get an heir. Both those women had died in childbirth along with their infant sons. Now Beatrice was the only heir remaining to King Helm, yet the way they sat together reminded George of the way things had once been with his father.

The entire dinner was spent in small talk, introducing George to various nobles of Sarrey. King Helm did not mention his daughter or invite her to speak. Indeed it was as if Beatrice herself were invisible. No, worse than that. It was as if she were a painting of a woman, meant to be seen and admired, but no more.

When the food was cleared, King Helm clapped his hands for wine, turned to George, and toasted him. "To Prince George and to Kendel."

George drank. Then it was his turn to offer a toast. He raised his glass and gestured to Beatrice. "To Princess Beatrice," he said stoutly.

King Helm laughed aloud.

Beatrice stared down at her untouched glass.

And George was left wondering how anyone could believe that Beatrice was not worthy of a toast.

As if in explanation, King Helm told George a story about Beatrice when she was three years old. "She was a spry little thing," he said, his eyes bright with amusement.

George tensed at the thought that Beatrice would be hurt once more. But this was not his court. He had no power here.

"I told her one day I was going out hunting." King Helm patted his stomach, and there were flickers of laughter about the hall. George could only guess that the courtiers were used to this treatment of the princess and knew that the king would reward them for their enjoyment.

A nod to Beatrice, who held absolutely still. "She said she would come with me. She insisted on it. She stamped her little foot at me."

He pointed down to her toes as if she were a child yet.

Then he straightened his shoulders. "But I sent her back to the nursery, where she belonged, and told her to play with her dolls instead. As everyone knows, a female on a hunt is a distraction at the best and bad luck at the worst."

Murmurs of agreement.

Which explained why Beatrice went out into the woods with her hound alone, George thought. She looked now as though she had gone to some other place inside herself, a place where she could not hear her father's words and thus could not be hurt by them. George wondered how often she was forced to go to that place.

"Her mother was so beautiful, you know." King Helm went on. "None of my other queens quite matched her in looks. Beatrice is a bit like her, about the eyes." But clearly he was displeased about the rest of her.

Did King Helm not see how much she was like him?

It seemed that she was rejected for any sign of feminin-ity yet also rejected for not showing enough femininity. How could she win?

"Well, what about tomorrow? Shall we have a hunt? If you are recovered from your journey, that is?" asked King Helm.

George unclenched his jaw and found his headache had become worse than ever. He had to get to the woods. The king's hunt was an opportunity, if not ideal. There would be a good chance he could at least play the role of the foolish prince and get himself lost. It seemed that King Helm hardly expected any different from him.

"Yes, thank you," George said automatically.

"Perhaps we'll find another man-beast," said King Helm jovially, looking around his courtiers for support. They showed it by hammering their fists on the table.

When the sound died down, King Helm turned to George and spoke as though George had come from a different world entirely, where animal magic had never been heard of.

"Now and again beasts come out of the great forest. Man-beasts we call them if they try to meet our eyes. For there are those who claim that it is only a man trans-formed to a beast with his own magic who does such a thing."

George was pierced with the thought of the bear he had seen so many years before. "And you kill such beasts?" he asked, horrified.

"Of course. It is a service, really. Put them out of their misery, hey?" said the king.

"But—" George stopped himself. Now was not the time. And King Helm was definitely not the man to ask.

Then George saw that Beatrice was watching him. Had he already revealed himself? But Beatrice was perhaps the last person in the hall who would pass on any suspicions to her father. And she did not look disgusted at all. Perhaps she was thinking of something else entirely.

"When we return, we shall have a marvelous feast. Beatrice will dance at it, won't she, good girl?"

Beatrice's mouth tightened. That was all the acknowledgment she gave her father's question.

"Ah, a quiet woman. What else could any man wish for in a bride?" said King Helm with a broad smile.

George could think of a number of things. A woman who had thoughts worth sharing, for one. But if one never asked, then one would never know if it was possible, would one?

What a kingdom.

What a king.

And what a princess.

Chapter Thirteen

FINALLY, IT WAS TIME for George to offer his gifts to King Helm and to Princess Beatrice.

George had the gifts brought in, then went to each box and presented them in the order that he and Sir Stephen had agreed upon.

King Helm accepted the delicately fashioned gold star and the precious gems. He sent the bottles of wine immediately to the castle kitchen, to be stored in the basement with his already outstanding collection. It was only the knife that he seemed to appreciate personally. He took it out of its sheath and admired the shine in the dimming light of the hall, then brought the blade down against one hand and sliced through the upper layer of skin so expertly that no drop of blood was drawn.

"A fine blade, that is," he said, looking at George with approval.

Then the knife was put away, and it was time for Beatrice's gifts.

George bowed before Beatrice as King Helm drummed his hands on the armrests of his throne in impatience. The beads came out, and Beatrice accepted them with a small murmur of thanks. She did not look at George.

Just as she did not look at her father.

She could not think him like her father, though!

But George realized in that moment he had given her a gift for a woman, a bauble that would mean nothing to her. A pretty thing, to be sure, but one to be worn with gowns of blue that were only a burden to her.

But how to make her see him true?

To show himself true.

It was that simple. And that difficult.

The headache throbbed behind George's eyes, and he felt a tremor of heat down his arm. But he forced his hand to feel inside his jacket for the leather pouch tied around his neck. With one swift movement, he broke the tie, then held out the pouch to Beatrice.

"For you, Princess Beatrice," George said with a bow. His hands were shaking, and he thought of the other things he could have bought her. Jewels. Fur.

But no, he could not. It was not what he was.

Beatrice's hands came up in a cupping shape. She showed no curiosity as she opened the leather pouch and put her hand inside. At last she pulled out the tiny, delicate object within.

"A glass hound," she said in such a muted tone that George still had no idea what she thought of it.

Then Marit danced to get a look, and Beatrice held it lower. Marit sniffed at the glass image, and her eyes went to George.

"Hold it up to the light," George said, his voice hoarse.

Beatrice did as he asked, and suddenly the hall swam in colors, in glints that turned and shook as Beatrice's own hand did. The glass hound not only had come alive but made the whole hall breathe with it.

"A glass hound that moves in its own way, with beauty to match a real hound's grace," said George. He stared at Beatrice, hoping for some sign of—what? She seemed so used to covering her emotions that George was not sure he could tell if she was pleased or not.

"Thank you," she said, and put the hound away. Her hands moved rapidly, and she did not meet George's eyes afterward.

Did she like it? Did she hate it?

It was Marit that answered his unspoken question, however. The hound came close to George to wrap herself around his leg once more, this time without pushing but with a simple comforting touch.

And George had to be content with that. At least it showed that someone knew he was not a man like Beatrice's father.

King Helm clapped his hands, and a minstrel came in then to sing ballads. At home in his father's court, George excused himself from such displays. But he could not do it here. He had to listen.

The minstrel began with the tale of a Sarrey maid who fell into the sea and then fell deeper still, to the court of the sea monster. She married the sea monster and gave him many children, but they all were sea creatures, none human like her. And so she pined for her world above the water, until at last she dared escape. She was found dead on the shore of her own kingdom the next day, a smile wide across her face.

Not a particularly encouraging story with which to begin a marriage, George thought.

The next tale had a happier ending, about two brothers who lived on the very edges of two different kingdoms. When war between the kingdoms was announced, both brothers laid down their plows and took up swords in defense of their lands. They were fortunate for many years, never facing each other directly across a battlefield. Then came the day the brothers had always dreaded, when they stood on the same field, on different sides of two armies. But the two could not even bring their swords to bear, and finally, when the battle was over, they alone were left alive. They returned to their fields, and when the story was known, the kingdoms swore that they would be as close as the two brothers were and never fight again.

George thought King Helm must have encouraged this story to be told, as a reminder of the real purpose of the marriage between George and Beatrice: to ensure that no war such as that one would ever be fought again.

The third tale, to George's surprise, was that of King Richon and the wild man, which the minstrel sang as George had always heard it, with one exception. In the end the wild man promised King Richon he would one day find a woman who would love him as he was, and then all that he had lost would be restored.

George thought the minstrel must have added this himself, but when he asked the man privately, he insisted it was the way the tale was always told in Sarrey. He was so vehement, in fact, that George believed him and wondered how this same story was told in other kingdoms. And what the differences might mean.

At last it was time to retire. George kept himself upright with great difficulty as he made his way back to the stuffy and ornately decorated bedchamber, then let himself slide onto his oversoft bed with a sigh. The headache raged worse than ever. He was exhausted, but he did not know if he would be able to sleep. He longed to sneak out again but doubted his ability to get outside without being seen, in a castle he was so unfamiliar with, fighting both the headache and fatigue.

No, he would have to wait for the hunt tomorrow.

Closing his eyes, he fell in and out of dreams until he

found himself in one that was like both his dream of the bear from childhood and the dream of the wolfish hound from the night before. It felt as real as his waking life, yet he knew it was a dream because he was nowhere in the dream himself.

He could see Princess Beatrice in what must be her own bedchamber. "He is not diseased," he heard the princess say, with a strange approbation, "and he does not seem unkind."

After a long silence she added, "How can I believe he chose the gift himself? It was an adviser, I think, who chose everything. That man I would like to know. He knows animals as few do. He sees us as living, thinking beings, not beasts to be killed in a hunt. He must, or he would not have chosen a gift like that one, so wild and free."

George felt a strange satisfaction in this, but it did not last long.

For the princess went on, brutally practical. "But what does it matter? A marriage is a marriage, and I do not care who it is with, not now. If it were you he were to have, I would be more cautious. I would look inside his jaw to see what his teeth have to say about him. And then I would smell him."

She turned and looked directly at George, who tried to wake from the dream, to get away from the determination there. But he could not move, not yet.

"You have smelled him. What does he smell of to

you? Might he be a man we could trust? Someday?"

And then George woke up, his head ringing, but not with the force of the night before. It was early morning yet, just barely dawn, and all hope of sleep had fled. He could go down to the kitchen to ask for food, but the headache had killed his appetite. Also, he did not relish the strained and curious company of the castle servants. Instead, he dressed himself and sat before the embers of the fire, wondering what the princess considered entrusting him with. He did not for a moment doubt that the dream was true, only whether or not he could tell his own truth in turn.

CHAPTER FOURTEEN

S OMEHOW GEORGE STILL managed to be late to the hunt. He stopped to grab a half loaf of bread and some apples in the kitchen and was slowed by the sight of a tomcat chasing a mouse. He wanted desperately to do something to help. He heard the mouse's calls for help and saw the mouse's eyes turn on him just before the end.

"My children," she said with her dying breath.

George could not help trying to track them down. He searched in every corner he could find, whispering in mouse language for "children, hungry children." He found two nests that seemed to be full of babies and empty of a mother. He gave them a portion of the bread he had and hoped he'd done enough. Then, with only a couple of bites of bread in his stomach, he went out to where he thought the stables were, to find he'd gone in entirely the wrong direction and had to run back through the castle at a very undignified pace.

By the time he arrived at the proper place, his pounding headache had made his eyes twitch and water so he could hardly see. Luckily, Henry had a horse waiting for him, already saddled. The horse was an extremely gentle mare, more evidence of King Helm's opinion of him. In another situation he might have been glad of it; as it was, this gentle mare would make it much more difficult for anyone to believe a story of his losing control of his horse.

"Your Highness," said Henry. He pointed back toward the castle gate.

George turned and saw Beatrice and Marit standing together, as if to see them off on the hunt. George waved, and after a moment Beatrice nodded to him.

"There is something odd about that hound," said Henry under his breath.

George dared not agree, so he pretended not to have heard at all. Henry did not repeat himself.

The other hunters, perhaps twenty of them, were already mounted, including King Helm, who was not the only one to express aloud a few choice words about the man who had made them wait.

For a moment George moved past his irritation at the man's treatment of his daughter to an appreciation of how well he ruled this rough kingdom. With a decisive nod King Helm indicated it was time to leave. The two young boys in page's uniforms ahead of him lifted their horns and blew the long, low sound of the beginning of the hunt. George scarcely had time to right himself before his horse moved forward with the rest.

Sarrey was a kingdom of few hills, with rivers and streams everywhere, crisscrossing fields and forests alike. It was lush with green this spring, the colors dazzling George's senses. He was sure that in colder, higher Kendel, some of those shades of green had never been seen at all.

It was a clear day, and the wind in George's face felt bracing. It seemed as though the chase would go on for a very long time, for the land itself stretched out toward the horizon forever.

At last the hunting hounds that had been released at the sound of the horns began to bark at the scent of certain prey. Wild boar, George guessed. He battled his headache, holding his face close to the horse's neck and searching for a place to escape. He was not assisted by Henry at all, who kept strict control over his spirited animal, holding directly behind George.

As they continued on, George was surprised to see no distinct woods here as he had expected, but rather bits of trees here and there, then open space, then more patches of trees. George could hear animal sounds now and then that were familiar to him and his headache decreased somewhat, but he knew he must wait for full relief until he had found some kind of shelter.

There: a larger group of trees, at least.

King Helm and the hounds rushed toward them. The hounds grew frantic in their barking, and George could see Henry taking more effort than before to keep his horse back.

Over a stream the whole group went. It was darker here, cooler. George pulled back on the reins of his horse, and suddenly Henry seemed to shoot ahead.

"Your High . . . ness," Henry shouted as George pulled back harder and brought his horse to a sharp standstill.

Some dozen riders stared back at George in mild surprise as their mounts led them ahead. George tried to put on an expression of exasperation, so that they would not think it their duty to come back after him. He was not injured, only a fool, or so he hoped they believed.

If Beatrice and her hound had been here with them, would George have been so eager to let himself be thought so?

Well, they were not.

He tossed his head angrily but regretted it as a new wave of pain and nausea struck him. He got off his horse. He thought a moment of keeping her with him but decided that would only make it more difficult for him to spend time with wilder creatures. And a horse alone would not do to stave off his fever. His mother had discovered that. No matter how often she visited the stables, she could postpone a visit to the woods for only so long.

What was it about the woods? The different animals

themselves? The many languages George would have the opportunity to speak? The smell? The very wildness of it? He did not know. It was part of the magic he did not understand and had never had a chance to ask about.

"Go on!" he said encouragingly to his horse, then patted her backside to get her started. It would not take her long to catch up to the others.

As for her, she did not even bother to give him a snort of disgust. Without a look back at him for confirmation, she cantered away, following her stablemates.

Allowing himself a long, low breath at the success of his hasty plan, George jogged away from the trail the hunt had been following and found a large hollow oak to rest against. This simple quiet of the forest was part of what he needed. At first he could hear only his own heart beating. Then slowly he came to an awareness of the other underlying sounds all around him. The life of the woods.

In what seemed mere moments, the headache had dimmed to a mere buzz.

Feeling stronger, George lifted his eyes to search the tree for signs of birds. There was a sparrow up above, circling her nest, and below that, a fox turning away as it realized that George was too big for its dinner. There were rabbits nearby that had frozen at the crash of horses but now came hopping out, one young one leaping directly over George's knee.

George had avoided a friendship with rabbits for a

long time, but as he thought it over now, it seemed a childish thing. As if he were punishing both himself and all rabbits for one that had died long ago.

"Hello." He greeted the small rabbit.

It was white, and it stared up at him with small black eyes. Its pink nose quivered, and the whiskers twitched as if it expected George to frighten it away again.

"Hello, friend," George said again.

The rabbit hopped closer to George, then sniffed at his leg.

George put out his hand, offering a bit of the apple he had saved from breakfast. That was all the rabbit needed, it seemed, to become George's trusting, eternal friend.

If only it were so easy with humans, George thought. But they were so self-interested, promoting their own purposes.

"My name is George."

"I am Hop," said the rabbit.

George smiled at this. All the rabbits he had met named themselves with a variation on some verb for their own movement. Hop, Jump, Lop, Bound, Leap, Skip—George had even met one ambitious rabbit who called itself Fly. Before it was killed by a boar, that is.

"Where do you live, Hop?" George asked.

The rabbit turned its nose in the direction the others had gone. "And you?"

George pointed south, to Kendel.

That was all the rabbit needed. It shivered. "Cold."

Hop nibbled a bit more of the apple, then seemed to decide it was full. He hopped away from George's side and toward his hole.

At last George stood up. How long until the hunting party missed him? Henry had seen him fall back, but even he would not be sure that George had dropped away entirely. George should have hours in here and could find the hunting party as they made their way back, after the quarry was killed.

Then: "Your Highness," George heard.

What could George do now? Run away from his own man?

"Here," said George, frustrated. He waved a hand.

Henry's face, drawn and pale, flushed. "I thought you were hurt," he said. "Your horse came back without you."

"Yes," said George. He could think of nothing to add.

"Didn't you want to stay with the hunt?"

George didn't answer, but Henry must have come to his own conclusion. He tilted his head to one side, then asked simply, "Why, Your Highness?"

Which was not something George dared explain, not today, or perhaps ever. He thought of two possible lies, telling Henry either that he had felt ill suddenly or that he had been insulted by King Helm's choice of a horse for him.

But when he opened his mouth, he said the truth, at least part of it. "Sometimes I like to be alone."

"Ah," said Henry. And his eyes kept watch on his prince.

"Are you ever like that, Henry?" George asked, wondering what in the world he was doing. He had tried so long to keep from getting close to others, for his safety and theirs. Why change now?

"At times," said Henry.

George waited for him to say more.

Then Hop came back to George, bringing a sister with a black patch over one eye. "Apple," Hop said.

George's shoulders twitched at the thought of what Henry might make of this interchange, but really, why should Henry think that the small sound a rabbit made meant more to George than to him?

George bent down and offered the remaining two pieces of apple to the rabbits, then stepped away from them.

Henry stared at George for a long while after that. Much too long.

"My mother loved rabbits," said George.

"Yet most people think that you do not care for animals yourself. Any of them," said Henry.

George shrugged.

"One can tell much of a man by his friends," said Henry at last.

CHAPTER FIFTEEN

"WE NEED TO get back to the hunt," George said. The encounter with the rabbit had dissipated the pain in his head—for now. It should last long enough to take him back to Kendel.

Henry nodded. "They will hardly notice you have been gone, I suspect. Too excited about the sight of the bear."

George's ears rang. "Bear?" he echoed, his body suddenly taut.

"Yes," said Henry. "A great black bear that has only recently appeared here in Sarrey, they say. Old, and alone, it is said to be angry and completely unafraid of humans."

George shivered. "We must get back to the hunt immediately," he said abruptly. "Where is your horse?"

"I brought back both of them, yours and mine," said

Henry. He nodded toward the way he had come. "I thought it would be better to tie them at the last place I'd seen you, in case I went in the wrong direction and you came back there."

George nodded. "We must reach them before they kill the bear," he said firmly.

"If you insist, Your Highness," said a bewildered Henry. "We will try."

No, thought George. It was not good enough to try. For this bear, he had tried before and failed. This time he would succeed.

George nudged his horse to go over faster through the woods. He hoped the horse knew the terrain better than he did, for he had no idea where there might be a pit in the trail, or a tree fallen in the way, or an old stream to leap over. Aware of Henry close by, George whispered in the horse's ear only now and again about the need for speed. By some miracle, the gentle mare was able to go nearly as fast as George wanted. Henry and his mount struggled to keep up, or so it seemed by the grunting and heavy breathing George heard behind him.

Drenched in sweat and dew, George emerged suddenly from around a corner and caught sight of the hunting party ahead. Many of the horses were shying away, despite their riders' attempts to keep control. King Helm was in the front, with a spear held up high, ready at any moment for the bear's throat.

It was the bear George had seen as a child; he was

sure of it. George could see the same coloring, the same terrible stature and girth. Most important, there was that same human look in its face.

Unmistakably human.

But that look did not stop King Helm, if indeed he recognized it at all. He shouted at the beast and maneuvered it this way and that, to make sure there could be no escape.

George, however, did not see that the bear intended any escape. It looked to him as though it were begging for death and had come precisely to this place to get it. The bear could have shorn off King Helm's throwing arm entirely with one swipe, if it had wished. Instead, it tottered back and forth, waiting.

"Stop!" George called out.

It was not enough to keep King Helm from releasing his hold on the spear but enough to alter its trajectory. Instead of striking the bear in the throat, the spear hit the animal's shoulder instead.

In a moment the woods were filled with a terrible howl of despair, a combination of human anguish and animal ferocity that George hoped never to hear again.

King Helm turned about, his face red with anger. "Mindless idiot! Why did you do that?" he demanded. Nor did he try to soften his words when he saw it was George.

George drew up to the king. "This is a bear from my kingdom," he said, mixing truth and bravado. "I claim it

137

for Kendel and for myself." He waved at the bear. "It is mine to kill or to let live."

"From your kingdom? How can you tell such a thing about a wild beast? Besides, if it has wandered here, then surely it is ours now." King Helm seemed to be torn between amusement and affront.

George dismounted and strode manfully to stand between King Helm and the bear. Strangely, he was not afraid of being attacked from behind. "I have hunted it several times," said George. "And I know its marking."

King Helm snorted. "Ridiculous." He looked back toward the bear, which had fallen to the ground in writhing agony. Then he sighed. "Well, then, finish it off, if you can," he said. He offered George the knife on his belt.

"No!" George said, shaking his head.

King Helm dismounted and faced George from his full height. "It is a man-beast. Did you know that when you hunted it in your own kingdom, if indeed you did? Infected with the animal magic. Look at it and see!" he said.

George did not look. "Nonetheless. It is my beast, and I say it goes free."

"With that wound in its shoulder?" King Helm was scornful. "You are simply condemning it to die in agony some days from now."

"And that bothers you?" George threw back at him. "Because you are so concerned about the pain of a man-beast."

King Helm's eyebrows rose in surprise. He might have said something then, but there came a distinct cry at that very moment. "Father, help me!"

"What?" King Helm seemed more irritated than afraid. "Beatrice?" he said. But then he turned to George and gave a tiny bow as if of acknowledgment. Whether what he did next was out of duty or merely to show up George, no one ever knew.

"Men, that way!" he called. He pointed to the west, and the hunting party followed him without hesitation, leaving George alone with the bear.

George should have gone too. His betrothed had called for help. Yet there had been something in her voice that made him disbelieve her need. And there was no question of the bear's need.

Hoping that Beatrice would understand, he bent himself to his knees and crawled forward, to show he meant no harm. And perhaps—could the bear remember him? "Let me help you," George said.

The bear said nothing, did nothing.

When George was close enough, he put his hands on the spear still embedded in the bear's shoulder and pulled on it, testing.

The bear gave a terrible whimpering noise but did not move. If that was not proof of its humanity, George could think of nothing that could be. But it did not help him move the spear, which had cut deep. King Helm was a strong man. Any smaller bear would have been pinned to the ground with the force of that

139

throw and certainly dead by now.

Could he pull it out?

He had to.

"This will hurt," George said, but not in the language of the bears. He knew already this animal would not understand that. He looked into the bear's eyes.

Then he planted his feet on the ground firmly, leaned forward, and took hold of the spear shaft with both hands. He breathed deeply, counted to three aloud, and pulled.

The spear shaft shifted, but it did not come out. There was blood all over George's hands and more blood pouring down the bear and into the ground. So much blood—how could anything live after losing that much blood?

"I have to try it again," said George aloud, to encourage himself. There was nothing else to do. He had thought he would save this bear, but perhaps King Helm had been right and the only thing to do was to end its suffering.

He leaned forward, gripped his hands so tightly his knuckles went white, and gave a grunt that sounded as if he had become a bear himself. Then he ripped, and the spear came loose in his hands. He careened backward with the force of his pull and stumbled a few moments before laying aside the spear and turning back to the bear.

It bled more, and then its eyes went dull. Slowly it fell forward, senseless, on the ground.

Would it live? Would it recover?

"Prince George, you have done all you can do, surely," said a voice behind him.

George looked up to see Henry. He had not gone off with the rest of the party after all. He was waiting for George. Until now, waiting silently.

What would Henry do? Well, George would have to see about that later. For now the bear was his priority.

After checking to make sure the bear still breathed, George considered his position. He had commanded the king of Sarrey, the man who could end his marriage prospects and bring a new war down on his head, not to kill a bear he had fairly hunted to the ground. He had done this for no good reason except what must appear either madness or boyish greed. Now what? He could not carry the bear all the way home. He could not nurse it back to health. He would have to leave that to the bear's own nature.

And try to save what he could of his own situation. Was there any chance that the marriage could go forward now? That there could be a lasting peace between the two kingdoms? Or had George ruined that in his rash decision to save this bear of his childhood dreams?

George patted the bear once, in encouragement; then he washed his hands in the stream and turned back to Henry. "We should go after the king now."

"As you say, my prince," said Henry, blank-faced. Together, Henry and George mounted their horses and followed the tracks that led them to King Helm and Princess Beatrice. And Marit.

When they arrived, King Helm turned back to George and threw up his hands. "Ah, the perfect match," he said disdainfully.

"Is the princess well?" asked George politely.

Beatrice looked flushed with exertion, and there was a tear in her riding habit, but otherwise she seemed as she ever was. George looked at the hound but saw no sign of an injury there.

"She is a woman," said King Helm with feeling.

Beatrice turned to George for sympathy. Or more than that? Assistance? Information? "I wished to join in the hunt for the bear," she said.

It suddenly occurred to George to wonder how she could have known of the bear and why she would have dared her father's displeasure by joining him on the hunt when he had expressly forbidden her coming. And by pretending to be hurt as well.

Daring indeed.

Or mad.

A madness like George's perhaps.

Beatrice turned and finished her story. "But then I fell—" She pointed to a tree root in the path. "And there was a fox." Her voice quavered falsely.

When George looked around, he saw no fox or any sign of one. There was only Marit, standing guard beside the princess.

142

"And that is why a woman is never welcome on a hunt," said King Helm in frustration. "She imagines danger at every turn."

"I am sorry, Father," said Beatrice, head bowed.

George doubted it very much.

"Next time you will do as I command you or I shall see you beaten," said King Helm. "Do you understand me?"

George twitched at the thought of how many times Beatrice had been beaten before, that she did not think this threat out of the ordinary.

Beatrice nodded. "Yes, Father."

And George remembered having said the same words so many times himself. In the same tone of abject humility. How could he not see the similarities in their lives? How could he not feel that they were meant to be together?

"The bear?" asked King Helm, swerving around, his eyes boring into George's.

"I chased it toward Kendel," said George, hoping it was true.

King Helm shook his head. "Your bear, your bear," he echoed in disbelief. "Ah, well, if I see it in my woods again, you can be sure I will not check its marking before I throw another spear at it. Your bear or not, it will hang on my wall."

"Yes, Your Majesty," said George.

The ride back to the castle was spent in listening to

King Helm complain about women in general and his daughter in particular.

"Ugly and ungainly. The least dependable creature you ever met. Just when you think you understand her, she changes. If only I had had a son," he said bitterly, each time.

Over and over again he disparaged her, and George would have thought that Beatrice would be so used to it, she could not be hurt further. But he saw her head grow stiffer and stiffer above her horse while the hound striding at her side began to move with a jerky uncertainty that seemed more human than hound.

CHAPTER SIXTEEN

*T*HAT NIGHT GEORGE dreamed again.

He was being dressed and primped before a mirror, in a confection of lace and ribbons. His red hair smelled burned from the attempt at curls, but they did not stay in well, and the maid was cursing the ineffectiveness of her efforts.

"Your father wants to see a beautiful princess," she said. "Why can't you be beautiful?"

It was only then that George realized the face staring back at him from the mirror was the face of a young girl, perhaps eight years of age. She was tall and awkward, and her eyes were filled with tears.

"No, no. Stop that. Can't have you crying. You'll ruin everything." The maid handed George—no, the girl—no, Princess Beatrice—a handkerchief. "Wipe your face. And be calm. We might have time to do something yet."

The maid stared at the hair for a moment and snapped her fingers. She moved away, then came back with something in her hands.

Then she was pulling and yanking at the hair until tears of physical pain sprang out of the princess's eyes. At last the maid was finished, and the hair had been teased into some kind of style.

It did not look right, George thought. It was the style of a much older woman, not a child.

"Your father will like that. You look like a woman nearly grown." The maid cinched up the laces at the girl's back till she could hardly breathe.

Then the maid led her away from the mirror.

George could feel how the tiny shoes pinched at his feet. If the princess was a woman nearly grown, why should she wear shoes this small?

They walked up several flights of stairs, then stopped by a door. A guard there nodded for the maid to leave. She kissed the top of the princess's head and whispered, "Be a good girl," and went on her way.

Then the princess was left to wait for what seemed hours before at last the door opened and she was admitted.

King Helm was inside. George recognized him, though he was much younger. He had hair as red as Beatrice's, and he was not as thick around the stomach, though still heavily muscled about his shoulders and chest. He did not look like a man a little girl could depend on for comfort.

"Beatrice, there you are," he said, as though he had been looking everywhere for her. "Come in and meet your new mother." He waved a hand toward the woman at his side.

Beatrice turned to her. She was a petite creature, hardly taller than Beatrice was now, though fully shaped as a woman. In fact her cheeks were bright, and her bosom seemed to flow out of the bodice of her gown.

"What a beautiful little thing she is," the woman said.

But King Helm shook his head at the lie. "I leave her to you," he said with a sigh. "If you can do anything with her, that is. Do not think that I expect much."

"I am sure she can be made to be an addition to you and not a detraction. Why, there is time yet to salvage whatever has been done to her before now. At least she does not talk."

"I do so talk," said Beatrice suddenly.

The woman's eyes widened.

King Helm laughed.

"I don't like you," said Beatrice. "I'll never like you." How must she feel, wondered George? "And you will never make me call you Mother. You're not my mother, any more than the other one was."

"You see?" said King Helm.

"I see," said the woman. "Well, I shall do what I can, but at the worst, you can marry her young, away from the kingdom, and no one will ever see her again."

"So long as you give me a son."

"I will give you more than one son," the woman said. She moved herself closer to the king, pressed her body against his.

With Beatrice, George looked about her father's chamber, and caught sight of a game board, with checkered squares. The figures on it were carved stone, in black and white, and they looked like little soldiers.

She stood there for a long while, staring at the game. George thought she must have wanted to make herself into one of the pieces so that her father would pay attention to her, as he did them. A good soldier, silent and cold and unmoving.

"My dear, the girl is still here," the king said a few minutes later.

"So she is. I must have forgotten her."

"Now what is wrong with her? She stands there staring like an animal in the woods, as if afraid that if she moves, the hunt will be on." The woman circled Beatrice, then stopped at last. "Well, I've seen enough."

"Don't say I didn't warn you, my dear." King Helm went to the door.

When Beatrice got back to her room, the maid scolded her as expected and gave her only bread and water for dinner, eating the rich pudding and fruits that had been sent for Beatrice.

But Beatrice had become a soldier and did not say a word.

George woke up dazed and fuzzy headed. At first he did not know where he was. He thrashed in his bedclothes, thinking he was trapped. But when he escaped from the confinement and fell onto the cold floor on the far side of the fireplace, he came back to himself.

He stood shakily, not understanding why he should dream of Princess Beatrice so vividly. He ate the breakfast that had been left on a tray by his door, then wandered through the castle in circles, trying to make himself lost. At least then he would have a puzzle he could solve.

If he were at home, he thought with amusement, he would have a full schedule, with no time to think of anything at all, let alone bemoan his lack of activity. No, at home he would bemoan how useless all the activity was and how he could never get out of it because he was prince.

Here, in Sarrey, he was more free than he had been in years.

Chapter Seventeen

IT WAS FAR TOO early for the formal breakfast to be served in the morning chamber, but George's stomach rumbled even after the early breakfast, and he went in search of the kitchen and food. On the way he bumped into Princess Beatrice turning a blind corner. They both were off balance, but Marit moved to Beatrice's side, and she managed to avoid falling. George had no such luck.

"I am very sorry," he said when he had righted himself again.

Beatrice pointed to a dusty streak down his side from where he had brushed against the floor, but George shrugged and ignored it. He was more interested in her.

She, however, was not similarly inclined. "If you don't mind, I shall be on my way," said Beatrice brusquely.

"Wait!" George called after her. He felt a sudden desperation to keep her by him. It was not at all what he had thought he would feel for the princess. He had told himself he felt sorry for her, that she intrigued him. But it was more than that.

"Wait!" he called again, louder.

She stopped, and Marit stopped with her. "Yes?" She only half turned toward him.

Why was she so cold toward him? What had he done to deserve that?

He was supremely conscious of the irony in this change in his attitude. He had told his father it did not matter what Princess Beatrice looked like or what her character was. He would marry her regardless, and no need for intimacy—indeed no wish for it.

How he had changed.

Might she also change if he seemed worthy of it?

Well, he would try.

"It is only—I thought I was to come here to get to know you. But we have had only a moment or two to speak to each other. I feel we are nearly strangers still." Surely there was a better way to say that he wanted to spend more time with her.

"You came to see me, to make sure I was neither too ugly nor too mad for you to marry. Well, now you have done that. I do not see why we must spend yet more time together." Beatrice spoke rather coldly.

George was nonplussed. But really, why should he be? She only said aloud what was the blunt truth, what he had felt himself. An arranged marriage such as this was for their kingdoms, not for themselves. And if

George had changed his mind, why should she do the same?

"It is not about 'must,'" said George cautiously. "It is only that I thought it would be pleasant. That is," he added, as he saw her frown disapprovingly, "I had hoped that we might at least be acquainted with each other's likes and dislikes. It would make for less friction in our marriage, don't you agree?"

George spoke to her as he might have to a skittish squirrel in the forest, offering what he thought she wanted, proving himself no danger to her. Perhaps there was some reason for a prince to know the animal language after all.

"Less friction," Beatrice echoed. "Perhaps." She turned back to face him fully. He had her full attention now, and Marit's. But he had not the faintest idea what to say.

Of course she would insist he begin. "What would you have me know about yourself then?" she asked.

George's mind was blank. "Tell me about yourself first. What is your favorite color?" What a stupid thing to say. She would think him an idiot now. What did her favorite color matter to her?

On the other hand, every lady he had ever met had had a favorite color and had made a point of asking George what his was.

"Black," said Beatrice, looking down at Marit.

"Ah," said George. He should have guessed that.

Marit nudged Beatrice's leg. "And your favorite

color?" she asked, as if prompted by her hound. As if Marit cared what George's favorite color was.

George sighed. He was used to this question. "Green," he said, for the main color of Kendel.

Beatrice nodded then. She looked bored. George did not blame her.

This time he thought wildly before he asked another question. He flashed over his memory of the dream the night before. "Have you played the game of kings before?"

Beatrice's eyes widened. "It is one of my father's games," she replied. "But I have never played it."

He had brought up something painful for her, and he had not meant to.

Then Marit nudged at her and whined. Beatrice seemed reluctant, and it was almost as if the two were battling. At last Beatrice said, "I have watched him play many times, but I have never found anyone willing to play against me. We could find a well-used board in the drinking hall, by the fire. It may be noisy in there, for that is where the soldiers congregate. And because my father's policy is to offer them as much beer as they wish, they do not have much self-control."

Was it a test of some kind? She was watching him closely.

"That sounds fine," said George. "I shall follow you there."

She nodded, but it was Marit who led the way.

George thought of all the favorites he could have

asked Princess Beatrice about. Her favorite season of the year? Winter, spring, summer, fall? Her favorite flower? Her favorite dance?

It might be useful to know those things, for when she was his queen. But what did that tell him of who she was?

On the other hand, Elin, the cook, might very much have liked to know if the princess preferred her meat rare or well done and if she had a favorite pastry that could tempt her even when she was feeling ill.

They walked down to the drinking hall, which was loud and filled with the smell of strong drink, murky with smoke from the incense burners spaced throughout the chamber. And no one had bothered to open a window.

George's eyes began to water as the door closed behind them, and his nose twitched with the desire to sneeze. He held it off, trying to prove that his self-control was as strong as hers.

And what of the game? Would she expect him to win? George was no expert at it, as he suspected her father was. He had played it against Sir Stephen, but he did not truly know if he was any good. Sir Stephen admitted it was not a hobby he thought much of, and everyone else George had tried to pit himself against let him win easily.

"I shall be black," said Beatrice, seating herself at one side of the board.

George sat at the other side. He noticed that Beatrice

had maneuvered so that he had to stare out at the soldiers while she faced the stone wall.

"Your move first." She prompted him.

George moved.

Beatrice copied him.

George moved again.

Beatrice did the exact same move, in mirror image.

George made a stupid move, just to see what she would do.

She had her hand lifted to do the same when she looked down to Marit. George was not sure what happened, but Beatrice moved her hand to another, more valuable player. George found himself in an unenviable position.

For the rest of the game George noticed subtle hints that Marit was guiding the princess, yet it was nothing he could point to definitively. Even if he could, what could he say? Demand that the hound be placed in another chamber because Beatrice was using her to cheat against him?

Finally, George sighed and tipped over his king to signal defeat. It was only then that he looked up and saw the audience of soldiers around him, now quiet and with full drinks in their hands. It was very warm, late into the afternoon. He was sweating profusely, and the soldiers were staring at him with wry grins on their faces.

He had embarrassed himself and his kingdom, being beaten like that. They all must see it that way, that he was weak to let a woman beat him.

But he could not regret it.

He stood and bowed graciously. "I thank you for the privilege of playing against so fine an opponent."

Beatrice nodded. Then, trailed by Marit, she walked with him to the door. They went on toward the stairs where they had met.

"You are angry," Beatrice said.

"No," said George.

"Men are always angry when they are beaten," she said.

"Well, I am not like other men," George replied.

"You would rather I had let you win."

"No," he said. He had had enough of that.

Beatrice was silent for a moment, her hand comfortably on Marit's back.

George felt a pang of envy at that sign of closeness. If he had not been so hurt by his first attempt with Teeth, might he have something of what Marit and Beatrice now shared?

"My father says that the only true woman's game is marriage," Beatrice said.

"And is it a game?" asked George. "To you?"

"It is far more than a game to me and to Sarrey," Beatrice said flatly.

"More than a game for both our kingdoms," said George.

There was a long silence, and George had the feeling

that Beatrice expected him to leave. But he did not mind silence, not when it was full of the hope of something between them.

"My father has always thought that I was of no value to him or to the kingdom."

George began to speak, to interrupt her, but she put up a hand, and he stopped himself.

"It is no secret that he wished for a son, to follow in his footsteps, to be a warrior as he was. And I could not be that son no matter how I tried." Beatrice stroked Marit.

"But I have done the one thing that he was never able to do. In one swift movement, I have won him all of Kendel. Through marriage to you."

George stared at her. Was that what the marriage was to her, a way to prove that she could succeed at something her father never had? He did not know whether to be affronted or impressed.

"I did not know that you were the one who had thought of the marriage," said George. He had assumed the idea must have come from King Helm. Or if not from him directly, then from one of his advisers.

But of course that had been before he had met her. Or her father.

"Oh, I had to make sure that he believed it was his own idea," said Beatrice. "He has been long looking for some way to rid himself of me to benefit himself."

What did it mean that Beatrice had offered herself to

157

him sight unseen? That she was more courageous than he had realized? Or more cold and indifferent than he dared see?

"And so you win at last," said George. "If not in one game, then in another."

Marit whined, and Beatrice had to stroke her even more than before. "My father does not see it that way, however. There is only one kind of battle to him and only one honorable way of winning. How he hates that he and the soldiers he trained himself have become too old for war."

George put his hand on top of Beatrice's and felt the warmth of both the woman and her hound pulsing through his fingers. "Just because your father does not see your victory does not mean that it is none," he said softly.

Beatrice's eyes jerked up to his.

He wanted to touch her cheek, but there was something in her stance that warned him away. She was not ready for that. Not yet.

He would content himself with sharing her hound, if only for a moment.

"And just because he will not play the game of kings with you, that does not mean you would not beat him at every turn."

Beatrice smiled at this, and George thought he could see something in Marit's jawline that was like a smile as well.

Then he moved away and made his retreat.

Chapter Eighteen

*T*HE NEXT AFTERNOON George was informed he was to meet with King Helm outside on the training grounds. George expected that King Helm would be showing off his best soldiers to warn George about the possibility of war beginning again at any moment.

But on the training ground, George remembered what Beatrice had said about her father's being too old for war. King Helm's grizzled beard was unkempt, and he wore a pair of leggings with holes at both knees and a short jacket over a top that showed the gray hair on his sagging chest.

It startled George to think that King Helm looked as old as his own father. But why should he not? The two kings had come to their crowns at nearly the same time, and had ruled for more than thirty years since then, including the ten-year war and the twenty years of unsettled peace.

Yet it seemed King Helm had to keep at something like war to be happy. Beside him was a row of weapons of various kinds, laid out carefully. They shone with oil, despite their obvious age.

King Helm turned toward George, looked him up and down, and handed him a padded tunic to put on over his own plain one. Then he looked at the weapons. "You'll start with this," he said, and handed George a wooden sword that looked as if it were made for a child. For himself, the king took only a long wooden staff.

He moved away from the weapons, out into the open ground of the field. Then he motioned at George. "Try me," he said.

George stared at the sword. He knew what to do with it. It was not as if he had never had any training. But it had been an hour a day for a few years and never with any opponent except for the assistant swordmaster. King Davit had never been a man of war either. He had left the decisions of war to the lord general and visited the troops only after a battle.

King Helm had always led his troops himself. Though George did not like the man in many ways, he could not deny that he was courageous or that he was a true soldier.

He told himself that for the first time in his life he had a chance to truly test his skills. King Helm would not be likely to let him win. For that George should be grateful.

"Go on. Do your best. You won't hurt me, I assure you," said King Helm with a gleam in his eye.

Nonetheless George's first stroke was tentative.

King Helm countered with a wave of his staff that took the wooden sword right out of George's hands and left his arms stinging with the jolt of the blow.

George was winded, but King Helm looked as though he had just finished his dessert, a fluffy cream confection. And his smile was very satisfied.

"Try again," said King Helm smugly.

George scrambled to get his sword, and this time he put all the power he could into his blow.

King Helm merely turned aside, and the force of George's movement left him sprawling in the dirt.

George looked up to see a very broad smile on King Helm's face. He gritted his teeth and went at it again. And again.

Until the sweat streaming down his face had soaked through the padding on his extra tunic and his legs were trembling with exhaustion.

"Two hours," said King Helm, looking up at the sun. "Well, I suppose you'll need some rest."

"Thank you," said George with as much dignity as he could manage. He stumbled away and leaned against the wall, nauseated and spent. But he couldn't maintain even that position.

Slowly, and utterly without grace of movement, George slid down. He wanted to put his head on the dirt, but he held it up. He gave himself some credit for that much, though he did not know if King Helm would.

"Here. Some ale," said King Helm. He passed a skin to George, who opened the top and sipped at it.

Not too strong, and not sweet either. It seemed the perfect thing to restore his spirits. What he would have to do after his spirits were restored, he preferred not to think about just at the moment.

"So, you are no soldier," said King Helm. He had knelt beside George — purely for George's benefit, it was clear.

"No," George said. Had that ever been in doubt?

"And you are no hunter either."

"No," George said again, his face turning red with embarrassment. Though he had claimed the bear his own quarry, he had let it go.

"What are you then?" asked King Helm. "What makes your people accept you as prince? Or your father as king?"

From anyone else, George would have been insulted at the question. From King Helm, it seemed reasonable. George sought to answer it fairly.

"He has a good mind," said George judiciously. "And a good heart."

"Good enough that his men are willing to die for him when he takes no risk of his own?"

"Yes," said George. He had never thought of his father as a coward, though he had led no troops to war, but clearly King Helm had.

"I have heard about his judgments." King Helm waved a hand negligently. "Far easier to settle things by a match of strength."

"Then the strongest always wins," said George.

"Precisely," said King Helm. "And a kingdom becomes very strong indeed when the weakest are winnowed out."

George thought about this for a long while. He did not mean to say that King Helm's way was wrong. But it was not his father's way or his own. "Those who are weak can sometimes offer things that the strongest lack," George said.

King Helm stared at him for a time. Then he said, "You truly believe that."

"Yes."

"Tell me what then."

Now George had to think of something concrete, not just the abstractness of right and wrong. He thought over his father's judgments.

"A man came to my father once. He had a dispute with a neighbor, a man who was much stronger than he was. Both men claimed that they had invented a new mechanism to make mill grinding more efficient. My father had to decide which one it was."

"And he decided it was the weaker man?" asked King Helm.

"Yes," said George, "though not because he was weaker. Because he could explain how he came to the invention, from another area of work entirely. From his work on trying to improve a plow, in fact."

"And the advantage to your kingdom was what?"

"The following year the man invented a new mechanism for a cannon," said George.

King Helm's face suddenly drained of color and he sank closer to George's position. "*That* cannon?" he asked.

George thought he must be remembering the rout that Sarrey experienced one year, a terrible loss of life, and even worse, an embarrassing end to King Helm's best-trained men. George's father had hoped it would be the end to all war between the two kingdoms, but the following year King Helm had found his own new cannon to use, and the war went on for two more years. All before George was even born, yet it was as real to him as if he had seen it himself.

"That cannon," said George softly.

There was a long silence between them.

"Will you let me try you again?" asked George. It was the last thing he truly wanted, to be defeated yet again by King Helm. Still, he was determined to show that if he could not win, at least he would not give up. That he could do for his kingdom and for its future.

"You are ready?" King Helm looked skeptical.

"I am ready," said George.

He ended another two hours later, badly bruised over his entire torso, worst on his back and arms. Yet with each blow George thought that King Helm's appreciation of him had grown. Not as a warrior but as a man . . . and a prince.

"Now it is time for dinner," said King Helm with a faint smile.

"Good," George said.

"Ha! That is what you think."

It was a comment George did not understand until he was sitting in the high-backed chair at the table with dozens. His body ached worse now than it ever had while it was warm on the field. He did not know if he could even move his head, let alone his hands. To chew was agony. To speak clearly: impossible. And through it all he had to smile, as King Helm smiled, as Beatrice smiled. Ignoring it all.

Too old for a warrior? George only wished it were true.

Chapter Nineteen

*T*HAT NIGHT AT DINNER George noticed, for Cook Elin's sake, that Beatrice ate her meat bloody rare, as her father did. George himself picked at the meat indifferently, trying only to eat enough to give no offense.

But Beatrice ate her meat with the same relish her father showed for his. And she offered a second portion of it to Marit, who was held on her mistress's lap and allowed to lick from the plate.

George saw more than one face around the table turn away from this sight, trying not to show disgust. Beatrice showed no sign of even noting the reaction.

Finally, at the end of the meal, one of Beatrice's women stood up and raised her glass. "I should like to make a toast," she said.

The servants scurried to make sure all glasses were full. George noticed that Beatrice's glass looked as if it had not been touched all night long.

"To the prince and princess," said the woman with a sudden giggle and a fluttering smile.

Was she drunk?

"May they make . . . beautiful hounds." She raised her glass and drained it, then fell into her seat.

In the stunned silence that followed, George tried to remember her name. She had a mole on her cheek and light-colored hair that was straightened back tightly to hide its natural curl.

Lady Dulen, that was it.

In the silence it seemed that no one dared look anywhere. Not at her, not at Beatrice or Marit, and certainly not at George or King Helm.

George was boiling inside. If he were in Kendel—He could not imagine this ever happening in Kendel. Surely there would be some punishment here. King Helm could not stand idly by and let his daughter be insulted in this way.

Yet when George looked to him, the king had a faint smile on his lips. And Princess Beatrice continued holding her glass, as if frozen.

"It was a joke, Beatrice," said Lady Dulen after a moment. "You must learn someday to take a joke."

Then King Helm added, "It was just a joke, my dear. Laugh."

If it had been a man who had said it, would King Helm have acted the same? Or was it only a woman who could speak to another woman this way?

King Helm raised a glass. "May they make beautiful hounds together," he repeated, and began laughing, quietly at first, and then roaring.

George looked around at those seated next to him. They were staring back and forth between Lady Dulen and the king. George realized then what he had not seen before, the possessive look on Lady Dulen's face as she watched the king.

As if he belonged to her.

He made it clearer by motioning her to his side and kissing her loudly on the mouth. Then the king turned back to the table. "Come, come, laugh with me!" he said.

He seemed to expect that even George would take part.

But George put down his glass deliberately and shook his head. He could not demand that King Helm punish the woman, and in truth he could not think of a suitable punishment. Besides, it was the king himself who had encouraged this attitude. If anyone should be punished, it was he.

George reached for Beatrice's hand. He wanted to do something to show his support for her, but she turned away violently. As if he were the one she was angry with.

What would she want then? What could he do for her? He could think of nothing. And yet he could not simply let her go on being ignored and abused by those around her.

He turned to Lady Dulen. "Hounds are loyal at least," he said.

Lady Dulen twitched a bit, but George wanted to do more. He looked back at Beatrice, who was glaring at him fiercely.

He had done it wrong yet again. How?

Was Beatrice trying to prove that she could take anything her father decided she should endure?

Hadn't she learned that she could not win with him that way?

"Excuse me. I think I am quite finished eating." George put down his napkin and turned to leave.

But Marit came after him, pushing at his leg, forcing him to go more slowly and then to stop altogether.

He felt a fool. Again.

"King Helm, might I interest you in a game of kings?" he asked, to save the moment—if that was still possible.

"You play the game of kings?" King Helm's interest was immediately piqued. "Certainly, certainly. I shall have my board brought in here, and we can play as entertainment for all of them." He waved around the room.

With those words the servants poured in to clear the huge wooden table of dishes and food, glasses and drinks.

"Shall I allow you the first few moves alone?" asked King Helm. "I should not wish to humiliate you."

He would wish to humiliate me, George thought. But he smiled coldly. "I'm sure there is no worry of that. Your daughter has taught me much of the game already. I think that after having lost to her, I will do very well against you."

"My daughter?" said King Helm, astonished. "Beatrice?" As if he had any other daughter.

"Indeed. She beat me in a whole room of your soldiers in the drinking hall yesterday. If you doubt it, you can ask any one of them."

King Helm turned to look at Beatrice. It were as if he was seeing another person entirely.

"Well, well, I am intrigued. I rarely have an opponent I can truly unleash myself on."

"Unleash yourself freely," said George. He hoped he was not idly boasting.

Still stiff from the swordplay as he sat down across from King Helm, he found that Marit remained with him. When he started to lift a player, she touched his knee with her nose, a subtle hint that he was wrong. He tried another player, and she did the same. When he chose the right player, she did nothing.

Ah, so this was part of Beatrice's secret.

George looked to her across the board, for she was on her father's side, and she smiled.

He did not know if she had trained Marit to do this or how Marit had come to understand the game of kings. In any case, George's play became more and more ruthless as she guided him.

By the end, not so very long as in the game with Beatrice, George was the winner.

"I shall have to think this over," said King Helm. He seemed on the verge of accusing George of cheating.

And perhaps George had cheated. But he would do it again if he had to. He touched Marit's head gently in thanks. She moved back to Beatrice.

"Perhaps you will permit me to play with you again sometime?" asked King Helm with more graciousness.

"Yes, of course," said George. "Sometime. But for now I should like to rest."

King Helm gave a wave of his hand in permission, then turned back to stare at the board.

George walked out, head held high. But a step later he turned back at the sound of Lady Dulen's voice. She was on the threshold of the room, her eyes flashing at Beatrice.

She pointed a finger. "You—you think you are a princess?" she hissed, this time softly enough that King Helm could not hear. "You are nothing more than an animal. You do not belong in a palace. You belong in the woods." Then Lady Dulen spat in her face.

George tensed. If she were a man, he could call her out to a duel. But even Beatrice could not do that. Women were not allowed to fight duels. Women did not use weapons. Only words.

Beatrice let the warm liquid drip down her chin and

fall onto her gown. Then, at last, she made her response. She moved slowly, so that not even Lady Dulen suspected what she meant to do. Certainly Lady Dulen did not move away from Beatrice's hand. It lifted from her side, then fell on Lady Dulen's shoulder. And there it pressed and pressed.

Lady Dulen gasped at the pain. Her eyes went fever bright, and her legs began to slump.

Yet Beatrice showed no mercy.

It was Marit that did, Marit, who barked and made Beatrice give up her grip.

Lady Dulen gave one look of sizzling hatred. "An animal," she whispered again.

"An animal is always dangerous to confront. Remember that," said Beatrice. And then she walked away without a backward glance at George or Lady Dulen. Marit strode at her side.

George stood still, until Lady Dulen turned on him. "And that is what you will marry?" she demanded, trying to win the last word on the matter.

George only smiled. "That is what I shall marry," he said. "And I would marry her a hundred times before ever I would deign to sit in the same room with you and sip soup."

Chapter Twenty

THAT NIGHT GEORGE had no dreams of the hound or of Princess Beatrice, which bothered him more than he could explain. He woke feeling leaden and empty, as bad as when he had a headache from the animal magic, but not like that at all. He dressed quickly and went immediately in search of Beatrice.

He needed to talk to her. And not merely because of that stupid woman Lady Dulen.

Knowing enough about Beatrice to guess that outside the castle was the best bet, after some wandering, George to his surprise found Marit alone by the training grounds. He was surprised to see the hound without the mistress, for he had thought them inseparable.

He approached the hound slowly, but so far as he could tell, she had no fear of him. On the other hand, she did not seem to recognize him as familiar or expect that she should go to him to receive a treat either. She simply stood and watched as he came closer.

At last he was on his knees and lifting his hand to the hound's nose. She sniffed, then stared at George.

It was the strangest look. He had not seen anything like it since he had first met the bear in the forest when he was seven years old.

"What are you?" George barked in what he recalled of the language of hounds from his days with Teeth. He hoped that wild hounds would speak as the tamed ones had and that it would only be that they did not lose their speech.

The hound's eyes went wider, and she stepped back.

Had he been wrong? Had she lost her own language, as Teeth had, by her long association with Princess Beatrice?

George was not willing to give up so easily, however. "Are you thirsty? Are you hungry?" he tried. The words came to him without a struggle. He had used them with Teeth, and the more he spoke, the more he remembered.

The hound barked tentatively—and wordlessly— back at him. He did not know what it meant. He hoped it was only surprise, and a little reluctance to speak with him.

So George tried once more. "Tell me of your mistress," he barked. It was the limit of his ability to speak in this language, but if only the hound would speak back to him, he could learn more.

But a hand on his shoulder made George's heart stop. He turned and saw the princess herself standing behind him, as fierce a look on her face as he had seen on any animal whose territory he had trodden too close to or whose young he had touched.

"What are you doing?" Beatrice asked.

Had she heard him barking at the hound? What could she possibly make of that? Nothing good, certainly.

What an idiot he was, to try such a thing where it was most dangerous. If she guessed at the truth . . .

"I was looking for you, but since I could not find you, I thought to make friends with your hound," said George quickly. "I thought that it would be well for me to begin now, since I expect you will not be leaving her behind when you come to marry me."

"No. Certainly not." She looked as though the idea had not occurred to her and, now that it had, shook her severely. Her father's power over her she had come to live with, but perhaps she had not thought what it would mean to be married and have a husband's demands to consider.

"She is not . . . as other hounds I have known," said George.

"She is the one living creature I trust wholly," said Beatrice. "She would never betray me."

George believed her. He turned to look at the hound's reaction, expecting her to be reflecting her mistress's distress. Instead, he found her circling Beatrice's legs, imparting calm to her as she had once done for George.

"What did you come to speak to me about?" Beatrice asked, forcing herself with some effort, it seemed, to speak politely.

Likely she would be offended if he tried to ask more roundabout questions. So he laid it out plainly. "I wanted to know how you and Marit found each other."

"Why do you wish to know? Do you think to find a hound for yourself?" She did not have her hands on her hips, but instead, her head leaned forward, her teeth bared in something like a growl.

"No, no!" George held up his hands. Had others asked her for that reason? Anyone who truly saw them would know that there was no way to duplicate their relationship. And who would want to? It was too close for George to feel comfortable with and yet not as close as others would want with a pet.

"I only want to know of you," George told her.

"Because we are to be married? My father never wished to know his wives beyond their beauty and their ability to make sons," she said.

"Ah." There it was, the old hurt. "I am not like your father," said George. If she had not seen that already, was there any chance she could see it now?

Beatrice considered this for a time. "Why?" she asked.

George did not know how to answer that, or was it only that he did not dare to?

"Is it because of the barking?" Beatrice asked suddenly.

George went very still. "Barking?" he echoed.

"The way you were playing with Marit. I have never seen a man do that before, with a hound. They expect hounds to answer to their language."

"That may be part of the reason I am different," George said, the words pressed out of his tightening throat.

"And the other reason?"

"Perhaps I was born different. Or made different by the parents who raised me," said George honestly. Did anyone ever know why he was the person that he was, animal magic or no?

"Yes," said Beatrice. "I can see how that would be. A different pack has different rules."

She had seen packs in the forest then, had watched them to know their customs. It was not a bad way to think of the world.

"Perhaps I also made myself different, because I wished to be," George added after a moment.

Beatrice looked at him then, and for a moment George thought he could see through her eyes to her soul, and she the same with him. It was a moment of pure understanding, such as George had never had with another person. It shook him, made him tremble at the strength of the connection, in fear and awe.

"Yes," said Beatrice. "That happens as well. Even in the wild, to animals who have broken from their packs." She paused and then, without another prompting from George, said, "I shall tell you of when Marit and I met."

George gulped in air, glad now that she was speaking instead of him.

"Beatrice was—I was fourteen years old and angry with my father. I fled the castle. I did not take a horse, or a blanket, or food. I did not want anything from him.

"I set out at night, so that no one would see me. By morning I was far away, so far south I did not know if I was in Sarrey anymore, and lost deep in a woods I had never seen before. I went toward the sound of water and fell into a stream. I twisted an ankle, and it was painful to stand on it, agony to walk.

"Then behind me I heard the sound of wild hounds, barking at the scent of prey. I thought they meant to devour me. I flung myself into the trees and ran, ignoring the pain in my ankle. The pack of wild hounds chased after me. I thought they were chasing me.

"At last I noticed that beside me ran a hound, chased by the same pack that chased me. Perhaps they chased her first, I do not know, but when I saw her, I knew that she and I ran for the same reason.

"We ran and ran, until at last we came upon a bear. The bear snarled at the pack of hounds and swiped at the lead male. He was wounded and called at the others to turn back, to follow him home. They snarled once more at Marit and me, and then they were gone.

"I was certain that the bear would devour us himself then, and I prepared myself for death. But it did not come. The bear only stared at us for what seemed a very long time, looking at one and then the other of us. But whatever it was looking for, it did not find, and it went on its way without touching either of us."

A bear again, George thought. His bear?

"We have never been parted since then."

Beatrice put her hand on Marit's head, and George was struck once more with how alike they were. The way they held their heads proudly, the way they had borne hurt and yet would not bow to it.

Still, Marit was softer than her mistress. She seemed not to have that ruthless streak George had seen with Lady Dulen. Perhaps that part of the princess came from King Helm, and Beatrice would one day set it aside if she became confident in her own strength.

"We have never told that story to anyone before," said Beatrice. "We did not think we would ever tell it to anyone, not even to you."

It seemed a gift, far more precious than the glass hound George had given her and far more personal. He felt ashamed that he had nothing to offer in return. Or did he?

"I am sorry that you never met my mother," George said at last. He thought again of the story of his mother and how she had at last told the truth to King Davit. Yes, he thought, that is the way it must be. Truth must come first in any real marriage. And he could not imagine wanting any less than a real marriage with Beatrice now.

She had been hurt too much before. She should not be hurt again.

"I never met my own mother," said Beatrice. "I do not think I know what I am missing. Perhaps it is better that way."

George's mouth opened, then closed. "That is not what I meant," he said at last. "That is—my mother was very much a friend of animals."

"Yes, I think I had heard that." Beatrice spoke with narrowed eyes.

Did she know? Did she guess? How much did George have to spell out for her? There was always the danger that she would be horrified. George's mouth went dry at the thought.

"She had a gift," George said. He could not stop now. She had shared with him. She deserved something in return. And truth be known, he was tired of always hiding himself.

"I have the same gift." George's voice was hardly more than a whisper.

He could hear Beatrice breathing and Marit breathing. They waited. Beatrice did not pepper him with questions but let him tell the tale his own way, as he had let her tell theirs.

"My magic is only that I can speak to animals in their own tongue." He stared intently at Beatrice's face and at Marit's. He could see nothing at all.

But at last Beatrice said only, "I shall not tell your secret."

George breathed heavily. He nodded. "Thank you."

Was that it? Was that how it was to end between them today? After so much sharing, polite nothings and then a parting?

"Good morning," Beatrice said, and walked away.

Marit looked back a moment longer, but then George was alone.

He had never felt so alone in his life.

CHAPTER TWENTY-ONE

THE LAST NIGHT that George was to be in Sarrey, King Helm invited a troupe of musicians in for dancing. Of course Beatrice and George were expected to lead.

George looked toward Beatrice and saw little interest in dancing before an audience, but duty called them both. He bowed to Beatrice. She looked to Marit, and George wondered for a moment if he would have two partners. But no, Beatrice came alone. She offered her hand, and George took it. As they stepped onto the open floor, the music began.

He bowed and motioned to the small open space available.

It was a languorous cat dance, which allowed the two of them to slide close enough to touch gently but never for long. George thought it strange that the hatred of animal magic remained so strong when so many dances were based on the movements of animals. Not all of them wild animals, but still . . .

The second one was a faster dance of a hunt. First one of them, then the other was the prey and skittered away with the music. It was meant to be a playful dance, but George did not notice any pleasure on Beatrice's face.

Then again, she did not smile often. In fact even the hound seemed freer in the castle than the princess was. Marit could move where she wished to go, could bark or express anger. Beatrice could not. Perhaps that made it impossible for her to feel happiness either.

Could he change that after their marriage? He promised himself that he would.

After a third dance, during which Beatrice stepped repeatedly on his toes, George pleaded exhaustion and sat. The truth was, she danced badly. George did not consider himself any more than proficient, but he had danced with some very graceful partners, and graceful Beatrice was not.

She was awkward, jerking this way and that. She remembered the steps. It was not that. It was that she seemed to have to think about them at every moment. They did not flow from her mind into her body. That consciousness was always a step behind the music.

George thought she was not even aware of how badly she danced, for she paid no attention to him at all, only to herself and what steps were coming next. She had no enjoyment in it, certainly.

Clearly dancing was not the thing to make her smile.

He couldn't avoid it entirely at their wedding, but he might be able to make it less obvious that she was so graceless. Would it be better or worse if he paired her with superb dancers? Much worse. A bad partner would be ideal, for all of Beatrice's mistakes could be blamed on someone else.

George had begun compiling a list of them in his head, beginning with Sir Stephen, when his attention was caught by one of the noblemen at King Helm's side. George saw the man's face go still, and then his hands went to his throat. Before they could reach it, his face turned very red, and he fell to the floor.

King Helm reacted quickly enough that the heavy man did not hit his head, while shouting for a physician. Two servants went running while the king shook the man and tried to get him to respond. He stirred as if in pain, but he did not revive. George thought the man's color was getting worse, more gray than red now.

The musicians had stopped playing, and the whole room was silent.

"Can no one help him?" King Helm demanded. George was surprised to see this distress from the king, whom he had thought removed from emotions that drove normal men. But there must be real warmth between King Helm and Duke Marle, the fallen man.

Moved by pity, George went to Marle's side and bent over him. "He is still breathing," he said. But shallowly and not with regularity.

George peered to see if something was caught in the

man's throat, but it seemed clear. "Perhaps turn him to his side, so he can breathe more easily."

Immediately King Helm did as George suggested. George could not help wondering why the king could not show even a tenth of this feeling for his own daughter.

In a moment the duke seemed a little better. He breathed more deeply, then looked up and said the king's name.

"Hush, my friend. Be still until the physician comes." The king held tightly to Duke Marle's hands.

Reassured, Marle closed his eyes and seemed to sleep.

King Helm swore violently. "Where is the physician? If he is not here before Marle is dead, I swear I will boil the man in his own medicines and feed him to the pigs for their supper."

The physician came at that very moment. He was young and thin and utterly unsure of himself. His hands trembled, and his knees knocked together.

"Your Majesty?" he said.

"Don't speak to me. He's the man who needs you," growled King Helm, gesturing emphatically to Duke Marle.

The physician knelt down and said exactly what George had: "He is breathing."

"I know that. What is wrong with him? Why did he fall? And what can you do to make him better?"

The physician swallowed hard. "It might be . . . an

ache in the heart. Or an imbalance of the liver."

"I do not care what it might be. It *might* be that I poisoned him myself, but that is not what it is. Tell me what it *is*, you fool."

"Your Majesty, if only Dr. Rhuul were here, he would be able to do more."

Out of the corner of his eye George noticed that Marit had twitched at the mention of the other physician's name and Beatrice had gone as gray as Marle himself. Whatever anyone else thought about the physician, it was clear that Beatrice and Marit considered him no friend.

"Dr. Rhuul, the foul-scented fool, is not here, and you are. Or do you wish to be sent to find him . . . less two eyes and a leg?"

"No, Your Majesty," said the young physician.

"Then tell me, what does Marle need?"

The young physician closed his eyes, then said, "Cool water, as much as he will drink. And a draft that I will send in but a few moments, for a man who has had an ache of the heart. I am sure it is no more than that, Your Majesty, for Duke Marle is of an age, and he is—"

The physician looked at the king and seemed to realize any comment he made on Duke Marle's size and tendency to indulge would reflect on the king as well. Instead, he coughed politely into his hand and said, "Give me time to go to my chamber, and I shall bring the draft back with me."

"Do not ask me for time," said King Helm. "Ask it of fate, for if he lives, then so do you."

The physician, in fear, did not move for a moment.

"Go, go!" King Helm shouted. "If you had been wise, you would have brought the draft with you when you came. Dr. Rhuul would have certainly."

"We all wish that Dr. Rhuul had not left us so suddenly last year," said the young physician softly. "He could diagnose any illness and predict some besides."

Predict them? George wondered at that phrase. It seemed ominous, though no one else remarked on it.

The physician scurried away, and King Helm sent one of the servants after him with a snap of his fingers.

"Water," the king commanded of his servants. They brought him a carafe.

King Helm poured it slowly into his friend's mouth. Marle licked his lips and swallowed once, then twice. He coughed suddenly, then jerked upright.

His color was improved.

"I suppose now that you will tell me it was all a farce. A terrible farce it was too for me to think of the loss of the only man who dares slice me on the practice field."

Duke Marle gave a faint smile.

George eased away from the two of them and toward Beatrice. He touched her arm. She did not resist him, but as soon as he let go, it fell back to her side. She was cold as stone.

"Who is Dr. Rhuul?" whispered George. His mind had twisted around the thought of the foul scent King Helm had spoken of. And predicting illness? Or creating it?

It made George think of Dr. Gharn's foul smell, and his unfortunate arrival just before the king fell ill.

George kept looking at Beatrice and Marit.

The princess said nothing, but the hound whined at him mournfully. They knew something about Dr. Rhuul, but how could he find out?

The young physician came racing back with his draft. Duke Marle drank it with a sour face. Then he threw it back up.

"You fool! I'll have your toes for this!" exclaimed King Helm.

"No, Your Majesty. It was supposed to do that. He will be better now. Ask him. Look at him. You'll see." The young physician's teeth chattered.

It was true. Duke Marle looked much better. He got to his feet and wiped his mouth. "What foul stuff that was."

"It has thinned his blood so that it can return to his heart. But he should be careful that he does not eat so much rich food, Your Majesty. And gets a little more gentle exercise. Walking perhaps." He bowed his head, as though he did not expect these recommendations to be accepted.

King Helm seemed chastened. "Is there anything else that needs to be done for him," he asked, "as he recovers himself?"

"Perhaps a little clear broth and bread for the next two days," was the response. "To clean out his stomach and purify his blood."

King Helm grunted at this, but he did not reject it. Then he looked to his friend and said, "Do you hear that? Mind you obey him as if your king had spoken."

"Yes, Your Majesty," said Marle hoarsely.

It was a miserable end to the dinner and to George's last day with Beatrice. He had no chance to speak to her again, but he told himself that Dr. Rhuul—whoever he was—did not matter now. He would let it go. There were greater things to be considered here and now.

"Your Highness, is there any way I can help you?" asked Henry when they were at the door to his bed-chamber.

"Do I look so bad as that?" George asked.

"Your Highness, you look tired."

"Tired I can manage alone," George said curtly.

Henry looked away, and George realized he had hurt him. That is what came of not having had experience in friendship. George did not know what was expected of him, so he would always be hurting people inadvertently, he supposed.

After a moment's hesitation he opened the door to his bedchamber and called Henry to him. "If you would get me a cup of hot tea," he asked, more because he wanted to give Henry some way to feel useful than because he wanted the tea.

"Yes, Your Highness." Henry seemed eager to help.

When the tea came, George was still sitting on his bed, fully clothed. The taste was better than he had anticipated and filled him with warmth. He lay back

189

when it was done and eased off his shoes.

He had forgotten entirely that Henry was still there, that he had not dismissed him properly, when Henry asked, "Is there anything else, Your Highness?"

George's first impulse was to say no, that he wanted to be left alone now. But then the back of his mind niggled at him. "Find out what you can about Dr. Rhuul," said George.

"Who?"

"Dr. Rhuul. The old physician to the king. Find out who he was and where he has gone. If you can, before we leave in the morning. If you can give me a description of him as well, that would be useful."

"Yes, Your Highness," said Henry. He looked as if he wanted to ask why, but then chose not to.

Not when it was the prince asking. No doubt he thought the prince must have some good reason for it.

Henry would likely spend all night on this mission and leave for Kendel in the morning swaying on his feet. But George had to know the truth of Dr. Gharn.

That night he did not dream much, only snatches here and there. But he saw one face more than once. That face stood over a hound and a woman with a sinister expression on his face.

It was the lined face of a man of less than average height, very plain features. He might have been a thousand men, George thought. He was the kind of man you forgot easily.

Except for his smell.

CHAPTER TWENTY-TWO

O N THE JOURNEY HOME to Kendel, George found himself thinking more and more about Dr. Gharn. He had never thought twice about the new castle physician before, but now . . . He wished more than once that he could bring Henry into his carriage with him to ask what he had discovered about Dr. Rhuul from those he had spoken to in King Helm's castle. Anything at all?

Near the end of the day, the carriage arrived home at last, and George alighted within sight of Henry. But just as he thought he would have a chance to ask the guard for a private conference, Sir Stephen stepped forward with a grave expression.

"What is it?" George asked breathlessly. He looked about. Was it his father?

"I wanted to ask how it had gone, that is all," said Sir Stephen. "Did you find Princess Beatrice as you expected?"

George spoke absently. "She was not as I expected."

Sir Stephen blinked rapidly, usually a sign that he was about to start on a long lecture.

George wished he could see Henry. Where had he gone? His horse was missing too. All the guards had already taken their mounts to the stables to be rubbed down.

"Were you pleased by her then?" Sir Stephen asked.

"Yes, I was," George replied. Then, finding himself warming to the subject of Beatrice, he added, "Sir Stephen, she is a woman unlike any other."

Sir Stephen's eyebrows rose. "You remind me of myself when I spoke of another woman . . . long ago," he said quietly.

George was nearly tempted into a longer discussion with Sir Stephen on the topic of love and duty. But first he wanted to see his father. Since Henry had disappeared, perhaps the king would be able to tell George about Dr. Gharn.

He gave his regrets to Sir Stephen, then hurried inside and bounded up the stairs.

Four-fingered Jack was waiting at the top. Inside, King Davit was sitting up, and his color was good. He smiled at the sight of George and gestured him to sit in the chair at his side.

George felt all his anxiety about Dr. Gharn and his father melt away. The foul scent must have been a coincidence. There was no sign of mischief here.

"You look very like your mother today," said King Davit.

George breathed deeply and settled himself. His father could not have known how much the words set his heart at ease. "And you seem . . . better."

His father stretched. "I think that Dr. Gharn must have found the cure at last. He has not been by in several days to check on me, but I believe when he comes, he must tell me that I will be able to go walking in a week or two.

"But I should not trouble you with that. I'm sure you are eager to share your thoughts about the princess with me. How did you find her? I expected resignation or coldness of heart, not the heat and eagerness I see before me now." His father smiled as if he had engineered it all himself. Perhaps he had.

George tried to think how to put Princess Beatrice and Marit into words. Finally, he said, "She knows I have animal magic."

He had not expected his father to start so. King Davit put a hand to his heart and went suddenly pale. "And do you trust her with that?"

"Yes," said George. "Absolutely." He had thought that was understood. If not, he would be telling of something else entirely, the beginnings of a new war.

"Good," said his father with relief.

At that moment Dr. Gharn interrupted them with a knock at the open door. "Your Highness, Your Majesty." He bowed.

The physician's face showed no sinister feeling. But like the man in the dream, he had unremarkable features. He had light brown hair and was of medium height and build, with eyes that seemed between blue and green. He walked lightly, as if to leave no mark behind him.

George felt confused. The physician did not make him feel at ease, and the smell—the smell was foul indeed. It made George want to turn away at every moment. Could it be meant to do that?

"How is my father?" George asked. "He says he feels very well today. Perhaps he will be ready to get out of bed soon."

"Oh?" Dr. Gharn came closer. He looked in King Davit's eyes and had him open his mouth to examine his throat. "Well," he said, "yes, I see why you would think you are better."

"Think I am better?" echoed King Davit.

Dr. Gharn opened his bag and laid out a small vial of elixir. "Yes. There are many who are afflicted as you are who have periods of near recovery and then relapse. Those who are tempted to do more than they ought relapse the worst. The others . . . do better."

"It is false, then, the sense that he is better?" George asked.

"Very false . . . and very dangerous, I am afraid," said Dr. Gharn.

"I suppose I am to take more of this then?" asked King Davit. "And feel as sick as ever when I do so."

"I know you do not care for the flavor," said Dr. Gharn. "And it may cause your stomach to be upset for a few hours, but it is all to the good. It is a purgative, you see. It will help ease the illness out of your body. As much as can be, that is."

"Ah." George reached for the vial and lifted it to the light. It was the same black stuff his father had been taking for months.

"Dr. Gharn, may I ask you a question?" George asked, probing.

"Of course." Dr. Gharn still looked not directly at him but at a place beyond George's shoulder.

"Do you believe that my father will ever be completely cured of his illness?"

"Well . . ." The physician hesitated. "That is very difficult to say. I do not claim to produce miracles, but I think I have shown enough of my powers not to be doubted at this point."

In fact George remembered the way the whole castle had been abuzz at the first appearance of Dr. Gharn. He had come without any letters of recommendation, without any personal tales. Yet within a few days there were dozens of stories of those he had healed. So of course when the king had a touch of stomachache, Dr. Gharn had been called in. And steadily the king had gotten worse, but never alarmingly so. Until now.

"But you have seen others with this same malady who have gone on to be fully well again? With your treatment, of course?"

Dr. Gharn turned to the side. When he answered, his voice was low and almost apologetic. "I have not treated a case as bad as your father's ever in my life. I am sorry to say that I cannot predict its end with any certainty."

This did not inspire George with any confidence. "And if my father refused your treatment? What then?"

"George —" King Davit tried to stop him.

But George was insistent. "What would happen to the king if you were no longer here to treat him?"

"I would not recommend that," said Dr. Gharn. "Not at all. Your Majesty —"

"George, what has gotten into you?" King Davit reached once more for the elixir.

George snatched it away. "What is in this elixir?" he demanded.

"I do not reveal my secrets to such as you," said Dr. Gharn stiffly.

Without a hint of what he meant to do, George dropped the elixir on the floor. The glass vial shattered, spilling the black liquid everywhere. If George had expected it to hiss or burn into the stone, however, he was disappointed.

"What have you done?" Dr. Gharn turned to the king. "Your Majesty."

"George, make your apology to Dr. Gharn immediately."

George, feeling utterly the fool, made a quick apology.

"I will get another vial, Your Majesty. Luckily, I made two up in my chamber this very day." Dr. Gharn gave a last look at George as he left.

"George, what is wrong with you?

George hesitated, then said, "I do not trust the man."

"Why not? And why so suddenly?"

"What do we know about him? Where does he come from? Why have you become more ill with his treatment?"

"Some illnesses cannot be cured," said King Davit, resigned.

"Father: After his medicines, do you feel better or worse?"

King Davit wrinkled his forehead in thought. "I hate the elixir," he said. "But it is as he said: It makes me sick to make me better."

"And you believe that?" George asked.

"Why should I not? When you were a boy, do you remember when your mother would make you eat greens fried with mushrooms?" he asked, his eyes bright.

"Yes," said George.

"You hated them, but she insisted you eat them. She said they would make you healthy and strong."

"She said that." George still disliked greens in any dish.

"But you did not like to eat them. You would hold your stomach for hours afterward and say that it hurt, that it was her fault that you hurt."

But Dr. Gharn was not his mother, George thought. And his father was not a child.

"Leave Dr. Gharn be. He is not an open man, I know, and there is little to like about him. But he is a fine physician."

What could George say to that?

He was about to leave, then turned back to his father with a wry expression. "You never made me eat greens after my mother was dead," he said.

His father shook his head. A cloud passed over his face, and George regretted having said anything. He had not meant a criticism.

"No," said King Davit. "I couldn't bear to do it. I was not a very good physician to you, I suppose. It was all I could do to be a father, and perhaps I was not so very good at that either."

CHAPTER TWENTY-THREE

AFTER ALL THE TIME he had waited to speak to Henry about Dr. Rhuul, George was a little disappointed at what he heard.

"They said that he was a man of few words," said Henry with a shrug.

"And?" George prodded.

"And he was not well liked by the servants. They said he looked down upon them, that he would not speak to them plainly or even allow them near him in the same chamber."

"And the others? The nobles?" asked George.

Henry sighed. "I did not have a way to ask them directly, Your Highness."

"Of course." George waved away this objection. "But did you have any impression from what the servants said?"

Henry shook his head.

"Did anyone give you a description of him? His hair color? His eyes? His height?"

"They said he was an ugly man," said Henry at last. "But I could not tell if it was from the way he acted or the way he looked. I'm very sorry, Your Highness."

George did not know what he wanted. He dismissed Henry with a hand and told himself there was far too much for him to do to keep the kingdom running while his father was ill; he had no time to keep at such a mystery. It likely meant nothing.

It was late spring when George returned home from Sarrey, and it was always busier in spring than in the fall at the castle. Sir Stephen seemed to have delighted in keeping a list of urgencies stored up for him while he was gone and then making sure that George took care of each one in the proper way. No shortcuts and no denials.

There were new uniforms to order for the guard, wedding invitations to be signed, a tax dispute to settle, aid for a town burned by lightning, and on and on.

And of course the judgment days to be managed, the everyday decisions of the castle to look over—who was visiting from where and what honor should be duly shown to them, which meals should be served and when. On and on.

So George went to the woods but once a month, to bleed off his need for an hour or two, enjoying the company of a family of sparrows that were as competitive as a family of ten sons of a baron he had dealings with. Diving out of their nest, each one trying to outdo the other. And all their names were Black. They seemed to have no understanding that perhaps they all should have different names.

Yet one day as spring was turning to summer and the warm judgment days seemed to be attracting fewer complainants, George had a session with Sir Stephen about the upcoming visit of Princess Beatrice. Suddenly George found himself asking, "What do you think of Dr. Gharn?"

After a surprised look, Sir Stephen said, "I must say I have had little contact with him. He seems a very private man."

"But surely you must speak to him about his treatment of the king?"

"The man keeps me very well informed in his written accounts. His expenses and his list of times for the king to be medicated, and with what."

"And you do not ask for more than that?"

Sir Stephen rubbed his red-veined eyes. "In fact I am glad that he does not ask for another part of me, Your Highness. I have much to do already, and speaking to a man when it is far easier and less time-consuming simply to read what he has written: What is there to complain of in that?"

George had not meant to scold Sir Stephen, who was clearly carrying far more burden of the king's illness

201

than George was. But he could not let it go.

"Is there no one who knows anything of him?"

Sir Stephen raised a finger as if to gather a memory. "You may ask Henry, of your own guard. I believe he was one of those who received some of Dr. Gharn's first cures."

"Oh? What was he suffering with?"

Sir Stephen shook his head and refused to answer. "I'll let him tell you himself."

So the next day, George went to Henry, who was in the stables tending to his horse, and asked him to walk about the moat. Staring into its dark water was a good reminder of the mistakes George had made in the past.

"Henry, Sir Stephen said that you were one of those cured by Dr. Gharn when he first arrived last year," George said. The sun was high overhead, and the moat stank almost as strongly as Dr. Gharn himself. George did not mind. Not so long as he was outside, in the fresh air.

"Yes," said Henry. He colored.

"Will you tell me what he cured you of?"

"I'd rather not," said Henry. His eyes would not meet George's.

Could George command him to speak? Perhaps, but then what? There would be nothing between them ever afterward.

Instead George asked, "Were you pleased with the cure?"

Henry hesitated for a long while before he spoke. "I could not say it did not work," he said, "so long as I was willing to take the medicine."

"Ah," said George. He was silent for long enough, to let Henry add more.

"He was . . . cold," said Henry eventually. "He spoke very little, and when he did, it was as if he was used to not speaking. As if he thought everyone but himself an idiot."

That was the same man George had seen indeed. "You saw others cured that day as well?"

"Yes, dozens," said Henry.

"Truly cured. Not gone home to discover their symptoms returned?"

"I suppose I would not know that," said Henry. "But there is another guard who said that his sister was cured of a blind eye she had had since a dog bit her in childhood. A magicked dog, he said. But I do not know if there is any truth in that."

"And yet he does not heal regularly in the palace now?"

"Well, he has the king's health to deal with," said Henry. "Of course he has no time for the rest of us. We would not want to take away his attention from finding cures for the king."

"Of course," said George, musing. "And do you think the king is getting better?"

"No," Henry said after a moment. "But what do I

203

know? I am only a guardsman—"

George put a hand out to stop Henry from going further. "You do not blame Dr. Gharn for this then?" he asked.

When Henry finally spoke, there were tears in his eyes. "Men die. Even kings. And even the best physicians cannot always heal them."

George turned to go, but Henry's voice stopped him. "Your Highness."

"Yes? Is there something else?"

"I—that is . . . perhaps I shouldn't . . . it was only a rumor." Henry looked miserable, his face twisting this way and that.

"Tell me."

"I heard that once Dr. Gharn was passing the king's own troops, who were holding a flag. He should have stopped and bowed his head, to do them honor, but he spat instead. Spat on the ground in front of the troops and said he hated the flag."

"A rumor," said George. Perhaps. But what if it was more than that? How could a man who hated the king's soldiers and the kingdom's flag serve the king without prejudice?

CHAPTER TWENTY-FOUR

F OR MANY WEEKS King Davit seemed better, and preparations for the wedding were so fierce that George let go of his suspicions about Dr. Gharn. But then George heard that Dr. Gharn had spent some hours tending to a family of peasants that had come to him from the north, begging for his particular assistance. He had gone to them, given them a few packets of herbs, and sent them on their way. But why? It seemed thoroughly out of character for the unpleasant man George had seen.

George decided in a rush of impatience that he would go to Dr. Gharn that very day. When he had a few moments between appointments, and the merchant he was to meet with was late, George disappeared.

"But your duty," said Sir Stephen.

"My duty does not include encouraging my own people to treat me badly," said George sharply. He slammed the door behind him on his way out.

So he went to the main hall and asked a few of the servants where Dr. Gharn was likely to be at this time of day. The physician was rarely out of his chambers, he was told. In fact the kitchen always sent his meals directly to him in the isolated tower where he slept.

Even at the bottom, the tower was hot and stuffy. George felt closed in as the staircase narrowed and the steps grew steeper.

Nervously George knocked on the door at the top.

"Leave the tray outside. I'll get it when I'm ready," came a distracted voice from within.

George knocked again. "It's Prince George," he said. "I would speak with you, if I may."

A short flutter of wings within, and there was a clicking sound as the door opened just enough to show Dr. Gharn's face. "I'm sure we have nothing to speak of," he said, not allowing George a glimpse of his chamber.

"Please. I should like to talk to you about my father's treatment." He tried not to breathe in the foul stench, but even with the door open a few inches, it was powerful indeed.

"Your father does as well as can be expected. Go talk to him if you wish," said Dr. Gharn.

George put his boot in the door before the physician could close it again. "I will speak with you." This time he did not speak tentatively. He used a deep, commanding voice, as he had on King Helm's hunt, and pushed firmly against the door.

Dr. Gharn stepped back, eyes wide for a moment. But very quickly they turned dark and cloudy. He waved George into his chambers.

Once George got used to the eye-stinging smell, he allowed himself to take in the details.

No one could say that the king's physician was overly indulged. There was but one small window that looked out to the east. The shelves on the walls were filled with odds and ends, and on the table by the bed were several vials like those that held his father's medicine and alongside them some dried herbs.

"Is this what you give my father?" George reached for a bit of the herb, and it crumbled in his hands. He smelled it, and his eyes watered at the sudden new and overwhelming odor.

"Yes," said Dr. Gharn. He offered no more than that.

The physician was standing beside a cage that held a small bird. A dove, in fact, the cause of the wing-fluttering sound he had heard at first.

"Your pet?" George asked, moving toward the cage. He meant only to look at the bird, for it seemed a very unusual creature. It held still when George came toward it and did not flutter even when Dr. Gharn snarled and held the cage away from him.

"Not a pet," said Dr. Gharn.

Then what was it? "You use the feathers in one of

207

your concoctions then?"

"Medicine, not concoctions," said Dr. Gharn. "And no, I do not use it that way. Not this bird. Not ever."

"Then it is—"

"What did you come for?" Dr. Gharn interrupted him, his tone belligerent.

"I told you, I came to ask about the king."

"And I told you, he is as well as can be expected."

George felt even more suspicious of the man.

"Dr. Gharn, can you tell me where you learned your medicine?" George decided to flatter him, though he doubted the physician would be fooled. "I ask because I should like to send others to train to be physicians as you are. We have need of many of your kind here in Kendel."

"I trained in many places," said Dr. Gharn. "I do not believe it would be possible to train another such as myself." He put a finger into the cage, and the bird stepped onto it. Through the bars he petted the bird's feathers.

"I do not doubt that is so, yet you seem very reluctant to speak of specifics. Is there a reason for that? A fear of something?" George pressed on, his heart in his throat. He was not used to wielding his power so directly.

"Perhaps you are the one who is afraid," said Dr. Gharn sharply.

For a long and terrible breath, George *was* afraid, that Dr. Gharn would accuse him of having the animal magic. That he knew the truth, had always known it, ever since he had entered the king's castle in Kendel.

The expected attack did not come, however. The physician said instead, "What do you know of being king?"

The implications of that fell on George slowly, producing a black heaviness in his heart.

In a hoarse voice, he asked, "Are you saying that my father will die soon?"

"I am saying that you are untrained, and you look for others to blame that state upon. You are so used to relying on others, so unsure of yourself. And yet—you are also a prince without friends, without any interests or passions of his own. A shadow of a man, one who does not know himself and does not wish to know himself. A man who is still a boy, truly."

"I—" George's voice broke and went high, as if he were a boy, as Dr. Gharn had said. If Dr. Gharn had seen this so easily, what about those at court? Did they all pretend that he was suitable as a prince because they had no other choice?

All except the lord general.

Dr. Gharn had one final salvo. "You, George, a king. Ha! I daresay that Princess Beatrice, even now on her journey here, is just as amused at the thought."

"What do you know of Princess Beatrice?" George demanded, distracted from his own doubts at the thought of her.

At this, Dr. Gharn's expression went very still, so that George was sure he was right.

"I have been sought in many courts." His voice dismissed the subject, but his eyes would not look directly at George.

"In Sarrey?"

Dr. Gharn shrugged. "Perhaps."

"Then you have met Princess Beatrice personally?" If Dr. Gharn admitted that, it would lend credence to George's suspicions about Dr. Rhuul. And then what? George's heart sank as he realized that he did not know what Dr. Rhuul had done in Sarrey. He had only Marit's and Beatrice's vague expressions of discomfort to guide him and Henry's report of talk of Dr. Rhuul's unpleasantness.

Then Dr. Gharn spoke. "I have met the princess." At first nonchalant and then filled with dark sarcasm. "What do you think of her, Prince George? Have you fallen in love with her already? She is so beautiful and so sad, is she not?"

Anger flooded through George. Dr. Gharn should not be allowed to discuss Beatrice in this way, as if she were some bit of flesh to be sold at a fair.

"Yet she can also be cold." The physician continued. "I wonder how it is possible that one woman can be so different. Have you heard the rumors that she is mad? Two women in one."

"What do you know of Princess Beatrice?" George

210

attacked in return. "She is not mad. Do not say that of her." His thoughts whirled. Beatrice was not like other women, but she had her sanity. More than most, he could argue.

"Do I hurt your feelings by speaking of your beloved? Poor prince, destined to be betrayed. And he does not even guess at the source."

George had his hands around Dr. Gharn's throat in an instant and tightened them as the physician struggled for breath. George pressed and pressed again.

And then abruptly let go.

He stared as the physician fell to the floor, gasping. Then he ran from the tower, afraid of himself more than he had been afraid of Dr. Gharn, whatever he had done. Was this the fault of animal magic, that he could let his anger take control of him so? Or was this simply his weakness as prince, as Dr. Gharn had said, never fit to rule?

CHAPTER TWENTY-FIVE

GEORGE FLED TO THE woods and to a family of possums, which chattered on about the way the sun moved overhead or underhead.

It was precisely the kind of contact he needed. Soothing, and without expectations. Later, shaking with cold from his own sweat, George made it back to the castle in the cool of the summer evening without being seen by the guard, sneaking in around the stables the way his mother had taught him so long ago. Only the lord general raised his head slightly.

George went back to his chamber to change out of his filthy clothing, intending to find a bite of food and then Sir Stephen, to offer an apology. Surely he had a long list of tasks that must still be done, as the princess was to arrive late the next day.

But before George could get out the door of his own bedchamber, he received an urgent summons to go to his father. He went immediately, taking two steps at a time, one boot still unlaced.

Four-fingered Jack stared down at the boot, but George refused to pay it any attention and stared at Jack until the door was opened and he was admitted.

Inside, his father was worse than he had ever seen him. He was pale and cold, but most terrifying was the fact that he did not seem to recognize George.

"Who are you?" the king demanded hoarsely.

"I am your son, Prince George," he said, leaning close to his father, trying not to show the terror that he felt in his heart. What was it Dr. Gharn had said: that he was afraid of his father's dying because he did not think he was ready to be king himself? Well, it was true.

"George? Don't be ridiculous," said King Davit, his mouth twisting to the side and a line of drool dribbling out of it. "My son, George, can't possibly be more than—" He stopped suddenly, and sweat broke out over his face.

"George?" he asked.

"Yes, Father. I'm here."

"So you are, so you are." And he dozed off.

That, at least, George had seen his father do before. And at the moment he was almost grateful. It gave him a chance to collect himself. His father needed immediate assistance, and much as George's encounter with Dr. Gharn had pained him, he had no reason to believe the man a danger to his father. He was a physician, and he might be able to give some ease.

So George slipped his hand out of his father's and opened the door to call Jack.

"Dr. Gharn has already been sent for, Your Highness," said four-fingered Jack, "at the same moment you were."

"Was he told it was urgent?" George demanded. Why was the man not here yet? His tower was no farther from this chamber than George had been.

"He was sent for immediately, Your Highness. I do not know why he has not yet arrived." Jack's expression was not at all happy.

"Has he been so late before?" George asked, dark suspicion growing in his heart once more.

"Never, Your Highness."

"Go after him yourself then, Jack," George said.

Jack hesitated a moment, looking back to the king.

"Go!" said George, using his commanding voice for the first time on Jack.

Jack started, eyes wide in surprise, but he did not object. Instead, he nodded briefly, then scurried down the stairs. In a moment he had gone from sight.

Immediately George regretted treating Jack so badly. It was hardly his fault that George felt the need to assert himself. And yet Jack would one day have to accept his authority too.

George waited what seemed an interminable length of time. At last Jack returned. He walked with his arms low, swinging randomly from side to side, and there was no attempt at speed.

"What is it?" George demanded.

"He is gone, Your Highness," said Jack.

"What do you mean? Gone from his tower? Then scour the castle and find him. He must have gone out for a walk."

But Jack only stared at George. "His tower is entirely empty, all his herbs and mixings gone, all his clothes, his trunk."

"Even his dove?" George asked in a low voice.

"Even the bird in the cage," said Jack.

George's head felt stuffed full of wool. He could not think. "But I talked to him only late this morning. There was no sign of his intent to leave then."

Jack merely shrugged.

"When did he last come to see the king?" George asked.

"But two hours ago," said Jack. "He brought him a triple dose of the black elixir and insisted the king drink all of it as he watched."

While George was in the woods, neglecting his duties. Again.

In a moment George could hear the low dong of the bells in the town of Wilbey that proclaimed it to be dark. Impossible to begin a search for anyone now. They would have to wait until morning. But Princess Beatrice would arrive the next day, and the castle would be far too busy with that to think about a missing physician.

No doubt precisely as Dr. Gharn had planned.

"How was the king when Dr. Gharn left?" he asked, though he thought he knew the answer already.

"He was . . . not well. He began vomiting soon afterward," Jack said, as if it pained him to admit his master's weakness. As if it were his own fault.

"And was that not alarming to you?" George asked. "That he began vomiting after the physician's medicine?"

Jack said, "It has always been so. Dr. Gharn says it is drawing the poison out of his system."

Or putting it in, thought George.

"Send for Sir Stephen," George said.

Jack went for a messenger, then came back and stood behind George's place at his father's bedside. "Do you think—will he die, Your Highness?" asked Jack.

"He can't," said George. "I won't let him." And he held tightly to his father's hand, hoping to make his words true.

CHAPTER TWENTY-SIX

*T*HROUGH THE NIGHT George kept vigil as the king slipped into a deeper sleep. He could no longer be roused by George's pricking a needle into his hand. And yet he breathed.

Sir Stephen had come in shortly after having been sent for, but he had said very little except to ask after King Davit's condition. Then he found himself a place to stand that was out of George's sight and remained there without a sound.

Once George turned and asked him, "Wouldn't you rather sit and have some rest?"

"No," said Sir Stephen. "I would not. While my king rests, I must be awake and alert." His voice was so prickly as to preclude any further comment on George's part.

So George let the man be, thinking that Sir Stephen, and Jack outside the door, and he himself were all the same in this. And why should he think that he was the only one who loved his father enough to watch every breath?

In some ways, it seemed unfair. If George's father were any ordinary man, then it would be his son alone who waited at his sickbed. But even in this, Davit was king, and so he offered his pain and his illness to all. George found his old childish anger bubbling, hot and volatile, back to the surface. Where was the man his mother had loved? George did not know if he still existed at all beneath the crown.

Wake up just once more. Let me make my peace. Talk to me again as George, he said in his heart. *That is all I shall ever ask of you.*

But come morning, the king was still in a black silence. And there were other things to be done.

"He is no worse," said Sir Stephen.

Yes, of course, Sir Stephen would feel obliged to put a good face on even the worst news. It was for the sake of the kingdom, and George thought that his father had never had a better student in keeping on a public face than Sir Stephen.

Four-fingered Jack brought in a tray of rolls and fruit from the kitchen. "It is the king's breakfast," he said as George's nose began to twitch in anticipation of one of Cook Elin's best pastries.

"Ah." George left the tray, untouched, on the table where Jack had put it. The king's breakfast indeed.

"Shall I call for something for you?" asked Jack.

"No, no," George told him, and Sir Stephen said the same.

Jack went back to his lonely post. George and Sir Stephen stared at each other.

"We cannot simply stay here. There are things that must be done to prepare for Princess Beatrice and her party. We must think of the future, of the kingdom and . . . and . . ." Sir Stephen went silent as he stared at the still form of the king.

Yes, what did any of it matter without the king?

The soft morning light grew hot on George's seat near the window. The king's lunch was brought in and the breakfast tray taken away. This time Jack did not ask if George and Sir Stephen wished anything. They were given bowls of soup and fresh rye bread.

George tried to talk to his father. It was useless.

His mind turned over and over all his failures, his weaknesses. Beatrice would see them surely as soon as she arrived. She would go back to Sarrey, and then George would be forced to admit to one and all that he could not take his father's place. His mind whirled with visions of what would happen to Kendel. Civil war, being swallowed up by Sarrey. Each thought was worse than the one before.

He turned at last to Sir Stephen. "Talk to me," he said. "Say anything you wish."

And perhaps because Sir Stephen was as desperate as George himself was, he did.

"I knew your father when he was first made king," said Sir Stephen. "He was hardly older than you are now. I was a page at the time, with no hopes for anything more than that."

"*Mmm?*" said George. It was not fair to make Sir Stephen carry the whole conversation, but for now George could not do any more than that one small sound.

"But still, I did not like him."

"Oh?" George felt terrible. Achy. Tired. Cramped. Thirsty.

"I did not think he had the qualities that make a good king." Sir Stephen went on. "He was not stern enough. He laughed too loud and too easily. The war was not going well. And then he married so far beneath his station."

George knew his father had been king for several years before he had married. "When did you change your mind about him?" he asked, surprised by his own voice, as weak as a thread.

Sir Stephen spoke as if in a dream. "I do not know when it happened precisely. When Elsbeth died, I was angry with your father. I thought it his fault in some way because he had not ended the war earlier. And though I was on his own council, I refused to speak to him directly.

"Time went on, and I could see the others around me change, as he took time to listen to them one by one and treat them well. But I did not see it in myself until the day you were born, just after the war was over. He sent someone for me, to come into the nursery where you lay, a few hours old.

"There he offered me the chance to hold you. I refused. I did not know how to hold a child. *Give me a child of fifteen,* I thought, *one who can speak and reason. I could deal with a child like that.*

"But your father insisted. He bade me sit in a rocking chair and showed me how to hold out my hands. Then he laid your tiny body in my arms. I was terrified that I would drop you, the heir to the kingdom. I thought the king was mad to insist upon this.

"But he told me that he trusted me with more than his life. He trusted me with his son's life. And when I looked into his eyes, I knew that I would never doubt him again."

Sir Stephen wiped his eyes. "I've watched over you ever since, George. Tried to justify your father's trust in me."

"Yes," said George, "I know."

"I wanted to make sure that you became a man your father would be proud of."

George stiffened. All his life he had tried to live up to his father's character, but no matter how he tried, he had always known he fell short. Flatterers told him differently, but Sir Stephen had never been in that category before.

Sir Stephen touched his shoulder. "You are, George. You are very like your father in many ways, yet you have strengths of your own."

"What strengths?" George asked, defensive, sure that Sir Stephen would not be able to think of even one.

"Courage," said Sir Stephen.

George could hardly imagine an answer that would have astounded him more. Courage? Compared with his father?

"Yes." Sir Stephen insisted. "In your honesty there is courage. You demand it of yourself and of others."

Honesty?

Sir Stephen went on. "And you give of yourself in a way your father cannot."

George had never heard Sir Stephen ever speak of King Davit's inadequacies.

"Ah, well. Enough of that. You will find yourself, as he did. But that will not mean it is easy. There are few things easy in life that are worth the doing."

This sounded more like the Sir Stephen whom George was used to. A few words of old wisdom to act as a palliative.

George felt steadier, and then a thought burst into his mind. His father could not die. "We must find a new physician."

"The other castle physicians were dismissed," said Sir Stephen. "But we might be able to coax them back with an offer of money. If you think they could do something—"

"No," said George. "No. We need another physician. Someone who can truly cure anything. Have you heard of such a man? It would not have to be in Kendel. In any land."

George would send out riders if he had to. He would mortgage the castle itself to the kingdom's noblemen or to King Helm to get enough money, if money was what was wanted.

Sir Stephen's red-rimmed eyes stared into George's. Then he said, "I know of no one."

"Think!" George commanded.

Sir Stephen was startled enough to say, "There is only—" and he stopped himself.

"Say it," said George. "Say the rest. Who is it?"

"I was thinking of Elsbeth's father. He was the finest physician I ever met. He disappeared after she died, but if we found him, if he is still alive . . ."

"You think he could cure the king?" asked George, breathless. This was hope, painful and sweet.

"If anyone could, he could," said Sir Stephen.

"But you have heard no hint of him in all this time? Surely a man so talented would be well known. Unless he wished to hide himself."

"I—" Sir Stephen paused.

"What?"

"There may have been tales of him. But I would not wish anything to happen to him." He looked meaning-fully at George. "Do you understand my meaning?"

George twitched. He was not sure that he did.

"Elsbeth would never say a word about his strange-nesses, but I could see they were there. He walked lightly, as if in a dance. A cat dance. He did not keep pets around him, but he would give medicine to animals. There were rumors about him—"

Sir Stephen looked at George and stopped.

So Elsbeth's father had had the animal magic. And Sir Stephen had been ready to marry his daughter. He had been willing to take the risk of her having it or of their children having it too.

Suddenly much of Sir Stephen's behavior to George made sense. His unwillingness to speak about the animal magic, but the way that he was unsurprised by hints of it.

All this time he had known.

Well, there would be time to talk of that later. Or perhaps not.

"Would you recognize him if you saw him again? Can you give me a description if I send out soldiers to find him?"

"It has been so long, and I have worked for so long to block my memory of that time. So painful. . . ," said Sir Stephen.

"Try, please try," said George.

"Medium height, medium build. Hair of brownish color. Eyes the same. Strong hands, long fingered." He shrugged. "It is not much. But I suppose he had his reasons for not wishing to stand out."

"Indeed." George's heart stopped. "What was his name?" he asked, and the voice sounded very distant, even to him.

"Raelgon Poll," said Sir Stephen.

"Rael-gon," George separated the two syllables, and said the last one as Sir Stephen had done, with a slight southern accent that added an *r*. It sounded exactly like Dr. Gharn. And Rael was not far from Dr. Rhuul.

Dr. Gharn had worked so hard to keep away from direct contact with Sir Stephen, with anyone, really. His disguise had been his smell and his very lack of distinguishing features.

The bird he had kept in his tower, George thought. That pointed to Dr. Gharn's having the animal magic as well. Why had George not seen it before? Because Dr. Gharn had turned George's thoughts to himself. And then to Beatrice.

"And you say that this man—his daughter was killed in the war."

"His only daughter," said Sir Stephen. "How he doted on her."

"Do you think he would have blamed my father?"

Sir Stephen shrugged. "I did for a time."

"And King Helm?" George asked.

"Perhaps," said Sir Stephen. George did not have time to explain it all, even if he could. The connections were so tenuous, requiring great leaps of the imagination. And yet they fit in a way nothing else did.

George let himself work it out in his mind. Raelgon Poll had wanted revenge for his daughter's death. He had planned for many years how to do it. He had gone to Sarrey. George was certain that he had done something

225

there, to King Helm or his daughter. And then he had come back to Kendel, to take out his anger on King Davit.

The black elixir. All along it had been poison. And three doses all together—would his father ever recover from that?

George began to search his father's bedchamber methodically.

"What are you doing?" asked Sir Stephen.

But George was too busy to answer. No doubt Dr. Gharn had very carefully cleaned the tower, but there might be something left here.

There!

Underneath his father's bed, an empty vial. George scrambled toward it, then came back out triumphantly. He held it high, then sniffed what remained inside.

"May I?" asked Sir Stephen.

George saw no reason not to let him.

But he did not expect the gasp that came afterward.

"Tell me," George said.

"There was a man." Sir Stephen spoke as if he had not thought of this memory for a very long time. "Raelgon found him in the forest. He had eaten some leaves. There were a few still in his hands. He was insensible and could not speak. But there was a strong smell, like anise and a bear's piss combined. A distinctive smell."

He held the vial to his nose once more. "This is it," he said. "I am certain of it. All this time the king has been taking it. And I did not know. I did not think to suspect—" He stared at George with tears in his eyes.

"What did the leaves do to the man?" George asked impatiently.

Sir Stephen shook his head.

"Tell me," said George. Then, more quietly: "Please."

"There was nothing to be done for him. Even though Raelgon was the best physician I had ever heard of, he said that he knew his limits, and some poisoning the man could never recover from."

George felt tears start out of his eyes. No! His father was not dead yet. And if Dr. Gharn had not known a cure twenty years ago, that did not mean there was no cure now.

"I'll go after him," said George.

"But Princess Beatrice's arrival—" said Sir Stephen.

Yes, of course. That was the reason that Dr. Gharn had left. Before he could be recognized and accused. George would wait to greet Beatrice properly, to see if she had information that would help.

George left his father's bedchamber to Sir Stephen and headed toward the stables. He could not leave today, but that did not mean he could not begin gathering what was necessary to leave as soon as possible. Supplies, for one thing. Men, for the other.

George could not do without Henry. The lord general would have to give suggestions for the others. And for the horses. They would have to go quickly. And in which direction? Where would Dr. Gharn go?

Not toward Sarrey: That was all George knew.

Chapter Twenty-seven

Princess Beatrice arrived with her entourage that evening. The royal trumpeters announced her arrival, and George stood in front of a veritable forest of nobles who had arrived purely to see the mysterious woman their prince was to marry.

They did not appear impressed by the small group that surrounded her. George counted four guards, the same number he had taken to Sarrey. She had no maid, no ladies-in-waiting, and no courtiers of her father's. She came alone, as George had gone to Sarrey, with the exception of her hound.

George smiled at the thought. Her hound was all the company Beatrice wanted, he was sure. The hound was also far better protection than any courtiers or ladies-in-waiting might provide.

After the trumpeting had ceased, George stepped forward and took her hand to help her out of the carriage. She allowed it but only for a moment. Then Marit leaped out, sniffed the air, and stared at the castle that would soon be her—and her mistress's—home. She did not seem impressed.

"How was your journey?" George asked politely.

"I'm sure you know well exactly what the journey from Sarrey to Kendel is like," said Beatrice in response.

"Ah, yes. I suppose I do. Just short of miserable."

"Long and unpleasant. I had rather walk it myself, but my father said it would be inappropriate to my station." She bared her teeth. "It would scarcely have taken any longer."

No doubt the king had had other objections, George thought.

He turned to Marit. "And how did your hound enjoy the journey?" he asked.

"She was eager for it to end," Beatrice replied.

George put his hand on her arm and guided her through the throng.

George nodded and smiled at the assembled crowd but refused to make any introductions to Princess Beatrice. Later perhaps. Now he must speak to her before he left on his mission to find the physician.

Sir Stephen would try to take her over, George thought. He would try to show her how things should be done, as he had with George as a young boy. But it would not be the same. George suspected that Beatrice would not take kindly to such attempts at training, here any more than she had at home.

Yet George did not think Beatrice was a bad choice for a bride. On the contrary, she made him think of how his mother had disappeared from her duties and been simply herself. Yes, that had left his father with more to do, but perhaps he had not minded, because even to look at her gave relief. So it was with Beatrice. She, too, was someone whose life was utterly different from his own, someone who could not be forced to do what was best for the kingdom.

Except that she was marrying George. He wished that he could say she had fallen in love with his patience and his perseverance with her father or even tales of his heroism with the bear. But he did not think it was so. If Beatrice thought of him at all, he had the impression it was as a suitable mate, no more than that.

He held more tightly to her arm, and she grimaced and yanked away from him, nearly stumbling over Marit in the process.

"Excuse me, Princess Beatrice," said George.

Beatrice said nothing.

George led her to the bedchamber that he had seen prepared the day before. But it was not as he had left it. He had specifically told Sir Stephen to keep it plain and simple, to leave the window open, and not to light the fire. But someone had come in and put heady flowers everywhere, lit a stifling fire, and filled the chamber with a sweet scent that made his nose twitch.

Beatrice actually sneezed, and Marit began to whine.

"I am sorry," George said, and went to open the window. He sighed. To take away the flowers now would do more harm than good. It would make Beatrice appear hard to please.

Beatrice leaned against the bed, and Marit made a small noise.

"How is your father?" George asked politely.

"He told me that I could do better at making you love me if only I would set my mind to it. He said that he knew I was intelligent enough but just too stubborn to do what would please you."

George flushed. He did not think he wished to know what King Helm thought would please him.

"He sent me with a gift for you, a small golden ball."

"A ball?" echoed George, confused.

"For our first child," said Beatrice. "Our son, as he put it."

"Oh." George did not know what to say to that. He could feel Beatrice watching him closely, though. Finally, he said, "I do not think of children when I think of you."

"No? That is what a marriage is for, is it not? To create children to bridge the gap between the two countries?"

"I suppose." Beatrice saw things so clearly and spoke so plainly. It was not that he did not like that about her, but somehow, it still surprised him.

"And how is your father?" Beatrice asked. "Is he still ill?"

"Gravely ill," said George. "In fact—" Now was as good a time as any. "I must leave the morning after tomorrow. To search out a physician for him."

"A physician?"

"Yes. I believe that he has been poisoned." He waited, then, ears burning, went on. "I am seeking a physician who will be able to cure him. A Dr. Gharn."

"Is that not the name of the physician who has been tending him these last months?" asked Beatrice.

George blinked in surprise. Then he thought of King Helm. Of course. Her father would have his own sources of information in Kendel's court. Spies.

"Yes."

"And you think this same physician has been poisoning your father? Yet you seek him out to beg a cure from him?"

Put that way, it did not seem sensible at all.

"Princess Beatrice, this man, Dr. Gharn, I believe he may be the same Dr. Rhuul who was but lately in your kingdom."

He stopped. Beatrice had gone very pale, and Marit had slumped to the ground in front of the fire.

"Dr. Rhuul?" Beatrice got out after a long silence.

"What can you tell me of the man?" he asked boldly.

Marit began panting heavily, and Beatrice moved to her side and knelt on the ground to rub her heaving ribs.

"Did this Dr. Rhuul do something to you?" George persisted.

232

"He is a horrible man," said Beatrice at last. "The worst of men."

"Yes." George did not ask for details. "Can you think of anything you know about him that would help me to find him?"

Marit and Beatrice seemed to shudder as one.

"I am sorry," George said.

There was a knock at the door.

Marit snarled.

George went to open it. Several of the young noblewomen were standing in front of him, and they seemed taken aback to see George.

"Oh, Your Highness," said Lady Teller, "I thought we might have the opportunity to speak to the princess." She stood taller, as if to get a glimpse around George.

"You may see her at the ball tomorrow night," said George curtly. "She is very tired after her journey and wishes only to rest." He closed the door.

Afterward he wished he had thought of a more polite way to do it, for it would reflect far worse on Beatrice than on him. They would think her snobbish and unwilling to make friends. He had been accused of the same things himself.

"He will be in the south," said Beatrice, to George's surprise. "And he will be with an animal."

"His bird, you mean?" George asked.

Beatrice shook her head. "Another animal."

"What kind of animal?" George was baffled by these

strange clues. What could they mean? How did Beatrice know they were true? Should he trust her at all?

"I do not know what kind of animal," Beatrice answered, irritated.

"Then how do you know the south?" asked George.

"He mentioned something to me once. That he would begin in the north and work his way south, until he was done with it all."

"All of what?" asked George.

"His revenge," said Beatrice.

"And the animal?"

"He likes to have animals around him. He enjoys commanding them." Beatrice spoke with bitter disdain.

Well, George supposed she would think her relationship with Marit different. But George had not seen that the doctor treated his bird so very badly.

"My father's closest adviser is Sir Stephen," George said, thinking ahead. "I shall make sure that you are introduced to him tomorrow at the ball. He will be eager to help you in anything you need while I am gone."

"No," said Beatrice. Marit began to pace the floor of the bedchamber.

"I have to go, and I know it is uncomfortable for you to be here alone," said George. It was worse than that. It was unconscionable.

And yet he had to find Dr. Gharn.

"I will not stay here," said Beatrice, "not if you are gone."

"But it will not be long," George said, though he

knew there was no guarantee this would be true.

Suddenly George found Marit's teeth on his leg, not tearing at the flesh, but digging beneath his thin leggings, giving notice.

"I will return as soon as I can. And I'm sure you will be well treated while I am gone." He hoped that his own noblewomen were better behaved than Lady Dulen.

"We shall go with you," Beatrice said.

George looked down at Marit, whose teeth were still firmly on his leg. He thought about what Sir Stephen would say. His guards. The lord general, who already thought George's adventure idiocy.

"You will come," George said.

Marit let go of his leg and went back to Beatrice. They stood together, and George realized how rare it was to see them apart.

"As for the welcoming ball, I do not see how we can escape from that," said George. But there was much preparation to be done in the meantime.

Beatrice's face went distant. "Must we dance?" she asked.

George hesitated. Sir Stephen had been so insistent on that point, even when George tried to explain about what had happened when they danced in Sarrey.

But Sir Stephen was going to be displeased about so much of this. He had best get used to it, George thought.

"We will not dance if you do not wish it," George told her.

Beatrice let out a long breath.

"Is there anything else I can get you? To help you to feel more at home?" George asked.

"A large haunch of raw meat," said Beatrice suddenly.

George's mouth fell open.

"For Marit," said Beatrice.

"Of course," said George. And he saw that it was done.

Chapter Twenty-eight

FTER AN EXHAUSTING day of secret preparations to leave, George sat in his bedchamber listening to the music for the ball being practiced. The musicians played the same eight songs over and over again, and he had become heartily sick of them by the time he dressed himself and combed his hair—five times.

Finally, on his way downstairs, he caught sight of Marit and Beatrice, wandering along the wrong hallway. He hurried after them, only to be told curtly by Beatrice that she and her hound must do "something alone."

It was but minutes before the two of them were to walk into the ball arm in arm. George was frustrated, but more angry at the way Beatrice spoke to him than about the ball's beginning late. What did he care about keeping the nobles waiting? It would just more thoroughly whet their appetites for the first sight of Princess Beatrice.

So he stood outside the door to the ballroom, back straight, head high, shoulders flat as any soldier's. Even the lord general would be proud of him, George thought. Sir Stephen was at his side. At the other side was a space for Princess Beatrice. And to her side, more space where her attendants should have been. The four guards from Sarrey, in full uniform, stood behind.

"Where is she?" whispered Sir Stephen, after the music for their entrance had been played twice.

"She will be here," George said with as much calm as he could muster.

"Where are her ladies?" Sir Stephen asked next.

It was evidence of how distraught Sir Stephen was over the king's illness that he did not know this about the princess already.

"She did not bring any ladies," said George, "only her hound."

"What?" Sir Stephen was astonished.

"She is more comfortable without them," said George.

"Without anyone?"

"What is wrong with that?" George asked quietly.

"To have no companions, no friends . . ." Sir Stephen said.

"She is who she is," said George.

"Her father could have demanded that she take someone with her. To put a good face on it," said Sir Stephen.

"I took no noblemen with me," George reminded him.

"But that was different. You are . . . a prince."

A man, thought George. *And so in need of no protection.*

"You should think of it as a good sign," George said. "If King Helm trusts us enough that he does not think she needs any attendants, it bodes well for the future."

"Or it means that he does not think we are any threat to him," Sir Stephen muttered sourly.

"Or that she argued her father out of them herself because she is so strong-minded." George tried again. "A good thing in a queen, that she thinks for herself and is unafraid."

"But no maid?" Sir Stephen protested one last time.

"She is not overly concerned with her appearance," said George.

Sir Stephen was not entirely satisfied with this explanation and became even less satisfied when Beatrice arrived at last, Marit at her side, both of them dusted with dirt and bits of leaves and flowers that they were trying to shake off.

George tried to cover a smile at the sight of them. Beatrice looked like a fierce little girl, determined not to be scolded. As for Marit, she held her head high and walked as a queen in her own domain. Confident and cool, though sniffing the guards as she passed by them.

"Go, go," said Sir Stephen when the music began again.

George took firm hold of Beatrice's arm and walked in. The ballroom was filled with more people than he had seen together in all his years as prince.

He forced himself to breathe deeply.

He searched for familiar faces to focus on, rather

than the whole of the crowd. Mostly he saw servants he knew. Elin, the cook, who stood by the tables of pastries with a challenging look on her face, in case anyone should dare not to finish a whole one.

And then . . . Peter.

George stopped short at the sight of him. He had not seen him in—how many years had it been? Eight?

He was taller than he had been, and broader. George suspected that most women would find him very handsome, with his blond locks and square chin.

"Who is that horrible young man?" Beatrice asked, following George's gaze.

For that alone, George thought, he could marry her happily.

"His name is Peter Lessing," said George. He struggled to recall his title. "Sir Peter Lessing."

"He looks as though he has eaten something very sweet," said Beatrice.

Indeed he did, smiling widely and moving forward through the crowd, raising a hand to draw George's attention.

George wished that he had Marit at his side, circling his leg for comfort, but she kept close to Beatrice, guarding her. George's hands grew sweaty, and he felt suddenly alone.

Peter stopped before them and bowed with a flourish. "My prince, would you present me to your bride-to-be?" he asked boldly.

Peter would take great pride in telling the story of

how he had been first to be presented to Princess Beatrice of all those who had gathered at the ball, George realized. And George, as prince, could do nothing to show his displeasure.

"This is Princess Beatrice of Sarrey," he said.

Peter took her hand in his and held it to his lips. "Very pleased to meet you," he said.

There was a moment of silence. Marit's hairs were standing up on her back, and she had her teeth bared.

Peter took no notice. "Let me tell you a story about George here. Did you know that he and I played together when we were young?"

Beatrice shook her head, her eyes on the floor.

"I shall tell you about the time that I convinced George to jump in the moat with me, shall I?" Peter said. His eyes flashed in triumph toward George.

George froze and suddenly felt as guilty and filthy as he had when fished out of the moat on that day so long ago.

"I told George that swimming in the moat at midnight was the one sure way to acquire the animal magic." Peter went on, his voice oozing charm. "And then I dared him to meet me there and jump in. Of course I let him go in first."

"You didn't jump in yourself?" asked Beatrice.

"No," said Peter. "No, I never did."

"Too afraid of the animal magic?" asked Beatrice after a moment.

"What?" asked Peter, stepping back and letting go of

Beatrice's hand at last. "No, of course not. That had nothing to do with it. It was a joke, don't you see?"

"A very mean joke, then, it seems to me. You were older than he, were you not? And he was your prince. Why would you tease him so?" she asked.

George put an arm around Beatrice to lead her away. He could see Sir Stephen motioning to him. This would be the perfect chance to exit.

And yet Beatrice froze at his touch.

"It was all in good fun," Peter continued, unrelenting. "George enjoyed it afterward, I am sure. Although the look on his face at the moment that he was pulled from the moat . . . priceless. I think he was really terrified that he had the animal magic then."

Had Peter been watching, hidden, all the time? As his prince nearly drowned? George burned all over again.

"You are an expert on such things yourself?" asked Beatrice. "On animal magic?" She nudged Marit, and the hound moved forward to flank Peter so that he could not escape easily.

"An expert on animal magic, of course not. No, no," said Peter hastily.

"Are you sure? I have heard it comes later in some, and they do not know they have it until it is too late and animals surround them."

Peter's eyes were wild. "I do not have the animal magic. I swear it!" His voice had gone as high as a boy's, and he put up his hands as if to ward off Beatrice's accusation.

Beatrice turned to George. "He should be sent away."

"Because you suspect he has animal magic?" asked George. It made no sense, not when she knew about him.

"Because he is evil," said Beatrice. "He stinks of it. Can you not smell it?"

George sniffed. He smelled fear, no more than that. But was it his own? Or Peter's?

"Please, Your Highness." Peter turned at last to George.

George wished that the moment were more gratifying. He felt a little sorry for Peter, and a little tired of him and his petty ways. Yet he was part of George's kingdom.

"Let him go," he said to Beatrice.

She shrugged and stepped back.

George stepped forward and put a hand on Marit's back, and she let herself be led back as well.

He nodded to Peter and did not see him the rest of the night.

Sir Stephen tried several times to get George to lead Beatrice in a dance, but George was firm on the matter. He listened to the music without complaint. He ate what Cook Elin expected of him. He greeted warmly all those Sir Stephen pointed out to him and presented Beatrice to every one of them.

Her pride, her stubbornness, her strength, and her refusal to be cowed: Those were all the things that would make her queen. His queen.

CHAPTER TWENTY-NINE

$\mathscr{I}$N THE MORNING George stood with the other guards, as well as the lord general, who had insisted on accompanying the prince on this "ridiculous advanture, if for no other reason than to prevent you from killing my best soldiers."

No mention of the lord general caring if George killed himself.

"Why are we not leaving, then? It is dawn, but perhaps you have not had sufficient breakfast?" the lord general asked.

"We are waiting for Princess Beatrice," George explained.

"Why?" the man asked, his twice-broken nose twitching in irritation. "Have you fallen so much in love with her that you can't stand to go for a ride without holding her hand?"

"She is necessary," George replied. As prince he should not have to say more.

"A woman is never necessary," said the lord general. "And the man who thinks she is will soon find out the truth of that for himself."

Another insult to Beatrice. This time George stared the lord general down.

But the lord general had his revenge when he sent Henry to bring their horses. Beatrice's was a fat white mare with a good temper. George's was a huge monstrosity of a beast, black and more than a hand above George's head. He stomped about, pulling at his bit, as Henry held him.

"He's called Ass," said Henry helpfully.

"And why is that?" asked George.

Henry swallowed, turned red, and said, "Because anyone who tries to ride him ends up on his ass."

George would not deign to ask for a different horse and hear the lord general complain of a weak prince. He reached forward to take hold of the lead and a moment later was flying through the air. He landed on his backside and got up with a glint in his eye. And an idea.

"Henry," he said, "take off all the gear, saddle, stirrups, reins—everything."

Henry looked as if George had suddenly gone mad.

George wondered at it himself. "Do it," he said again. "And make sure you stay with the princess."

"Yes, Your Highness," said Henry. He did as he was commanded.

Ass was quiet.

But George was not fooled.

At last Beatrice arrived, Marit at her side.

"Wearing something suitable, at least," the lord general muttered.

She was dressed in men's riding trousers and riding jacket. George found it strangely appealing, though it did not emphasize her femininity. It made her eyes seem darker, her cheeks broader, and her whole body stronger.

"Good morning," said George. "Will this horse suit you?"

She looked the mare up and down. "Of course," she said, without much enthusiasm.

George looked down to Marit, but she seemed as comfortable as her mistress and, if he was not misinterpreting her look, was watching him with something like laughter in her hound's eyes.

George nodded to her with a wry smile of his own and turned away. He walked once around Ass, then leaped suddenly from the side and landed on the animal's back. It took all the courage and strength he possessed to hold on to Ass's mane for the next several minutes, speaking quietly all the while in the language of horses.

At last Ass slowed.

George held as tightly as ever to the mane.

Ass gave one last great shiver to dislodge George. It did not work.

Beatrice and Henry were far behind him, but they caught up as George rode to the edge of the forest, where the lord general and the others of his men were waiting.

"Still intent on this foolish chase, Prince?" asked the lord general.

"Yes," said George. He spurred Ass onward, and by the time he made it across the forest, he was sore in places he had not known were his before, while Ass seemed to be enjoying his every twitch.

It was far from dark, but he dismounted and waited until the others caught up. Then he instructed the lord general to make camp there at the edge of the forest. He walked around the camp to ease his aching muscles and found Marit at his side. She was a comfortable companion. She matched strides with him, and there was about her presence something that soothed him.

When he realized how rare it was for Marit to be away from her mistress, even for a short time, he felt honored that she had chosen to come to him. He took in the smell of her coat, the feel of her eyes on him. He did not know if he had ever felt so rested in the company of another. It was no wonder that Beatrice loved Marit so. At first he had thought it was because Beatrice was so remarkable a woman. But that was unfair. Marit was at least as remarkable a hound.

Finally, he went back to check on Beatrice and her tent. The princess did not seem very impressed with it but had made no complaints.

Just then the lord general himself came to see the princess. He stared at her rather rudely, then turned to George. "She looks pretty enough and strong enough to bear you several children," was his blunt assessment.

Beatrice hesitated a moment, looked down at Marit, then faced the lord general directly. "When you speak to me, speak to my face," she demanded.

The lord general's face was a study in surprise. "I do not take orders from women," he said. He could have taken a step away from her and retreated to save his pride. But George was sure the lord general had no intention of showing even that much weakness to Beatrice. So he held his place, and she held hers.

Beatrice's lips were firmly set together. George almost expected her to growl. She said, "You will not dismiss me. I demand your recognition."

The words were awkward, yet George silently applauded Beatrice.

"You are a woman," said the lord general, with a dismissive wave of his hand.

"I am Princess Beatrice." She took a small step closer to him.

The lord general stepped back at last. His head bowed, and he moved around her. "Prince, we will be up early in the morning." He glanced at Beatrice.

"I am sure the princess and I will be ready to leave when you are," said George.

The lord general gave a curt nod and walked away.

"You were right to insist he treat you well," said George.

Beatrice said nothing.

"Is there anything I can get for you?" he asked.

"What could you get for me?" asked Beatrice quizzically.

What indeed? "I meant, are there any comforts you would prefer to have? I might be able to find a cushion for you or an extra blanket," George said at last. "Or perhaps a candle if you wished to keep your tent light in the dark."

"No," said Beatrice. She had her hand on Marit.

Of course, with Marit, she did not need George for company.

Still, he stood there, thinking.

"Did you wish to offer me a prize of some sort?" Beatrice asked, her head tilted to one side as if she were studying him. "You have already presented me with your betrothal gifts. Surely that is enough for the sake of the custom."

"It is not about a custom." George had become impatient with this conversation, but he did not know how to end it.

"You are not afraid that I will marry another," said Beatrice. "I have told you already my reasons for the betrothal, and those have not changed."

"Yes, you have." Cold-blooded reasons, all of them.

"Then what is it?"

"When you were a girl, was no one ever kind to you for your own sake and not your father's?" George finally asked.

Beatrice took a moment to think that over. "I do not know. I do not think so, but it is so difficult to be sure."

George sighed deeply. And was he really any different from her? His life too had been the closed and private life of a prince. It was why they were to marry after all. Yet if he could erase his place as prince and hers as princess, if they could meet as only a man and a woman, what then? Would they do better or worse?

George had to believe better.

"I am sorry to have bothered you." He turned on his heel, expecting her to let him go.

Nothing could have surprised him more than when she spoke back softly into the night. "I am sorry I cannot accept more from you, Prince George. It would be unfair when I am already taking more than you know."

"Taking what?" George half turned back, but he could see nothing on her face that gave him a hint of a clue. She was speaking in riddles again. She seemed to be speaking in riddles always.

No, that was not true. Now and again he had a sense that what she said was absolutely true and from her heart. But he thought he could count those times on one hand.

Well, there was nothing to be done about it now. She did not offer any more.

"Good night," said George.

CHAPTER THIRTY

*T*HAT NIGHT GEORGE dreamed of Marit, instead of Beatrice as he had before. He watched as the hound ran through the forest, chasing down a fat partridge. He tasted the hot blood in his mouth and the warmth in his belly. He danced in the cold stream and back out again.

Afterward George saw the castle in Sarrey, now through Marit's eyes, as she ascended the steps in front and sniffed along the corridors. He felt her sense of confinement in this place. She was restless to be out again as soon as she entered it. Yet she made no sound of complaint.

It was more restraint than George had ever seen in a wild creature before.

Then Princess Beatrice came into focus in the castle. The hand on the back, the warmth shared. And so she stayed. Duty and love tied her.

George understood both very well.

He woke feeling as tired as he had when he went to sleep. It was still dark, but he could not sleep again. The restlessness of the hound in the dream was part of him now. He quietly dressed and crawled out of his tent.

He looked across the camp and saw Marit staring back at him.

He went toward her, thinking perhaps he could offer her something. If the princess would not accept, then the hound?

He put out his hand to beckon to her. But she did not move from the door of the tent.

He moved closer, then knelt down. "We'll go out running, you and I," he whispered. "Wouldn't you like that?" He remembered from the dream the way she had felt with the wind blowing in her face, the feel of the moss beneath her paws as she pressed and moved as a hound was meant to.

Still, she would not come to him.

So George sat morosely on the ground, hands on knees, and thought on the matter. Why would she deny herself what she loved?

There was a rustle inside the tent, and before George could stand, Beatrice was there, a dark shadow in the open flap.

"She woke you too," she said flatly.

"I suppose. After a fashion."

"She does not sleep well these days." Beatrice seemed on the edge of tears, something that George had never seen before. Yet he dared not offer her anything, not even a chance to unburden herself.

"Do you share her dreams as well?" George asked instead.

"No. I have not your gift," said Beatrice. "It is one of the things I envy you."

George had the feeling that the list was not very long. "Would you like me to tell you what she dreamed?"

"I can read it in her eyes and in the way she stands," said Beatrice. "She is unhappy. But I am unhappy as well."

"Will you ever let her go?" asked George.

"When she lets me go," was the cryptic reply.

"It has not always been like this between you, though," said George.

"No," said Beatrice. She seemed about to add more, then shook her head.

"A hound should have a pack," said George suddenly.

Beatrice looked down at Marit. "And a woman should have a family that loves her," she said.

George granted that with a nod of his head. "I feel as if we are pieces in a game of kings," he said. "Moved about this way and that, coming close together, then moving apart once more."

"Who is moving us?" asked Beatrice.

"I don't know. I cannot see that far."

"And if you could, would that change the power that works you?"

George did not answer this. There was nothing to say.

"If you were a hound, I should say that you needed to make a kill," said Beatrice.

"And is that what you think this hunt for Dr. Gharn is? My chance for a kill?" asked George.

Beatrice shrugged. "Is there pleasure in it for you?"

George thought back to the dream he had shared with Marit. She had been hunting for a small thing, a partridge, yet her joy in the catch had been so pure. Would he feel that same joy in catching Dr. Gharn?

No, because it would not be finished then. There would always be another step and another.

"Is there pleasure in anything for you?" Beatrice asked. "Without thinking of the future or of others, only of yourself?"

George tried to think. There should be one thing in his life that was for him alone. He was a prince, of course, and he had his duties. But even the animal magic that was his alone was not something he found joy in. It had always been a source of shame, and fear, and constant thinking, to make sure that he was not gone too long or did not meet with any other humans while he was out or did not come back too obviously from the woods.

"Perhaps not," he said.

"My father always loved war," said Beatrice. "He did not like the idea of giving it up, but he still has the chance to practice in the yard, with the soldiers. I think that will be enough for him."

As for George's father, he had had his queen. Even

when she was gone, he could remember her. George had come upon him often enough, distracted, his eyes cloudy in the past.

"And you, what gives you joy?" asked George.

Beatrice met his eyes squarely. "In that, you and I are alike," she said. "Duty moves me wholly."

"Duty does not force you to speak to me like this, in the middle of the night," said George. "You could have remained in your tent."

"No," Beatrice said. "You are right."

"Then we can be friends? Or if not friends, then at least we could walk together in the dark, while we are not sleeping."

"We could do that," said Beatrice.

That was the trick, George thought. To make sure that she did not think she was receiving an undue gift and to keep her from giving more than she wished. They walked around the camp, Marit keeping pace with them, then around it again in a wider circle. Suddenly Marit went very still.

"Shh," said Beatrice, and put out a hand to catch George's shoulder.

He stopped, and Beatrice pointed. There was a flash of white not far into the woods, and then it disappeared in a sudden movement.

Marit raced after it, and George and Beatrice followed. As they chased, George realized that the animal was no hare. It was a fox, full grown, far too big for a single meal for Marit. Yet Marit was eagerly playing the game of the hunt with it.

In fact it was all George could do to keep pace with them. His heart pounded, and his legs ached with cramps, but he could see a smile on Beatrice's face, and it seemed contagious, for he knew he too was smiling.

In the end, Marit caught the fox by the tail and worried at it. The fox turned and scratched at Marit's nose.

George thought that Marit would use a paw to stomp on it. She had it now; it could not go free.

But she let it go, and it ran off into the woods.

George thought it strange that after all the hours he had spent in the woods, he had never had such joy as this. Was it because he had not used his animal magic enough? He was inclined to think that it was Beatrice and Marit. They knew a secret he had never thought of: Sometimes it is better not to think of tomorrow, but only of today, of this minute, of now.

The sun was rising behind them, just a touch of pink in the sky. In a few minutes the lord general would be out of his tent and rousing the rest of the party. George did not care to imagine what the man's reaction would be if he found the prince and the princess missing from their tents without a word.

They had to go back.

George touched Beatrice's hand. "Thank you," he said.

It broke the spell that had been between them. She stiffened. "I did not even know you were here."

Yet it had been as if all three of them had been hounds. Interesting, that with all his animal magic, he had never before been able to forget how human he was. He had talked to the animals, learned from them, even seen their way of life, but always from his perspective. It had taken Marit and Beatrice to show him a new way.

He bent down and looked at Marit. Perhaps he would get a better reception from her. "Thank you," he said.

She came toward him until her muzzle touched his nose. She did not bark or whine, but simply held there. A moment of recognition, of acceptance, George hoped, that they were more than they had been. Friends indeed.

Then they went back, and George wondered if it all had been a dream. It did not seem quite real, but he still had a scratch on his hand from a tree that Marit and Beatrice had avoided but he had collided with.

It would fade in a few days' time. And then what? Would their shared chase also fade?

No, he promised himself. He would remember it. Even if Marit and Beatrice did not. Like his father, he would go away in his mind and let his eyes go blank, so that he could take out that memory and relive it. A pleasure for himself, and fairly earned.

CHAPTER THIRTY-ONE

*G*EORGE BROUGHT BEATRICE'S breakfast to her tent, then sat with her while she ate it in the cold morning air. She fed Marit bits directly from her hands.

"Do you know why Dr. Gharn — Dr. Rhuul to you — would want to take such revenge on your father? Or on mine?"

"It has something to do with the dove in the cage, I think," Beatrice said after a moment.

How had she gotten that idea? George told her about Sir Stephen and the physician's daughter and how the war had killed her.

But Beatrice shook her head: "It has to do with the dove."

Her certainty almost made George doubt himself. But it made no sense.

"He spoke to it constantly," said Beatrice, for evidence. "He asked it questions and then waited to hear an answer."

George had not seen this himself, but he did not doubt that Beatrice had. Still, what did that prove? "Perhaps his revenge and his isolation have made him mad." But as soon as George said it, he remembered that he had been certain that Dr. Gharn was not at all mad, merely determined.

He had no desire to argue with Beatrice any longer, so he shrugged. "It doesn't matter why, I suppose. We can ask him that when we find him, if we wish. But the important thing is to capture him—and soon."

Beatrice nodded, and George went away quite unsatisfied. What did he feel for her? Something strong and warm, but he had no name for it. Not yet.

The next day George and Beatrice rode together. The lord general set a cruel pace, and while Marit might have been able to keep up if left to herself, Beatrice's mare lagged far behind. Ass tried to get ahead of her and snapped at George when he put his heels deep into his sides.

By late afternoon, when they reached a deep forest in the south that was the last part of Kendel, George was exhausted. It was, George realized, the forest his mother had mentioned when he was but a boy, the forest she had meant to take him to.

The lord general asked, "Shall we go around the forest and make camp on the other side? I believe the trails inside the forest are too overgrown for such a group to travel safely."

Perhaps he did not want to force his men, who looked terrified of the rumors of the forest they must have heard. Even Henry seemed uneasy, his mouth twitching at one side as he watched George.

George turned to Beatrice. He wondered if she would demand that they make camp directly by the forest, just to be contrary, but her face wore a strange expression, half dreamy, half defiant. At last she said, "Yes, we will go around."

Marit, however, kept wandering to the edge of the forest as they skirted around it, daring to go in for a few yards and then coming back out when Beatrice called for her loudly. George did not understand it.

He nodded to Beatrice, then pulled Ass back and around her, toward Marit. Was there something in the forest she had seen and they had not? Suddenly Ass was galloping, and George could see a branch looming ahead, as wide around as George's head and right at the level of his throat.

George ducked just in time to miss it and didn't get his head up again until much later, when he was utterly lost in the depths of the forest.

George had never in his life been lost. It was a strange sensation.

Finally Ass slowed nearly to a stop, and George took the chance of sliding off his bare back to stretch his legs.

He heard a whinnying sound, then remembered Ass had not been tied to a stake or corralled in a pasture. By the time he looked around for the horse, Ass had disappeared into the trees.

This wasn't a familiar forest, but the sounds weren't entirely alien either. It was not light enough to see much more than the outlines of trees and plants, but George had only to listen carefully to catch the sound of running water. He headed toward it, thinking that if he followed the water, it eventually would lead him out of the forest.

He hoped.

Or at least to some animals to which he could talk. Perhaps they would know the way out. If he could get them to tell him in a way that made sense, then he might have a chance of getting back to the lord general and Beatrice. And of finding Dr. Gharn.

The water was cool on his face and in his mouth. George didn't even bother taking off his trousers before sitting down in the middle of it. He leaned back and fought the desire to sleep.

Then he heard what sounded like a pack of wolves readying for a contest. He slipped out of the water and moved toward the sounds of growling and encouragement. He pushed past the reeds by the stream, then reached for the first branch of an oak tree nearly as large as his palace. He pulled himself upright as silently as he could, edged toward the trunk, and climbed until he could see the wolves beneath him.

No, not wolves. Wild hounds. A pack of twelve or more, and they surrounded a large black hound.

It was Marit.

She had been drawn to the forest in some way. George had noticed it just as Ass went wild. But why?

"Our territory," growled the lead male in the language of hounds, swiping at Marit with one paw.

Marit didn't move, though the paw sliced within inches of her face.

George didn't know what to think. She had to have smelled the wild hounds about. She had to have known she was headed for them. She had endangered herself deliberately.

"Don't belong here now," snarled the lead female as she nudged her way to the side of her mate. She leaped toward Marit, and this time it was no feint. The two bitches flipped end over end until the lead female landed on top of Marit. Her paw raked Marit's side.

And still, Marit did not struggle. She was so limp she might have been fighting a bear.

But wild hounds would not accept surrender as a bear would.

I have to do something for her, thought George. *But how?*

The lead female did get bored, tangling with an unwilling enemy. At last she got up and sauntered away, leaving Marit behind, bleeding and unsteady. But Marit would not leave. The pack had turned their backs on her, but she would not take an easy escape.

Did she want to die? George wondered. It reminded him a little of the way Beatrice treated the women in her father's court. She made no attempts to secure their affection, and when they insulted her, she did not turn away from the fight.

Now Marit howled after the pack.

The lead female turned and came back, this time with several others at her side. The lead male turned up his nose and watched her. This had apparently become a matter for the females and something he would not meddle in.

The lead female nodded at the others to stand to the side and approached Marit, this time with teeth flashing.

But Marit did not pay any attention to her. She seemed to have eyes only for the young bitch that had just emerged from the pack, a little smaller than herself with the same color coat, though she did not walk with the same proud, defiant stance that Marit had.

Still, it was Marit's daughter. George was sure of it.

The lead female tore another gash in Marit's side, but Marit seemed only distracted. She hissed and tried to lick at the wound herself, then turned back to the young bitch.

But how had it happened? The only bitch in a pack of wild hounds that had a child was the lead female. What had happened to Marit and to the pack to so change things now? The lead male George had seen showed no sign of a bond to Marit. Perhaps her lead male was dead. And if she had been chased from the pack following that tragedy, then her child was no longer her own. No matter how much their shared scent and features made Marit still feel a connection, her child now belonged to the pack.

Ah.

How human of her to refuse to give up that child. Perhaps she fought within herself, the wild hound and the part of her that had learned human ways, coming back to her child to claim her. If she could.

George felt for her and tensed at the danger to come.

The lead female attacked again, this time cutting at Marit's face. George's shoulders twitched at the strangled sound of pain, but when the lead female growled, "Leave," at Marit, she did not seem to hear.

Marit whined at the young bitch.

As if deciding at last that she had to make some response, the young bitch turned her head toward Marit and answered directly, "Not my mother." It was clearly said, and the effect on Marit was immediate and devastating.

As much as if she were a human mother.

Marit let her head bow at last, then turned away from the lead female, who gave her a final swipe across the flanks as she moved away from the pack. George dropped to the forest floor and waited only long enough to be sure that the pack of wild hounds were eagerly moving away from the place of conflict before he ran toward Marit.

She was limping noticeably now, as if the pain that had passed her by before had returned in full force.

She looked up at George, seeming ready to snarl at him as well. He held his hands up in surrender, and she began walking again. He let her lead him, hand on her back, out of the forest and to the camp.

It was not as far as he had thought, but he would never have been able to find the way himself, even if it had been full light. She led him directly, without any apparent trouble. So much for her having turned human. Still, the way that she held her head down, defeated, seemed very human indeed.

She had lost a child not once but twice now.

When they emerged from the forest at last, George could see the moon just beginning to rise in the sky. He let his hand fall from Marit's back and walked the remaining distance to the camp on his own.

"You are here," said Henry, sighing with relief. He stared down at the hound. "I told the lord general you would catch up, that you must have fallen off Ass." He gestured toward where all of the horses were tied. Ass was indeed among them.

"Did he believe you?" asked George.

"He didn't doubt it for a minute," said Henry with a grin.

George was sure he hadn't.

Chapter Thirty-two

ARIT MADE HER WAY to Beatrice's tent. She poked her head in, then lay down halfway across the threshold, as if she could make it no farther.

George heard a yelp of anguish from Beatrice, then saw her form at the flap of her tent as she struggled to pull her hound inside.

He went to her assistance immediately, but she would have none of it. George suspected she blamed him for what had happened to Marit, for not protecting her while they were together.

Why hadn't he? He had felt that Marit's business with the hounds was her own, not his. Even if he had tried to intervene, he could not have changed the outcome in the least. Oh, perhaps he might have kept her from being injured physically, but he did not believe that was where the true injury lay.

"She was attacked by other hounds," George said, standing just inside the tent.

"I can see that. Do you think I am an idiot?" asked Beatrice tartly.

"No," said George. He was taken aback, but he would not be so easily chased from this scene. "Do you know that she has—had a daughter among them?"

"She should never have gone back there. I have told her it is not her business. A pack is not kind to those that are set outside it. They are worse than strangers."

It sounded as though Beatrice understood the pack mentality of the wild hounds better than Marit did. Perhaps Marit was too close to it, and Beatrice was not.

"I do not think she will go back again, though. She has learned her lesson," said George.

Beatrice's head jerked up at this. "You are so sure of that, are you?" she demanded.

"I—well, I trust in Marit's judgment. She is no idiot either," George answered.

"No?" Beatrice's sharp, gleaming eyes turned back to Marit. "Are you not?"

Marit tried to lick at her wound, but it was too far up her back for her to reach it. She tried again.

George reached for her, to ease the cut himself. Beatrice snarled at him until he backed away.

"She is my hound," said Beatrice.

"Yes, I know. I am sorry—"

Beatrice began to weep, great racking sobs that

267

shook her whole body. While she wept, she tended to Marit's wounds, getting out a packet of supplies she had brought with her. It was well planned, George thought, as good as anything Dr. Gharn might have had. A poultice that smelled of herbs and oil, narrow strips of cloth for wrapping.

George stood nearby, thinking himself entirely useless. Marit and Beatrice both would be more comfortable if he left, and yet his legs would not move. He needed to be here.

He should do something then. Offer to help wrap the bandages, or put on the ointment. Anything!

At the very least, he could put an arm around Beatrice to comfort her. But he was so sure that it would only make her think he believed her weak. And he did not want that. What was between them seemed so fragile, and he would do much to keep it from breaking.

So he listened to her weeping until, as she finished wrapping the wound, her weeping stopped.

If he thought Beatrice would thank him then, however, he was mistaken.

"How was she?" Beatrice demanded.

"Who?"

"The hound. Her daughter."

"Oh. She looked well. A little smaller than Marit, but otherwise full grown."

"And the others in the pack? Do they treat her well? Did she have injuries?"

"No," said George.

"Any sign of illness?"

George shook his head.

Beatrice took a breath and then let it out. She did not ask any more. "Dr. Gharn told me there was a woman who had accused him and his daughter of animal magic," she said.

The hair on the back of George's neck stood up.

"He said that he would have his revenge on her as well. That is why I brought you south. This is where he said he would find her."

"He told you this himself?" George asked in surprise.

"He told it to Marit," said Beatrice.

"And you can speak with her?" George asked.

A bleak expression crossed Beatrice's face. "After a fashion," she said. "We have worked out our own way of communication, but it is not as you can do." She sounded jealous. Of him! George could hardly believe it.

"I can speak to other animals," said George, "but not to her." He nodded to Marit.

"But you can," Beatrice said.

What could she mean?

"The dreams," said Beatrice.

But George shook his head. Somehow she knew about the dreams he had, but they had been almost entirely of her. Not of Marit.

"But—" George protested.

"Tell me what you have dreamed."

So he told her. Since he had left Sarrey, it had only been in bits and pieces. One dream showed her caught in her father's bedchambers, playing with his soldier pieces, and being punished by missing two meals in a row. As soon as she had the chance, however, she had gone back to them, again and again. Until her father had locked the pieces up in a chest to which only he had the key, which he hung around his neck.

She had gone to the woods then, to make herself pieces out of clay and dry them. But they were never good enough for her, and eventually she despaired of it.

He had dreamed of her being dressed to go to one of her father's weddings, then running away before it started and being chased by her father's guards and dragged back.

George had dreamed of the days when the new queen was laboring to bring a son into the world and then of that stillborn child, bloody and pale, next to his dying mother. He had seen the pyre that had burned both of them and Beatrice's refusal to cry for ones who were so weak.

George had become so used to the dreams that he no longer thought it unusual when he fell asleep and saw things through her eyes. Yet the dreams were all of the past. Nothing from the last year and certainly nothing of himself. Or was it too arrogant to think that she would ever dream of him?

"They give me glimpses of you that let me see how you have become who you are. And why."

Beatrice smiled a strange smile. Then she glanced down to Marit and sighed. "The dreams are not from me," she said. "They are from her."

"What? How?" He was baffled.

Beatrice gave him an odd look. "Have you not guessed it yet?" she asked.

"Guessed what?" George's mind whirled. Was it possible that Beatrice had told the hound so many stories of her childhood that Marit dreamed them real in her own mind?

But that was not what Beatrice explained. "It must be part of your gift," she said. "Not only do you speak the language of the animals, but you can become one with them. In their dreams."

George thought of his dreams of the bear so long ago. Part human, part bear. Those dreams had confused him.

He took a sharp breath, then stared at Beatrice and saw somehow beyond the shell of hardness to the fragile shape within. A strange, struggling shape.

Two women in one.

That was what Dr. Gharn had said.

Why had he not understood it then?

Dr. Gharn had worked his revenge on King Helm's daughter, but he had not tried to poison her. What had he done to her? What terrible thing?

George looked at Beatrice, at the hound, and back at Beatrice.

The answer was in her eyes. And in the wild way she held her head. In the way she sniffed at the air.

Answers everywhere, if only one thought to ask the right question.

Memories came tumbling over one another in his mind, in case he did not see the truth clearly enough already.

Wild hound though she was, Marit did not understand the rules of the pack. He thought of Beatrice's strange behavior. Her inability to dance. The way she spoke. Her growling stance with the lord general. So like a hound's.

How could he not have guessed?

The woman he had thought he was coming to love, the woman from his dreams, that woman had been transformed into a hound, while the woman who stood before him, the woman who was called Princess Beatrice and whom he was expected to marry, was no woman at all. Though she had the figure of a woman, and the hair, the eyes, and the voice, inside, she was a hound.

George found he had no words.

"I am sure that you wish to be gone now," said Beatrice stiffly. Marit had moved to her side, rubbing against her leg as if to ask for comfort, but Beatrice would not look down at her.

Neither of them came close to George.

"That is not true," said George. But he did not even know whom to speak to. Marit or Beatrice?

"Stay then." It was not spoken with any kindness. She turned away from him. They both did.

George's hands were sticky with Marit's blood. The bitch hound in the forest had been Beatrice's daughter, not Marit's. But Marit, human as she was in her heart, had sought her out for Beatrice. To see if she could still be her mother, and if not, at least to bring back news.

And Beatrice had scolded her. Beatrice, who understood what pack meant all too well.

George licked his lips and found he could speak, though hoarsely. And slowly. "When I was a boy, my mother would tell me stories of those who had animal magic in the old days. They had such power. And we had so little. I thought that it was gone now. I thought—" The truth was, he had not thought of it much at all.

A darkness swept over him.

He was failing. Far worse than he had before King Helm with a sword, far worse even than on that distant judgment day.

Dr. Gharn had been right. He was not fit to be king.

He was not fit to have animal magic.

He was not fit for anything.

"You are afraid of your magic," said Beatrice as he stepped back toward the tent flap.

George stopped.

"As much as any of the people from whom you hide it." Beatrice went on, not even looking at him, but at Marit. As if she were voicing what Marit thought.

"What do you mean?"

"You believe you will betray it. It is in everything you say about it."

"Surely I am afraid of its betraying me," said George.

But Beatrice shook her head.

George thought of the owl in the story his mother had told him, the owl that no longer wished to live after his family had died. It meant he had an obligation that came with his magic, as much as the obligations that came with his crown. But what could he do? She had not taught him enough.

"I am sorry," George said. Sorry for so much that he could not begin to list it.

There was silence behind him. He listened for a long while, and then he went to his own blanket, rolled up in it, and stared at the stars the rest of the night. He could not sleep, and he was glad this time. At least that way he knew he would not dream.

CHAPTER THIRTY-THREE

THE NEXT MORNING Marit and Beatrice came out of their tent later than usual, Beatrice standing taller and straighter than ever and Marit hardly noticing the small bandage on her back as she strode toward the breakfast fire.

No one asked what had happened the night before.

George walked around as though he had a stone in his throat, blocking the passage to his lungs. He struggled for every breath and felt his heart pounding in his head, as if it had swollen to ten times its normal size.

He worked hard to focus on his food, on the daily tasks of the morning routine: feeding Ass, rolling up his blanket, and then coming back to where the lord general stood, to discuss the day's journey.

"So, now we are just out of Kendel and into Thurat. Do we go farther, Prince?" asked the lord general. "Or do we stop here and wait for the physician to come to us?"

George turned to Beatrice.

"To the next village," she said coldly, her eyes looking beyond George.

The lord general bowed with some irony and said, "As you command."

That day Beatrice contrived to keep at least one other rider between her and Marit and George, with little difficulty. George noticed that the guards hardly showed her more respect than the lord general did.

They stayed with her if commanded. They brought her food when commanded. They cared for her horse when commanded. Otherwise they kept their eyes from her and their thoughts as well. She might as well have been a ghost riding with the company.

As for Marit, they treated her worse than a stray cat. They did not even offer her little bits of food from their plates. Instead, they kept away from her as if she had some disease. As if she had the animal magic herself and were not the victim of it.

It made George furious. Yet he could say nothing aloud. It would only make it worse for them.

If only he had done as he had planned. Marry the woman and feel nothing for her. Not try to love her. Not even try to know her.

It would have been so much easier.

But he could not wish it for very long.

When they stopped for lunch, George ate with Henry. The guard seemed to sense how upset George was and tried to distract him by telling George about his childhood in the smallest village, he claimed, in Kendel. It was so small it didn't even have a name until Henry's younger sister decided she couldn't keep calling it "that" and officially named it Georgeville.

"After you," Henry added.

From anyone else, George might have taken it as an attempt at flattery, but not with Henry. "What does your sister know of me?" asked George.

"Only that you are the prince and that she wanted our village to sound important. She is very proud, my sister. My father says no man will ever have her."

"And why is that?" George asked politely.

"Because she is as loud as a chicken and as stubborn as an ox."

George could see the love for his sister shining in Henry's eyes. He wondered what he had missed, never having had a sibling. His father had been urged over and over again to marry a second time, but he had always refused. George had always thought it was because his love for George's mother had been too immense to allow another in her place. But what if there was another reason? What if his father had not married again because he had been protecting George? If another son had been born, one without the animal magic, would he have felt obliged to set George aside as heir?

"You have other sisters?" asked George.

277

"No," said Henry. "Just the one. And she is plenty."

They stood as the lord general declared it was time to ride once more.

"Do you wish to marry Princess Beatrice?" asked Henry suddenly. As soon as he spoke, his face went crimson, and he bowed his head. "I'm sorry, Your Highness. I should not have asked such a bold question."

"And what will you think of when choosing a wife?" asked George.

"Oh, the most important thing is how she smiles when she looks at me," said Henry with certainty.

"How she smiles?" echoed George.

Henry nodded vigorously. "And how she smells, like lavender and wood pine. And how she dances barefoot in the woods when she thinks that no one sees her. Or how she holds the hand of a young child when the wind blows in a storm."

"You know her, then, the woman you wish to marry?" asked George, though it was not really a question anymore. The look on Henry's face told all, except for her name. She must be a girl he had left at home, in "Georgeville."

Henry's open face seemed to close as George watched. "No, Your Highness. Not at all. Why should you think so?"

George said no more, but wished he knew enough of Henry to offer help in some way. He should have happiness. He deserved it, far more than George did.

They rode again for a time, until they came to a hill. At the top George could see the lord general and the others waiting. George slowed his horse to let Beatrice and Marit catch up, but Beatrice was too stubborn to allow it and went more slowly still.

When he reached the top, it was nearing sunset, and the lord general asked permission to set up camp. The evening seemed to stretch on for a long while. George watched Beatrice go into her tent alone, watched as stew was brought to her to eat, watched as she went out alone with Marit to hunt for fresh meat.

When she came back, it was dark, but George was still as far from sleep as the night before. She motioned to him, and instantly George was out of the simple blanket he had insisted on and hurrying toward her.

He said nothing and stood before her tent flap. Marit was inside and did not deign to come out.

"Lady Fittle," said Beatrice shortly.

George started at that old awful name.

"That is the name of the woman he said he would take his revenge upon. Lady Fittle of Thurat."

Lady Fittle? George had never thought to hear that name again.

"We should ask after her, for I'm sure that if we find her, he will be close by," said Beatrice.

"Yes," said George. It was all he could get out.

Beatrice squinted at him. "Do you know the woman?"

"She is . . . a hunter," George said, "of those with the animal magic. I thought once that she was hunting me."

"Ah," said Beatrice.

What if Lady Fittle accused George on the spot, in front of the lord general and the other guards? In front of Henry? There would be more than rumor then. It would come down to a full trial, and George did not know if he could withstand it. He was sure that his father, in his current state of health, could not. The judgment day so long ago had nearly killed him. Now this?

No.

But what was more important? Finding Dr. Gharn and having the hope of forcing a cure for his father—and Beatrice and Marit? Or hiding the truth of his animal magic?

He knew what he had to choose.

"I shall tell the lord general," said George.

Beatrice nodded and returned to her tent.

Their conversation after that was limited to a few formal greetings in the morning and at night.

For days they went from village to village in Thurat, asking for a Lady Fittle, for a hunter, for information about animal magic. George would go with one guard or another, or the lord general would go, never all together and never under their true identities.

George was full of hatred. Of his own weakness and stupidity, of his magic, of the stubbornness and pride of Beatrice and Marit, and last of all, hatred of Dr.

Gharn, who had begun it all.

But the hatred swayed to pity. And then to hopeless-ness. And back to anger.

Every once in a great while, he felt a moment of peace, usually when he caught a glimpse of Beatrice and Marit together.

He had loved them both in different ways. But that could not be.

He turned away, and the cycle began again.

Henry tried to talk to him, to no avail.

One evening, the lord general made a joke about the prince needing a dip in some cold water to cure his bad temper.

George had his sword out to challenge the man before he could think twice.

The lord general took out his sword as well.

George thought of how badly he had been beaten by King Helm. And here was an opponent who was, if any-thing, more skilled.

Was he mad?

"I shall give you a chance to take back your chal-lenge," said the lord general.

But George only shook his head. His anger roared in his ears.

At the word from the lord general, George lunged.

The man was bleeding from his face in another moment, and George stepped back, ashamed of himself.

This was his own man. He could not do this, no

matter how angry he was. His father was right. He must think of others first. Duty first. Not himself.

He put his sword down. "I—" he began to apologize.

But the lord general held up a hand. He seemed pleased with George, and the blood dripping from his cheek. "First time I've ever seen backbone in you, my prince," he said, and walked away.

George stared after him, speechless at the compliment.

How to think of all this?

But there had to be a solution. Once he had found Dr. Gharn, he would find it, wouldn't he?

Would he give up the woman of his dreams?

Men had done it before him, surely. And would after.

But those dreams . . .

Finally, after going through the nearest villages in Thurat a second time, the lord general nodded toward a tavern and told George he would go inside and hear what gossip he could. George and the rest of the company were to stay outside and wait.

"And be quiet," said the lord general, glaring at Beatrice.

As though she ever spoke too much.

"We will all be as silent as we can," George said in her defense.

"It is the 'can' that concerns me," said the lord general tartly. He had given George more respect since their confrontation, but so far, that had not extended to Beatrice.

He gave George no chance to say more, for he kneed his horse and they were off.

The lord general had been inside the tavern for more than an hour when George saw a drunken pigkeeper careening toward them, holding a caged bird in one hand and driving a sow before him.

"The dove," said a soft voice in his ear. Beatrice's voice.

George stared at the drunken pigkeeper and held very still. Could this be Dr. Gharn at last?

"I'm going to get closer," he announced softly. His heart beat so loudly that he could hardly hear his own words.

"I'm coming," Beatrice said as George moved forward. She and Marit were as silent as George had promised the lord general they would be.

There was a small footpath that led away from the tavern and into the dry plains beyond. It wasn't wide enough to be used by hunters or riders. The pigkeeper weaved this way and that along the path, often kicking at the sow.

It was the name he called her that made George shiver.

"Lady Fittle," the pigkeeper said, kicking at her. "A fitting fate for you at last. Don't you agree?"

Before the sow could grunt in response, Marit

attacked. One moment she was just ahead of George and Beatrice. The next, she had leaped into the drunken man's path. She was big enough to pull him down with her.

George half expected that she would tear the man's throat out and claw his remains until they were bloody shreds. But as soon as she was on top of him, Marit went quiet, only a low, gravelly hum in her voice as she waited.

The sow ran off, squealing. George had no interest in pursuing her. He had known Lady Fittle too well to feel compassion for her. Let her find her own cure—if she could.

"Get off me! Help! I've been attacked!" called the pigkeeper frantically. His hands worked to reach the dove's cage, but it had been kicked out of his reach. He did not sound drunk any longer, and all trace of a peasant's accent had disappeared from his voice. Now he spoke in the accents of a well-traveled, well-educated wealthy man.

Beatrice moved forward until she stood over him. "Dr. Rhuul," she said.

The physician did not deny it. "Princess Beatrice," he said, "and her hound," with a disdainful tone.

George wanted to kick him. Instead, he picked up the cage and held it over the man's head.

"Prince George." George could now barely recognize the man who had taunted him in the tower chamber, who had been in the shadows in his father's rooms time and time again. He was a master of disguise, George thought, though it helped that he was very ordinary-looking to begin with.

At least he did not smell so pungent now as before.

"Dr. Gharn," said George.

He did not argue with that either. In fact he seemed utterly unsurprised that he had been discovered.

"Change them," George demanded. "Now." He did not know when saving Marit and Beatrice had moved ahead of his father's condition, but it had.

This was the moment of truth. George could hardly breathe for hope and fear. He could not even look at Beatrice or Marit as he spoke, for he could not bear to see what might happen to them if he failed. He could not fail them. Not again.

Yet Dr. Gharn's eyes filled with tears, and Marit allowed him to sit up, his arms around his knees. "If I had the magic for that, do you think I would not have done it long ago for her?" he asked plaintively, pointing to the dove in the cage. What did he care about a dove?

"Her? The dove?" George asked.

"My daughter," said Dr. Gharn harshly. "Surely you have figured out at least that much by now."

"Your daughter?" echoed George. Not wanting to understand.

"The dove in the cage is my daughter," he said bitterly. "Of course."

"Your daughter is dead," said George. Surely that

was the reason for this revenge plan.

"Her body is destroyed, yes," said Dr. Gharn. "But she lives still, in the dove. I changed her when I saw she was dying. And now she will never forgive me."

George stared at the dove in his hand. It appeared just like any other dove he had seen. Except—no. It was not ordinary at all. There was a human look in its eyes. Angry. But not at George. At Dr. Gharn.

At her father.

But if Dr. Gharn could change Beatrice into Marit and Marit into Beatrice, if he could change his own daughter into a dove, why could he not undo the change?

George staggered back.

This was not possible. It could not be true.

But there was no reason for Dr. Gharn to lie. His own daughter—a dove? Of course he was not lying.

He was as devastated by the truth as George himself. Only he had been living with it for twenty years or more. No wonder he was bitter and half mad. No wonder he had had wanted revenge.

George felt a terrible sympathy for the man, though he did not want to. He wanted only to weep in despair. All was lost.

He would marry a woman who was a hound. And his true love would be lost to him forever.

"George," said Beatrice. "Now is not the time."

Yes. The hound was chiding him for his emotions.

And Marit?

She got off of Dr. Gharn and slowly moved away, as stunned as George himself. Her eyes seemed darker now than ever before.

Was this the end? Would she take herself into the forest and never return?

George expected it. He steeled himself to feel nothing. To be as unfeeling as Beatrice so often was.

And then he felt a warmth on his hand. He looked down and saw that Marit had come back to him.

She was not yet ready to give up hope.

Or him.

George breathed deeply and regained some modicum of self-control.

Jus then he heard Henry and the others arriving from behind. George did not wish them to hear any of Dr. Gharn's talk of animal magic. Thinking quickly, he grabbed a bit of cloth from his pocket and shoved it into Dr. Gharn's mouth.

"Go get the lord general," George shouted at Henry.

Then he gave over control of Dr. Gharn to Beatrice and Marit once more.

When Henry and the lord general returned, George took a small, sour pleasure in seeing the lord general's surprise at Beatrice's strength.

She insisted on hogtying Dr. Gharn herself and throwing him over Ass's back.

George secured the dove's cage on one of the pack-horses. He noticed that the dove did not flutter or frighten as other birds seemed to. He stared through the bars, and the dove stared back.

Once that was done, George forced himself to act as normally as he could. He packed things up, spoke of riding order and night guards with the lord general, and stole glances at the stolid Beatrice and the wounded Marit.

He had found no solutions in Dr. Gharn, after all. He felt as if he were just beginning a new quest. But perhaps he knew now at last what it was he quested for.

Love.

Chapter Thirty-four

George took the less fractious horse the lord general offered him. He had done something, it seemed, to raise his position in the lord general's eyes. But not in his own. They rode hard for home, though they had to stop another night by the great forest when it grew dark.

George thought of how tightly bound Marit and Beatrice were now. And he with them. How could he love the one and not the other? How could he love either?

It was too much. Dr. Gharn. Sir Stephen. Elsbeth. Would he tell Sir Stephen that his beloved had not truly died, that she was a dove? What possible use could that be? Kinder to let him believe she was dead, that Dr. Gharn's fantasies about the bird were no more than that.

But would he believe? Or would he always be haunted by guilt about what he might have done?

The truth was not always a gift.

In the evenings on that long journey home, George made a point to visit Beatrice, if only for a few minutes at a time. He spoke to her briefly of the day. But it was Marit he went to see, and Beatrice knew it.

When she had listened, she would wave to Marit and suggest that George might take her hound for a walk. And George always did.

Then George had the chance to touch her on the head. To feel the beat of her heart beneath his fingertips. To stop and look into her eyes and know who it was he saw in them.

He brought her back to Beatrice afterward, and all three of them were as silent as she.

Nothing was resolved between them, but there was honesty, at least, and George clung to that.

Dr. Gharn endured at first the silent scorn of the soldiers, and then, as the lord general did nothing to curb them, less subtle torments.

Meat so oversalted he could not eat more than a bite.

A leg held out to trip him, and he could not catch himself, for his hands were bound behind his back.

George put a stop to it when he saw Dr. Gharn forced to stand for hours on end.

"It sends no good message to other criminals if this one is given ease," warned the lord general.

George shook his head. "Justice is not ease."

The lord general grumbled over this but did not defy the prince.

But if Dr. Gharn noticed the change in behavior toward him, or to whom he owed it, George could see no sign of it. Dr. Gharn only looked at George suspiciously, if he looked at anyone at all.

At last, one morning, George smelled his own familiar forest and was reminded of his mother and the way she had first introduced him to his magic. Might George one day do the same thing for his own child?

He turned to Beatrice and Marit, but they were far behind and he could not share the moment with either of them.

"I will take him to the dungeon," the lord general announced the following day, when they arrived back at the castle.

It was now long past noon, and George was half asleep on his feet and half dead in mind and heart.

But there was duty waiting for him again. "Give me an hour to eat and change my clothes. Then I will be down to speak to him myself," he said.

The lord general made no protest.

George took the cage, but Beatrice came after him, Marit trailing. When they were alone, he turned on the stair and stared into the princess's eyes. "I shall find a chamber for you to rest in."

He glanced down at Marit. Marit? Or Beatrice? By which name should he call her? He had been introduced to her as Marit. Marit she would remain. Until— unless . . .

He turned back to Beatrice. This was impossible. Worse than impossible.

"I cannot believe I did not guess it earlier," he said at last. What a fool she—they—must think him.

"We did not mean you to," said Beatrice.

Which did not make him feel any better.

"We could not take the risk, you see. Because of the kingdom."

George set down the cage, tired. "Even after I told you about my animal magic?" he asked. Had that not been the proof that he was trustworthy?

"Even then," said Beatrice. She looked at Marit, and George wondered if there had been disagreement between them about that choice. If so, there was no sign of it now.

"Did you ever mean to tell me?" George asked at last.

"No."

"I see."

Marit gave a small sound, and Beatrice's head turned slightly to the side. "And there was her father as well," she said, as if making an admission. "Can you see what it would have done to the king if he had known the truth?"

So she was asking him still to keep this quiet. Of course he would. What kind of man did she think he was?

"You care for him more than he deserves, I think,"

George said at last. And yet he would have done the same for his father. Was it more than his father deserved?

All his life George had tried to live up to his father. But it suddenly struck him now that King Davit, for all his kindnesses in private, was not so very different from Beatrice's father in public. All these years King Davit had made George keep his magic secret. He had refused to let George be who he was, just as King Helm had refused to see Beatrice as she was.

King Davit had not meant to harm George. He had meant to protect him. Perhaps King Helm had meant the same.

It was scarcely relevant to the damage that occurred. In fact the love that was between them made it worse.

"I shall send for you," he told Beatrice.

She bowed her head. She did not ask for more than that. She did not beg him to continue their betrothal. She had too much pride for that.

George went to his chamber, set the birdcage on his wardrobe, and sat on his bed. It felt very cold there.

He changed his clothes, moving woodenly, trying to think of nothing else. Foot here. Leg there. Arm there. Then he was done.

He took a few breaths, then prepared himself to go to the dungeon. Was he ready to face Dr. Gharn?

No.

He should go see his father.

But was he ready for that? To see King Davit would mean facing the realization that had just come to him. All this time, since his mother's death, since the judgment day on his twelfth birthday, his father had spoken about the animal magic in whispers here and there, but no more than that. He had made it seem that there was no other choice, that George could not possibly allow anyone to know the truth about his animal magic.

But if just once in all that time his father had stood up and declared that his son had animal magic, how different it all might have been.

It would have been harder in some ways. But it would have been true.

George stared at the dove. What would she say if she could speak to him? What would she wish for, for her father? For she too had been harmed by a man who had meant to show his utmost love for her.

It made George wonder why love was supposed to be such a wonderful thing. As far as he could tell, love was just another excuse for causing pain. It was just as well his marriage with Beatrice would be without it.

CHAPTER THIRTY-FIVE

GEORGE CHECKED ON his father briefly and spoke to Sir Stephen. Then he bathed and changed. It was evening when, holding the dove's cage, he forced himself down to the dungeon. It was built directly beneath the castle, but the only way to get there was to go out and around the moat, then descend by a hidden staircase near the stables. It was cold, and the stone walls sweated black drops. The stairs were uneven and treacherous, and George nearly tripped more than once.

The sounds of the place were eerily inhuman. It was only after George had descended all the way, ducked his head through the first arch, and begun down the long corridor that led to the row of closed stone doors that he could hear voices.

They came from inside the first chamber, where George was surprised to find not only the lord general, but Sir Stephen inside as well. George looked through the bars to see the two arguing, while Dr. Gharn kept silent, a strange grimace on his face.

He looked now much less like the man whom George had seen as the physician in his father's castle, but also very little like the drunken man with the sow. Yet his basic features were the same. Medium-length hair of indeterminate color, medium height, a face of no distinguishing characteristics.

The smell was gone, George thought. That was part of it. It kept George from always wanting to turn his head away.

More than that, something in the man's eyes had changed. He seemed defeated now. But did that make him any more likely to give George what he wanted?

George lifted the birdcage and set it down at the barred door to the chamber. The dove made no sound, nor did Dr. Gharn. But the two were instantly aware of each other. Now the despair on the physician's face was mingled with something else. Softness from a face that was used to being hard.

George left the cage where it was and knocked on the bars.

The lord general hesitated a moment, then shrugged and took the key off his chain to allow George inside.

"But I see no reason to believe you will have more luck convincing him to cure the king than I have."

The king, yes. His father was the only part of this the

lord general knew about. Best to keep it that way.

"You must let me talk to him. He will say more to me than to you. I know him," said Sir Stephen, nodding to George, but keeping his attention on the lord general.

Neither of them seemed to think that George had any part in the argument. They would not have treated his father so. He had half expected such treatment from the lord general, but Sir Stephen was supposed to be his friend and guide. For all he had said that day in the king's bedchamber, he did not think of George as the man who was to be king.

Well, would he?

"That is precisely why you should not speak to him or even be anywhere near where he is. He will trust that you will protect him," said the lord general, "and then I will get nowhere with him."

George's head turned back and forth, from Sir Stephen to the lord general, watching their game as if it were King Helm's board of pieces, and he himself but another one of them.

"You mean you intend to torture him?" asked Sir Stephen. He moved closer to the lord general, pulling himself to his full height, some inches taller than the lord general.

"I will do what I must to get what I need," the lord general insisted, his eyes blazing. "Do you argue with that? Do you believe his comfort is more important than my king's very life and the good of the kingdom?"

"A lack of comfort? Is that all you intend toward this man?" demanded Sir Stephen.

"Well, what is pain but the loss of comfort?" replied the lord general.

The two men were talking about what might be Dr. Gharn's last moments, but George noticed that the physician seemed hardly aware of their battle. His eyes were on the dove in the cage. And George.

"You are . . ." Sir Stephen sputtered.

The lord general seemed to take pleasure in Sir Stephen's inability to find words to match his emotions. "Despicable?" he said. "Heartless? A blackguard?"

George was tired of the competition. He was even more tired of being ignored.

"Lord general, you are dismissed," he said shortly.

The man turned and stared at George, his mouth open wide.

"You may complain to my father if you wish," said George. But he would have to get through four-fingered Jack first, and George did not think that would be easy.

"You will regret this," said the lord general, and stalked off.

"And you," George said to Sir Stephen, nodding toward the door.

Sir Stephen looked stunned. "No," he said. Then he added, "Please. Please let me stay. I swear I will stay silent if you ask me to. I will do whatever you say. But I must stay—" His eyes went to the dove and then away, as if they had been burned.

George sighed. So someone had already told Sir Stephen the truth.

"All right then. Stay," he said. He turned to Dr. Gharn and asked, "Have you spent all these years planning this revenge?"

Dr. Gharn looked up at him. "No," he said slowly.

"Then what?" asked George. "Tell me."

"I spent many years wandering in the eastern countries, searching for one who had the other half of the animal magic. I thought I might undo what had been done — to her. It was all I thought of then."

George's heart sank. If Dr. Gharn, with all his single-mindedness and all that time, had been unable to find a way to turn his daughter back into what she had been, what hope could there be for Marit and Beatrice? And George?

"Then I found a man on the edges of the great Salt Sea, a learned man who owned as many books written on animal magic as I had ever seen and knew even more stories of it. He told me that there was no hope for my dove, even if I found one who had the other magic. Because her body was gone. He told me that I might be able to give her another body, but that she could never again be the girl I had known."

The physician was weeping, George realized, but hardly seemed to notice it.

"I spent some time simply wandering then, with no

thought except to feed myself and my dove. I worked here and there, at this court or that one, each more opulent than the last."

His gaze caught on George for a moment, and there was a hint of disdain once more.

No doubt there were greater places than Kendel, but George had no wish to see them. They were not his.

"It came to me slowly, the thought of revenge. I moved from court to court, and my reputation followed me. Emperors asked after me, and I healed them. I should have been proud of it, and yet I felt nothing at all."

He took a great, shaking breath.

"A lesser king died after I had given him the wrong medicine. I was hunted from the court, in danger of my life. I had to go without my dove, but I came back that night, in disguise, and got her. I saw then how I could be unnoticed by those who had seen me but days before. A few changes to my hair, leaning to one side, talking differently. It was not much, but they did not pay attention. And that was the beginning of the idea for my revenge.

"It did not take much more for me to see how I could most thoroughly destroy two kings. One through his daughter, and the other through his son." He looked at George and sighed.

After this boldness, George did not want to feel sympathy for the physician, but he found it was there nonetheless. And yet he could not forgive him.

Sir Stephen glanced at George, eyebrows raised, as

if to ask permission to speak.

George nodded.

"Why did you never come to me?" he aske[ ] physician quietly. "All these years I thought you [ ] dead too."

"And what could you have done?" Dr. G[ ] demanded, shaken out of his memories to a sharp, [ ] anger. "To help me or her?" He waved at the dove.

"I—I suppose nothing." In a distant voice, [ ] Stephen went on. "Do you know, I have never been a[ ] to love another? She was superior to all the other[ ] have ever met. I could never see their faces witho[ ] thinking of hers, and how much more beautiful she w[ ] or how her laughter was more infectious, and her w[ ] more quick."

He looked down at Dr. Gharn and added, "[ ] thought, if you were alive, that we might weep togethe[ ] for her. I thought that might offer us both some relief."

George thought then of what the houndmaster had once told him: "There are hounds for whom gentleness is the worst punishment. They have not been trained to it. They want to be hit and pained with every movement. They expect it."

It seemed that Dr. Gharn expected pain here, too. And Sir Stephen giving him gentleness might well prove his undoing.

"There is no relief for me," said Dr. Gharn at last. "Not while she breathes. And yet, I cannot kill her myself."

"Does she wish it, do you think?" asked Sir Stephen.

Dr. Gharn's hands began to writhe. "I don't know. How can I know what she thinks? She cannot speak."

"But surely there are other ways?"

"Do you think I have not tried to speak to her in other ways?" Dr. Gharn's voice was hoarse. "With notes? Asking her questions that she could choose to respond to in one chirp or two? Questions that she could fly to, or peck at my eyes to—or anything at all? She will not answer me. She hates me."

There was a moment of silence as the dove made a small sound of distress and began to fly about in the cage.

George could hardly breathe for the swelling in his throat.

"She could not hate you," said Sir Stephen with certainty. "Not the woman I knew. She could hate you least of all. After all you have given up for her. She must see that."

"Must she?" said Dr. Gharn. He watched as the dove settled once more. Then he shook his head. "She is no longer the woman you knew. Or the daughter I loved. She is a dove. And yet, she can never be content to be only a dove. Do you see the position I have placed her in? If I let her go, she could never find a place among the birds. She does not know their ways."

George thought of the bear, whose dreams he had shared. There was still a man inside the animal. Just as

there was a woman who remembered being human inside Marit's hound body. "She can remember," he said softly.

Dr. Gharn flinched at the words as if George had shouted them. "What do you know? How do you know this? Do you speak to her? Do you know her mind?" he demanded. His eyes were wild, and his body trembled.

But George just said, "She is not the only human so changed."

Dr. Gharn began to shudder in great spasms.

Sir Stephen embraced him.

"What shall I do?" asked Dr. Gharn. "Tell me what I should do. You are the only one who can help me, who can know what she would wish better than I. If I had known you were here— No. I would not have come for you. But now you will help me, won't you?"

He was asking Sir Stephen to decide if the dove should live or die. George could not bear it. He sagged against the stone wall and let its chill wetness soak through him, as if that would take away his fear.

"Do you let her out of the cage?" Sir Stephen asked.

Dr. Gharn shook his head. "Not anymore. Not for a very long time. I am too afraid that she would not come back. Or that she would be harmed while she was away.

"Years ago I did let her out, and she did not come back for three days, and then it was with a broken wing and a fever that I spent many weeks curing. I used all my physician's skill to keep her living, and I did not dare let her go again after that. What if I did not have enough skill to cure her the next time?"

"You must let her go," said Sir Stephen at last.

"Is that not the coward's way out? For then I could tell myself, when I wished it, that she was still alive. This way I have to look her in the eye day and night and see her contempt for me. It seems much more just."

Dr. Gharn gave himself no mercy, George thought, so why should he give it to anyone else?

"It is not your choice. It is mine," said Sir Stephen tightly. "I claim it by right of our love. She was to be mine. She would have been mine—"

Dr. Gharn looked up at him and held his hand tightly. "Yes," he said. "Yes."

"It is what she would have wanted," said Sir Stephen. "If she had to live as a dove, she would want to be free as a dove, to enjoy the wings that a dove is given for flight, and to see the world from above as only a bird can. Even to experience the dangers that a dove must face."

Dr. Gharn had closed his eyes and was so still that for a moment George wondered if he had poisoned himself and died. Then he nodded, just the slightest nod.

Sir Stephen bent to take the cage, then opened the barred door of the cell.

When he was gone, George turned back to Dr. Gharn. "My father?" he asked. The physician had already answered the question of Beatrice and Marit. Twice over now.

Dr. Gharn only shook his head. "There is no cure for the black-green leaf," he said. "At least, there is nothing

I have ever heard of, in all my years of travel. It is ideal for that reason. Even the wealthiest man in the world can have no hope of recovering from a slowly given dose, day after day, for months on end."

George did not disbelieve the physician's answer, for the man spoke with such bluntness and seemed so little interested in mercy. And yet it was all George could do to keep his hands clenched at his sides, away from Dr. Gharn's throat. After a long moment George recovered himself enough to ask, "Is there nothing you can do for him then?"

Dr. Gharn's head jerked up at the question as if he had never considered it before. "Oh. Well, yes, of course I can give him ease from his pain. I cannot save his life, but I may be able to prolong it. By a few days, a few weeks." He shrugged with a very small motion. "I do not know how long." He turned to George. "Is that what you would wish me to do?"

George closed his eyes, wondering if Dr. Gharn would not kill his father with some other elixir he offered. Why should he trust him?

But, then, why had he gone after Dr. Gharn if he had no intention of allowing him to come near his father again? He had to choose, the hope of helping his father against the chance of hurting him.

The weight of the decision settled on him, and George had the first taste of what it would be like to be king.

Was Dr. Gharn lying about the black-green leaf?

Was there a cure after all? George did not believe it, for if the man had intended to lie, surely he would have said that King Davit could be cured. That would make him far more valuable, would give George a reason to keep him alive.

But the man did not care. Now that his dove was gone, he had no reason left to lie. Or to take his revenge.

George looked at Dr. Gharn and saw a different man. He was sure of it, as sure as his father must have been when he saw four-fingered Jack and offered him all that he had. He had to believe in Dr. Gharn, for that was the only way that he could also believe in himself.

"I wish you to help him all you can," said George.

"I will then," said Dr. Gharn, "for my dove's sake."

After a long moment Dr. Gharn spoke once more. "The scholar in the east," he said, "the man of the animal magic, he told me many stories. One of them was very like our tale of King Richon and the wild man, except that it promises a different ending, one that is not told either in Sarrey or in Kendel."

George listened breathlessly for the rest.

"It promises the magic will be broken when there is a woman to love an animal and an animal to love a man."

There was a rushing in George's ears, and when he next opened his eyes, he found he was on the ground, with Dr. Gharn's head above his.

"It would take great magic," said Dr. Gharn. "Great magic indeed. But they say that the greatest magic often hides as long as it can. Hides and waits."

Chapter Thirty-six

GEORGE SLEPT THAT night in fits and starts, dreaming of Marit and Beatrice and of the bear. They were not the true shared dreams he had before, just repetitions of what he had already seen. When morning came, his eyes were red, his ears rang, and his body ached with the slightest movement. He felt old already and too worn out for more. But there was no way out of it. He had to see his father, and soon. He was king yet, and a report must be made in person.

George thought of stopping to see Beatrice first but told himself he had no time. The truth was perhaps more cowardly than he cared to admit.

Climbing the stairs to his father's chamber, he realized the enormity of his having come here. This was not just coming to see the king. This was coming to see his father, knowing everything had changed between them.

He did not know what to do or what to say. He felt as though he were meeting a stranger for the first time.

As if he himself were walking up to the judgment seat to face his punishment.

And yet nothing was truly different. He was still the prince of Kendel, betrothed to the princess of Sarrey for the good of his kingdom. And his father was still dying.

George took a moment to catch his breath at the door to his father's bedchamber, where four-fingered Jack waited, as always.

"Jack," said George at last with a nod.

"He is asleep," said Jack.

"Then I shall sit by his side," said George.

Jack made no complaint.

George stared first at his father's wasting gray form, then out the window at the distant woods. Was it any wonder King Davit had not known what to do about his son's animal magic? It was nothing he'd had any experience with. It took George into dangers his father could not protect him from, dangers of which he knew nothing. Of course he had wanted to deny it existed or at least to ignore it as much as possible.

And now? The full story of Dr. Gharn, of Beatrice and Marit, was so complicated and so disheartening. Did his father truly need to know it?

Suddenly the king spoke. "In a fit of anger I once asked your mother a terrible question." His eyes were only partly open. He seemed almost to be speaking in his sleep. To touch him would wake him further, and that might do him more harm than good. So George stayed back and held himself as still as before.

"I asked her"—the king went on—"if she would choose her woods and her animals over me." He paused, breathing heavily. "She told me . . . only if I forced her to the choice." A longer pause then. So long that George began to wonder if that was all.

"And then she said that there was a part of her I could never understand, just as there was a part of her no animal could ever understand. She was two women, she said, in one body."

George's throat tightened.

"George, that is what you have always been, I think. Two boys, two men in one body."

Was it true? It was what Dr. Gharn had said of Beatrice. And Marit.

George had always felt as though one side of himself had been suppressed, made to hide away. He was both the prince who lived in the castle and the boy who wandered in the woods. Was he any different from the princess and the hound?

It occurred to him suddenly that perhaps he had begun to love her—them—because he had sensed that division and known it matched his own.

"I think I was jealous of you, that there was always something in you I could never be part of. Just as I was jealous of the magic your mother had. It took her away from me, and it bound you two closer together in a way that I could never understand."

Jealous? King Davit? Though George might not have felt close to his father, it was not because he thought that his father was wrong.

Now—

"It's hardly something to be jealous of," George said. "If you knew what it was like . . ."

With great effort, his father took hold of George's wrist, leaning in so that their eyes were very close. "Tell me what it is like," he said.

George opened his mouth and only one word came out: the word *hop*, in the rabbit tongue. George realized that it was not something he could explain, any more than he could explain what the color red looked like to someone who was blind.

"I knew it," the king whispered, despondently. "Even when your mother died, I knew that she had lived more than I ever could. It is not so hard to give it up now as I thought then. I am so tired of seeing myself wanting. It is time for a better to take my place."

"No," said George. "I cannot lose you too. Not yet."

His father smiled on only one side of his mouth, as if he were too tired to move the other. "We do not decide whom we lose, or when. That at least is the same for both of us."

It isn't fair, thought George. He knew he would sound like a child if he said it aloud.

"Dr. Gharn said—" George said at last.

"Ah, Dr. Gharn? The lord general came to beg of me permission to see him hang."

310

"But you did not give it," said George.

"No."

"Father, he has lost so much. I do not believe he will try to hurt you again."

His father sighed. "I suppose it makes very little difference if he does. I have no hope to live long after this. I might as well give him one more chance. Why shouldn't he have that too?"

George did not answer.

"George, listen to me." This time his father spoke as the king. His voice was soft, but it was commanding. "I will not let you have regrets when I am gone. We must say what we have to say to each other before then."

"I don't know what you are talking about." George did not want to know.

His father's mouth worked furiously, but then he spoke instead of something new. "I have never told you of the way your mother died in my arms."

"In your arms?" George had always assumed that his mother had been brought back from the woods dead. He had never thought there might have been a chance to see her one last time. . . .

"Yes. My jealousy again, you see. I wanted to have her to myself at the last. I pretended to agree with those who told me that a boy your age should not see his mother covered in so much blood, that it would be better for you to see her clean when she was gone, to say good-bye to her then."

George had not known that talking of his mother

could be still so painful.

"But of course I knew in my heart that you would want to be with her, as I did, in the last moments of her life."

A long, ragged breath.

George held himself very still. Was this what it would have been like if he had been allowed to see his mother dying? Would it have hurt so much? Would it have made him wish to be sent away?

At last his father went on. "The truth is, I did not want you with me. I hardly knew you. My own son, but I had spent so little time with you I felt you would have been a stranger there. And I was afraid."

"Afraid?" asked George. "Of what?" Surely his father did not mean he was afraid of himself as a young boy.

King Davit gave a small, silent laugh. "Afraid of failing you. And being afraid, I did fail you. Over and over and over again."

Yes, George thought. He had.

"After your mother died, you changed. I saw it before my eyes. You became less than what she would have made of you. But I did not know how to stop it. I could not take her place. I could only try to banish her from your thoughts, to make you think more of me. You learned duty from me then. You learned to be a king. At least that is what I told myself."

"You were right," said George, desperate to give his father some small peace.

"No," his father said. His arm jerked across his

chest, and the motion exhausted him. He had to breathe quietly for several minutes afterward.

"No," he said at last. "I taught you to be me. There are many kinds of kings, but I only knew how to be myself. I thought if I showed you that, you would be safe and secure. You would forget about her, about your animal magic, about that whole part of yourself."

If only I could have, George thought. He would have done exactly as his father said. But the animal magic could not be set aside so easily as that.

"Then came the night of the fire, after my failed judgment of the man with the animal magic. How you must have hated me that night, yet it was no more than I hated myself.

"Did I change then? A little, I think."

George would never have allowed himself to judge his father as harshly as King Davit judged himself. In a way it was cathartic. It let the anger out without destroying him. He could remind himself that there was still love between them.

His father had given him this one last gift. It did not make up for what George had lost, but it was wonderful in its own way.

"Tell me about her," said George. He felt free now. He had never talked to his father so openly before. "When she was dying. I want to know."

King Davit nodded. His face relaxed, and he thought for a long while. "She did not know where she was. She thought she was still back in the woods. She spoke as if in a dream. I tried to get her to recognize me, to talk to me. I wanted to tell her I loved her one last time, but she would not see me. She would not see any of us.

"That was another reason I told myself it was just as well that you did not see her. Because I thought she would not have known you. Or maybe—maybe I did not want to see that you were the only one she would know." He gave a small shrug.

George put his hand out to his father's shoulder and held it there. It felt good to be offering his father strength for once in his life, instead of the other way around.

"She spoke as if I were the bear. I think that was it, although it made no sense at all to me at the time. She spoke sometimes in another language and sometimes in ours. When I understood her, she told me I should not worry, that my time was coming. That the pain would be gone soon. That wearing a skin had taught me much. She said—the last thing she ever spoke—she said that even a beast could be loved for who he was."

George's heart nearly stopped as he heard this. It sounded so much like what Dr. Gharn had said about the end of the tale of King Richon and the wild man. Could that be what she had meant? But why would she have said it in her last moments?

"Was I right? Was she speaking to the bear that had killed her? Or did she mean—was it you she was speaking to all along and I never understood it?"

"No," said George. "No, I do not think it was me she meant."

314

"But if I had brought you to her then, you would have known. You would have understood her."

"Would I?" George was not so sure. His mother's story of the owl that had lost his family was only now starting to make sense to him. It had taken all these years before he knew what they had meant and whom they had been spoken to. It might well have been the same with his mother's last words.

"She was speaking to a bear," George said.

"The bear that killed her?" asked King Davit.

"No," said George. "I don't think so. A bear she had been searching for, one that might have looked like that bear. But not at all the same."

"Ah. And this bear, it is special?"

George nodded.

"Is it possible—do you think you might find it? And tell it what she meant to say? If it still lives?"

"Yes. I will," George replied.

His father seemed to sink then, and George was terrified that he had stopped breathing altogether. But when he put his head to the sunken chest, there was still a faint rise and fall.

Wiping his own face, George kept his hand on his father's shoulder. He knew what the story of the owl meant at last.

CHAPTER THIRTY-SEVEN

GEORGE STAYED WITH his father the rest of the day and into the night. The next morning Dr. Gharn came in to relieve him. Sir Stephen had gone back to let him go freely from the dungeon, and the lord general had not stopped him.

No one else in the castle had been informed about what Dr. Gharn had done to the king. It was a good thing, perhaps, for George did not doubt that if four-fingered Jack had known the truth, Dr. Gharn would not have escaped from his sight with less than several broken limbs. And there were others who would have taken the rest, if given the chance.

George himself did not leave as Dr. Gharn examined the drowsy, weary king. He did not trust Dr. Gharn that far after all.

"How is he?" George demanded as the physician stepped back from the bed.

Dr. Gharn put a finger to his lips and motioned to George. He closed the curtain to give the king some quiet, then answered: "Not well, but not as bad as I feared."

"No?" George felt a desperate hope rise in him.

"The poison has not yet dug deep inside him, or he would not be breathing so easily."

"Then you can flush it out."

Dr. Gharn looked up at George, "Your Highness, I told you already I cannot do that."

It was hard for George to remind himself that this was not a new betrayal. This was what was expected. "Then what?" he asked, trembling so he had to reach for the wall to lean against.

"He will die, but not as soon as I thought," was all Dr. Gharn said, in his blunt way. Then he went to work with the herbs he had brought. A new elixir was soon ready, this time green and yellow-flecked, but pleasant smelling.

Dr. Gharn offered it to George to taste, and George felt it his duty to do so.

Then he watched as Dr. Gharn showed himself willing to do the same. "You see? It is no poison this time."

George nodded. He checked Dr. Gharn's supplies and saw nothing there but what he had put into this new elixir. If he was going to let the man try, he must leave him to do his work. He decided he must be satisfied.

George too had work to do that he had been putting

off. As he climbed down the stairs and outside, he thought once more about his mother and her animal magic. Small magic or great?

Outside the castle he stood by the moat and remembered all those times when he had wished he had never been born with the animal magic. Why hadn't he seen that it was something to be cherished, not hidden? He felt rain fall on his head and welcomed it.

And then he reached deep inside himself, where the animal magic was.

Yes, there.

A great magic indeed.

It was so enormous that George had always been afraid to see it. And yet it was so clear.

He looked, and this time he saw with his magic.

There in the kitchen was Fat Tom, licking his paws and waiting for a bit of fat from the spit. A chicken in a cage, waiting to be served for dinner. And beyond the kitchen, the family of mice he had tried to save. Not young any longer and scattered throughout the castle, but George saw them as individuals, brilliant lives of color and joy.

When he looked outside the castle, his ability to sense the animals around him increased. And became overwhelming.

Birds overhead. So many of them, calling to one another. Calling to the sky itself. Calling to him.

Fish in the moat. Diving, turning, twisting, sliding, with a language all their own, not sounds at all, but scents. George had never thought to wonder how fish spoke, and now it was so obvious.

It hurt to be so aware of everything at once, yet George could not push it back now that he had started. He was not with his body now. He was with the creatures around him.

Ants dancing everywhere, in red and gold. Worms beneath the dirt. Beetles and moths and crickets and slugs. And on and on.

Even if his mother had known this part, she could never have taught it to him as a child.

Now, where was Beatrice?

There. Not in the castle at all, but wandering about the stables. How to call to her?

George was vaguely aware that his body was soaked with cool rainwater and the ground around him had turned to mud. He had to speak to Beatrice, had to reach her somehow, without words.

Ah, that was it. He had to stop thinking of her as a woman. She was a hound.

"Beatrice, come to me!" he said.

In his mind, he could see her image start, her head lift like a hound that has heard a distant call. In a moment she was coming toward him. The hound at her side came as well. In his mind, it was not a hound at all, however. It was a human woman.

George stared at the shape for a long time. This was his first chance to see the girl from his dreams, the girl who had become the woman Princess Beatrice and then the hound Marit. He had always known there were things about her that were not houndlike. Just as Beatrice had never been comfortable in her woman's body.

Now, though, George could see that both of them fit the images in his mind perfectly. There was a wonderful peace in that moment, but it did not last long.

When the two arrived, Marit stared at him with a hint of distrust.

"Did you call for us?" She seemed unsurprised.

"There is something in the woods I wish to show you," said George. "Will you come?" Now it was he who was not telling all that he knew. He did not want to get their hopes up for no reason.

"I will come," said Beatrice. She looked at Marit.

Marit said nothing, but Beatrice interpreted. "She will come as well."

"Thank you," said George. Despite all, there was still that much trust between them. He hoped he did not kill it after this.

"One more moment please," said George. "There is another I must call."

"As you wish," said Beatrice.

Marit looked as though she were straining to hear him with her own closed eyes.

Without knowing why, George was certain she would not hear him. Even another hound would not have heard his specific call to Beatrice. If he called all

320

the wild hounds in the kingdom, they all would come to him expecting to be the only one. That was part of the magic in that place deep inside him, that crystal-clear place that had been there all along, waiting for him to wake to it.

Now he reached out to call to the bear his mother had meant to speak to as she lay dying. The bear he had tried to help as a boy, that had lived all these years. The bear he had saved from King Helm. The bear Beatrice and Marit had already come to know, impossibly gentle. A bear that was not a bear.

Inside his magic, George stretched and stretched but could not find any sign of the bear. There were several bears in the forest near the castle, but none of them was the right size. He looked farther abroad, seeing bears now and again but not the right one. He went all the way to the woods in Sarrey where he had last seen the bear, but still no sign. And then south, as far as he could go.

So, north again? George felt at a loss. The world was very large indeed, and he was not sure how far this sense of creatures went. There were limits to it, though. He thought that it did not work far from his own kingdom of Kendel.

"What is wrong?" asked Beatrice.

Her voice jerked George out of his trancelike state. He stared at her and did not know what to say.

"Wrong," he echoed. Suddenly he knew what it was. He held up his hand to stave off Beatrice, then closed his eyes again. Into the forest by his own castle he went once more. This time he searched not for a bear but for a man. A wounded man, very old.

Yes. There he was. Hunched over close to the ground, moving slowly, lumbering along.

"Meet me at the edge of the woods," George said to him.

The man looked up at once, as if searching for the source of the voice.

"I will do at last what you wanted me to do so long ago," George told him.

And then the man, the bear that had been a man, began to move quickly without any regard to whatever injuries remained from the day of King Helm's hunt. He would reach the edge of the forest before George and Beatrice and Marit did no doubt.

"It is time," George said, and began to run.

Beatrice pushed herself behind him, but Marit was right at his side.

A woman to love an animal and an animal to love a man. That was what Dr. Gharn had told him.

George himself was presumably the man who could love an animal. Could King Richon love a woman who was also a hound? What of Beatrice? Could a hound that had been a woman also love a bear that had been a man? He did not know how to ask her such a thing. Or if there was anything to ask at all.

George was running so hard that he had difficulty

thinking more than one thought in a dozen strides. The rain had made the ground wet, but not until they came close to the edge of the forest was the grass high enough to make George and Marit slow down. Beatrice came up swiftly behind them, never complaining of their pace or her own inability to keep up with it.

George stopped.

Was that the bear he could see pacing to and fro like a man behind the first trees? The smaller animals had fled, for George could hear no sign of them. And when he blinked, he was also aware that he could not see them with his other vision either.

"What is this?" Beatrice asked.

And he had to tell her something. "Could you love a man?" he asked bluntly.

"A man? What man?"

George shook his head. "Could you?" he insisted.

Beatrice's face tilted to the side, a very houndlike expression. "I do not think that I can love as a human loves," she said.

George's heart sank.

Then she added, "But perhaps I have learned to be a little more human since I have worn this body. I don't know, it might be possible. I did not think truly that I could ever give myself again as a mate to any hound, after what was done to me before and the loss of my daughter. Still, if it were not a hound at all but a man, then it would be different."

George thought of the bear he had seen in his shared dreams. His gentleness. His struggle to be human in some way, despite the bearskin he wore. He thought of the man he had watched, the king who ruled long ago, unsure of himself, cruel and hasty.

He thought of Beatrice, with her temper and her pride. Her refusal to be hurt.

Perhaps there was a match to be made there. He could only try.

At last he turned to Marit. This was the hardest part. He saw her with his own eyes as a hound. She smelled like a hound, breathed like a hound. She could not speak to him with a human's voice or in the language of the hounds. They were as separate as ever two beings could be.

But he had to do this. He knelt on one knee. He closed his eyes and blocked out all his other senses so he could see her as she truly was. The resourceful, self-sufficient girl from his dreams, who had become a woman undamaged by her father's mistreatment. And then a hound, warm and giving as a hound could be.

He loved her. As much as his mother had ever loved his father, he was sure. And more perhaps. For he shared more with her than his father and mother had.

It was not only that he trusted her or that he understood her and she him. It was not only that he thought her beautiful and courageous and strong. She was unique, but that too was only part of it. There was no one thing that he could point to and say, "This is it." But all of them together, yes.

"I love you," he said. There, was that so hard to say out loud? It felt as though something had been wrenched out of his heart. He knew men who had had teeth pulled out, but those teeth were usually partly loose and rotting away. Perhaps this pain was something like that one, magnified a hundred times.

"Can you love me?" he asked. That was the one that should have been harder, but strangely it was not. He thought a moment and realized why. He could withstand it if she hurt him. He did not want to be hurt, but he was willing to take the chance of it. After all, he had withstood it before and survived. They both had survived.

With his magic's eye George could see Marit move toward him. Marit, the woman, in her true, beautiful human shape. Her red hair, her square jaw, so much like her father's, her eyes flashing defiance, her lips showing vulnerability. All he had seen in his dreams. And more.

Yet she did not touch him. Her mouth opened. Her lips moved. "Yes," was all he read. But that was enough.

He sagged, relieved. Really, this was only the beginning of the magic, if it was a beginning at all. But it felt to him as if nothing else could matter more. He put out his arms to embrace her.

She fell toward him.

Their faces touched, and he felt her warm, wet cheek against his. It was a hound's fur that touched his skin,

325

but he did not notice it. To him, it was a woman who touched him. His magic told him it was true, and he found that he trusted his magic at last.

George breathed deeply and felt as though something inside him had been filled, something he had never realized was lacking before.

Chapter Thirty-eight

"WE GO TO meet the bear," he said at last.

"The bear?" whispered Beatrice behind him.

"Yes. The one who saved your life once. And whose life you saved when your father was hunting him. You are linked already. It is time now for you to be linked even more."

"But how?" asked Beatrice.

"I do not know," said George. He only knew that it would happen—or he knew nothing of his magic at all.

Beatrice did not ask more, for they were under the trees, and then the bear leaped toward them, roaring incoherently, claws showing, the signs of unhealed wounds on his shoulder and face. He oozed blood and pain. Yet he had been called here by a voice he could not resist.

Now it was the time to tell him why.

George was still thinking what to say and how to convey it when the raking claw hit his side. He was stunned. The bear had had chances to attack him before, but never had. Why now?

"Stop!" George exclaimed, not using either human or bear language, but the pure, clear language of the magic.

The bear fell down on all fours and, moving away step by step, panted.

But before George could try anything more, Beatrice was between him and the bear. She stood as a human but snarled like a hound. And she showed no sign of any fear of what the bear could do to her.

"Stop!" George told her.

This was not what was supposed to happen. They should not be attacking each other. That was not love — or was it?

They were staring each other up and down, sniffing the air, sizing up. George was reminded of a wolf mating he had seen when he was nine years old. It was after his mother's death, and he had had no one to explain to him what was happening. At first he had thought that the two animals were intent on death. It seemed unfair to him that the one was so much larger than the other, but the wolf bitch had fought fiercely to the end, until she was subdued. It was then that he had seen, and understood, the true purpose of the battle.

So George held his breath, and his commands, while the bear and Beatrice continued their silent battle of wills. The bear began to move again, in a dancing circle that inched forward and then back, around Beatrice. Beatrice moved with him, her eyes never letting him go.

Marit came to George's side and whined quietly. He bent down so his face was next to hers. "It must be this way," he said, and hoped it was true. If this was all for naught, then what was his second choice? He had no backup plan. There was no other bear in the woods that had been a man, and he and Marit would be forced to live with her current form forever.

Somehow the horror he had felt at this before left him. Whatever her form, she was the woman he loved.

Perhaps the kingdom of Kendel could not accept Marit as queen. But he had lived for duty all his years. If Kendel demanded he choose between Marit and his place as prince—or king—he knew what he would choose. He would not disguise himself any longer to fit another's mold.

The bear moved closer, and Beatrice howled.

What was it that had led to the mating of the two wolves he had seen before? Was it merely a matter of the strongest female and the strongest male coming together? But Beatrice had had that once, and it had given her no satisfaction. She had been a woman now and had seen what a woman looked for in a man. She might not agree with it entirely, but she had been changed.

This dance of power and love would be unlike any

other. As the bear leaped forward and tumbled Beatrice to the ground, George realized there was no way for him to know what would happen. This was not his choice. It was the bear's and Beatrice's, and while he could force them to do as he wished, he could not force them to love each other.

Now, when he had discovered the extent of his power, he could use it least. "Stay," he said to Marit, and pulled on the nape of her neck.

She dug in her feet, but when the bear and Beatrice emerged from their tumble and began to touch each other, Marit moved and hid her head in George's side.

So soon? Could this be the end?

Yet George did not breathe relief.

He sat beside Marit, let the hound put her head in his lap, and stroked her. And now and again, he looked up to see Beatrice and the bear, slowly moving closer together.

A man who had been a bear might never be a man fully again. But he would also never be an animal, content with an animal's life. There was something human in the way the bear touched her, but without the full gentleness of human love. Perhaps Beatrice would not want that.

George got to his feet, and Marit followed him to a discreet distance from the bear and Beatrice. He did not know when he was sure that it was the right time or if it ever had anything to do with him, but suddenly there was a difference in the air, a waving in its fabric.

A change was coming.

He reached for Marit, took hold of one of her front paws, then the other. He stared her in the face. "Ready?" he asked hoarsely. Or perhaps he only thought he made a sound with his mouth at that point.

In any case, she nodded at him. Her eyes in his eyes, her paws in his hands, her life in his power.

And it began.

The whole world seemed very far away. He could see nothing but Marit. He felt nauseated and could not stop himself from vomiting on his boots. She looked up at him in concern. Then she began to change.

There was a blur around her, and an aura of bright red that he dared not penetrate. Suddenly all was clear, and he could see her as she began the transformation.

A paw lengthened, grew fingers. Then ears retracted, the snout shortened. Fur disappeared into pale human skin.

There was a flash of blue, and George could see the hint of fabric on her body, a gown like the one Beatrice had worn that very morning. How the magic worked with clothing George did not know, but all magic was a mystery to him, so why not this one bit as well?

Marit's eyes turned from black to blue, almost finished, and so it must be for Beatrice too, but George could not see her clearly through the magic mist. The bear stood guard next to her, like George, and not enveloped in the mist. But George trusted the bear more than he would have trusted any man he knew to keep Beatrice safe.

And so George was free to watch the rest of Marit's miraculous change. She seemed dazed, as if dreaming and unaware of the magnitude of this event.

Her hands were held at waist level and she did not notice how the hair disappeared from their backs, or how the fingernails, pink and new, grew in perfect moon shapes above the tips of her fingers. She did not see how her feet shrank into the delicate skin that was then covered in the black, poorly shined boots that Beatrice had worn that morning.

Eyelashes.

Wrists.

Ankles.

Toes.

George marveled in all of them.

The tip of her nose.

The curve of her hips.

The dimple in her cheek.

The length of her thigh.

The turn of her knee.

All was as it should have been. And it was perfect.

The sensation of nausea in George's stomach turned to one of empty terror. What could this woman want with him?

"George" was the first word she spoke. She looked

at Beatrice, who was now a hound, tucked close to the bear.

The bear had not been changed, thought George dizzily. Had that not been part of the magic's promise — that King Richon would be returned to his former shape?

Then—"George," Marit said again. "What have you done? You've taken her from me forever." And she wept.

CHAPTER THIRTY-NINE

*I*T WAS TRUE. George had not thought it through carefully enough when he began this magical transformation. Had he expected Beatrice to remain a woman? Of course not. She was a hound. But if she loved a bear who became a man once more, where could they go?

No, the magic was right to leave them like this. They must remain in the words now. Apart from Marit. Yet how wrenching that loss must be to her.

"We could come visit," said George. Even as he said it, he could hear how human the word was and how it belittled what had been between Marit and Beatrice, a love that he could not supplant or step between.

"Visit," echoed Marit blankly.

George had thought it would be a triumphant moment when he succeeded in finding a way to make Marit human again and to transform Beatrice as well.

Now it seemed cruel.

"What day is it?" Marit asked suddenly.

George had to think to answer. "The thirtieth day of summer," he said.

"It has been a year, then. It was the twenty-ninth day of summer that we were changed. I remember the summer sky and the smell of cherries and peaches in the air."

George looked back to Beatrice and the bear, King Richon who once was. They seemed more comfortable with each other now, in some ways, than George and Marit were.

So perhaps the bear was not disappointed in the magic after all. He was loved now, as he had not been in his man-form.

"We should let them alone," said King Richon. It was more a question than a statement, but truly George did not know what to do next, and he had the feeling that the longer they stayed, the more difficult it would be for Marit to leave.

Marit flashed George a look of pure dislike. "Do you feel nothing for her anymore?" she demanded in a low voice. "She was the one you were to marry. She was the one you thought you loved."

George felt a wave of heat cover his face and neck. "No. It was not that way. The dreams—"

Marit waved them away. "It was her words you heard, always, never mine. She was the fierce, strong one. Of course you would love her. How could you not?

How could you ever love me?"

"I—I always felt more at ease with you," George said. "Always." Would she believe him? It was Marit who had been the comforting one. Beatrice had been strong, it was true, but in a way that had seemed strange even at the time. Not human, somehow. Not quite in keeping with the hurt child he had seen in the dreams.

"I wish . . ." Marit said.

"It is as it must be," said George.

He looked at Marit, waiting for her to slap him or spit at him. Instead, she simply sighed and turned away.

"I cannot stay here," she muttered. Then she began to walk away from Beatrice and the bear, out of the forest, toward the castle.

George hurried to follow her. Halfway back to the castle, Marit still had not turned to look at him or speak to him. The bear and the hound had fallen together so easily. Why could it not be the same with Marit and him?

Or was that fair? Perhaps Beatrice and the bear would have their difficulties. Certainly they would in time. A bear and a hound, a difficult combination to sustain. But were Marit and he any easier?

No.

Love was a terrible, messy thing. And yet George could not go back, could not even want to go back to the man he had been. It would have been like wishing to be a shadow again, like asking the night to stay forever so that he never had to see the brilliant color of summer green in the full light of the noon sun.

He had been starving and had never tasted food. Now he had.

"Marit," he said, reaching for her.

She stopped and turned to him, a hint of hope on her face.

But the thought he had been holding to desperately went suddenly out of his head, and he did not know what to say.

Her face faded.

George sighed. "Wait a moment. Let us rest for a bit," he said, his tone polite, distant, cool, as if he were speaking to an utter stranger.

Marit responded in the same way. She nodded her head slightly, then followed his lead. They sat on the ground some three feet apart from each other, each looking in a different direction.

"I—" He tried again.

"I—" she said at the same moment.

And both stopped.

"Please, speak," said George.

But Marit bit at her lower lip. "I have been a hound too long," she said. "I do not know how to act like a human woman anymore."

"Well, I have no excuse like yours," said George. "But I cannot see how living as a human for seventeen years would have prepared anyone for this. Certainly I was not prepared. How could I be?" He allowed himself a small smile. If they could share a smile, surely that would be the beginning of the healing.

But she did not smile. She seemed to have lost her anger and turned to despair. "You were blinded. If you had known, if I had dared to tell you—"

"Perhaps you would have trusted me if I had been more worthy of your trust," George interrupted.

"You did nothing but prove to me your worth every moment that we were together," said Marit bitterly. "And I did nothing but continue to deceive you."

"You and Beatrice," said George. "It was not as if you could have spoken to me directly."

"But I could have—no matter what Beatrice believed was right. We had the dreams together. I could have spoken to you then."

"I do not know if that would have been enough."

"If once you had suspected, you would have understood it shortly. You are not a stupid man," said Marit.

Which was not as much of a compliment as George might have hoped for at this juncture.

"I do not blame you," George said.

"I do not blame you either," said Marit.

But that did not bring down the barrier now between them.

George was struck with a thought. "Let us begin again then," he said, "as if we had never met before now, before this very moment. We shall forget everything, good and bad." He moved closer to her.

"How can we forget?" she asked solemnly.

Too solemnly. That was the woman who had been made out of the broken girl. But was there any bit of that young girl left over, the determined child who would do whatever it took to get what she wanted? The girl who had seen her father's game of kings and been determined to learn to play it? George had to reach that girl, somehow. He wanted to play with her again.

"Magic," said George softly. If it was a lie, then it was one meant with kindness. "If you close your eyes, I will work it on you, and when you open them again, it will all be new."

"And on yourself?"

"I will do the same magic on me. You will see," he said.

"Your animal magic does not extend that far, I do not think," said Marit flatly.

"Close your eyes," George said. It was meant as a game. Did they not deserve that after all this?

At last Marit gave him a ghost of a smile and did it.

Now what? He tried to think of some ridiculous rhyme to say but gave it up. Instead, he brushed his fingers over her eyes briefly, then said, "Open."

She stared at him.

"My name is Prince George of Kendel. I was passing through the woods today and found you here. Are you in any distress? May I help you?" He could not help how stilted his words sounded, as if he were in some minstrel's tale, the stereotypical knight offering his assistance to the maiden in the woods.

"You can help me stand," said Marit. She gave him her hand.

It wasn't working. He did not know what else to try.

He was ready to give up when Marit at last said, shyly, "I am from Sarrey. My father is King Helm. My name is . . . Marit."

George bowed over her hand and kissed it. "Princess Marit, it is good to meet you. I have heard of you before, but you are not at all what I expected."

"I hope it is a good surprise then," said Marit.

"A wonderful surprise," said George. "I knew you were beautiful—"

Marit blushed at this.

"But I did not know that you were also a lover of the woods and of animals, as I am. Perhaps we will find we have more in common."

"Perhaps," said Marit. Then she said, "I believe in magic of many kinds."

"And so do I," said George. "So do I." He allowed himself the luxury of looking at her for a long while. It was not something that Beatrice would have allowed, but now he could see the differences in them. Marit blushed, for one. Beatrice had never done that. Marit spoke softly, with hesitation. Beatrice had always known what she thought, but there was strength in being unsure too.

"I think that I could love you," said George earnestly.

And held his breath as he waited for Marit's reaction. Would she turn away from him? Was it too much too soon? Damn.

"So soon to speak of love. Do you always tease women so?" asked Marit.

George shook his head. "It is not a tease."

"Then it is flattery," said Marit.

"No," George insisted.

"But . . . we have just met." She at least was playing the game.

"Yes," said George, allowing himself to fall back into it. "We have. But it feels as if I have known you forever. It happens that way sometimes, don't you agree?"

Too much, too much, George warned himself. But it was too late to stop now.

"Yes, I know what you mean," said Marit, and, all shyness gone now, looked him in the eyes.

"Will you follow me back to my castle?" George asked, offering his arm.

She took it, and they went on their way.

The silence between them then was not the same as before. It was not a lack of something between them; it was an agreement. Why should they need words when they had the sights and sounds and feel of the woods to share?

CHAPTER FORTY

*I*T WAS PAST MIDNIGHT, and the moon was shining bright as Marit and George approached the palace.

"Can you see her still?" Marit asked. "With your magic?"

George closed his eyes. Yes, there she was. In the woods with the bear. They had not yet retreated to a cave but were washing in the stream.

"Is she well?"

George smiled as he saw the bear push Beatrice into the stream. She righted herself, then leaped out, circled the bear, and this time he fell in.

"She is happy," said George.

Marit winced a moment, as if Beatrice's happiness hurt her. Then she sighed and nodded.

Did she expect that Beatrice would not go on with her life? Did she expect her own life to be at an end now?

"She is a hound at heart," said Marit. "She does not let wounds fester. When they are healed, they are done and gone."

"Yes," said George. That did seem to be part of the Beatrice he had known. It had been something he had admired about her and would miss. But it belonged more in the woods than in the human world.

Humans did not let go easily. And there was something wonderful about that. The way Marit had, after all these years, not given up on her father. Perhaps not on George either.

"I shall see you in the morning," George said firmly, daring to touch her arm.

She nodded and moved away. She turned back a moment later. "Will you dream of her?" she asked.

"I don't know," said George. He thought now that the dreams had been the way for the other part of his animal magic to bubble up, to communicate with him when he would not see it true.

"I envy you that," said Marit.

"I will share them with you as much as I can," said George. But of course that would not be enough for her.

Marit nodded, biting her lip, and turned away once more.

"We will visit her," George told her. He did not think she believed him until he added, "And take the game of kings with us, to see how well she does."

Then Marit smiled. "Yes, let us do that."

That night George slept like a rock, dreamless. In the morning he felt so refreshed that he smiled at his reflection in the mirror. He would go and talk to Marit, invite her to sit with him at breakfast. He would have amusing stories to tell her, and there would be always a bit of truth in them so that she would see he was not a frivolous man.

He had almost reached her chamber when he heard the noises outside: voices, shouting, and the sound of a cannon.

"Prince George?" asked Marit formally, peeking out to see him. Her lips trembled, but she held them tightly closed as if to conceal her concern.

"I'm sure it is nothing to worry about," George said. "I shall be back in a moment."

When he had started down the stairs, he realized she was following him. The noises had grown louder and more ominous. Where were his guards?

George set his jaw and went outside to the drawbridge. Marit had caught up to him by then, and when he stopped to see the guard, her hand was resting on his shoulder.

"What is this?" George demanded. He did not recognize any of the guards. He should, he knew. He needed to take time for these details. His father did.

"Your Highness," stuttered one of the guards, with a bow.

George turned to see the crowd gathered around the moat, shouting and jeering. "Burn him!" came the shout of one man, his fist raised.

"No animal magic at the court!" shouted another.

Marit's hand on his shoulder tightened.

George turned to her. "You could go back in," he said.

She shook her head, and it gave George renewed courage to know that she would not desert him now, despite all.

He turned back to the crowd. It was time for him to face this alone, without his father.

Somehow the knowledge of his animal magic had come out. He would not deny it this time. It was time his people knew the truth, and time too for the whole kingdom to be changed, as changed as Marit and Beatrice had been. But not by magic. This time the only power he had to use was the power of his persuasion.

George stepped forward, determined not to show fear. "What is this?" he demanded. "Why do you come here in this way? Since when do we solve problems in Kendel this way?"

A whisper seemed to spread through the crowd, and George heard his name. "Prince George, Prince George is here!" It did not make sense to him. Hadn't they expected that he would come answer his accusers?

"You!" George said at last, pointing to a man near the front of the crowd. At his side was a young boy, limping, a bloody bandage around his leg. The boy stared wide-eyed and pale at the castle.

345

"Tell me what this is about!" George demanded.

The man stepped forward tentatively. "My son," he said, then swallowed.

"Yes." George tried to look at the boy kindly. Did the boy truly have something to do with all this?

"He saw a man in the woods. Dressed in the livery of the king's guard. He used animal magic."

What? One of his guards was accused, then, and not he himself? For a moment George was tempted to let it go as it was, not to admit anything. But that was the man he had been, not the one he had become. Moreover, if he put this off for another day, it would not get any easier. It would only force him to hide himself more and more deeply.

He was tired of hiding who he truly was. All his life—it had been far too long.

"Tell me what this guard looked like," said George.

The father looked back at his boy. "Young," he said. "And—" He faltered.

George pointed to the boy. "Bring him here."

He was perhaps ten years old. George remembered that age very well. Of course he was afraid. And he had no idea what any of this meant. Later, perhaps, he would understand it more.

"Tell me what he looked like, this guard you saw." George coaxed the boy. He held out his hand, the one not holding Marit's, and pulled the boy toward him.

The boy moved jerkily and looked about wildly for his father.

But the father could not speak against the prince.

"Was he tall? Short? Young? Old?"

"Young," said the boy at last.

That helped George but little. All his guards were young. If they grew older, they became trainers for the younger guards but rarely moved outside the castle itself.

It was really a matter of mere curiosity, for George had never suspected that any of his guards had animal magic. If he had, what would he have done? Anything at all? Perhaps not. He would have been afraid of the connection, much as he also would have longed for it.

And now?

Now he refused to be afraid any longer. Still, he wished to know.

"And the color of his hair?"

"Br-brown," the boy answered.

"His eyes?"

The boy shook his head, trembling from head to foot. "I don't know. I don't know," he said. "I don't remember."

"Do you remember anything else about him? Anything to tell me which one it was?"

"You could bring them all out, Your Highness," the father said, "and let him look at them one by one. He could tell you which one it was then."

George said, "I think I shall do just that." He motioned to the guards at the gate, and one ran forward. George gave a whispered command, and the guard stared out at the crowd, whitened, and nodded. Then he ran back.

Marit was holding George's hand so tightly that he could no longer feel his fingers. Did she trust him to do what was right here? It seemed a test, and not merely for the guard.

George looked down at the boy. "They will come out, a group of twelve. All with brown hair, as you said. All young. You look at them carefully and tell me if you see the man there."

What would George do if the boy did not see the guard he had met in the woods? What if it had not been a guard at all but someone else in a uniform? The whole castle might have to be searched before they came to him. And if they did not, then what?

Then what? It would not be as easy for George to proclaim his animal magic. Another temptation to wait, to take the easy course.

Only half the guards had come out when the boy shouted out, "There he is." He pointed, and George turned to see who it was.

Henry.

Henry?

George moved to his side, shielding the guard who had become his friend.

Henry stiffened. "I shall tell no one, Your Highness," he promised in a mutter that did not move his lips.

He did know of George's magic, then? He had

known that they shared that one thing all along. And he had never spoken of it, had allowed George to think it was still his secret?

"This is the man?" George asked the boy, nodding to the other guards to go back behind the gate.

The boy shivered, then nodded, and his father came to lift him up and carry him off.

As if the animal magic, like a disease, could contaminate them.

George turned on Henry. "Will you confess?" He shouted loudly enough for all in the crowd to hear.

Henry, confused, stared at George. "I have the animal magic if that is what you mean," he said.

"Yes, and tell us all how this boy came to know it of you. Speak your piece as the boy has already spoken his," said George, borrowing his father's words from judgment day. He saw backs straighten and knew there were many who recognized those words and knew what they meant.

CHAPTER FORTY-ONE

"*I*—I went into the woods. I was there because I needed . . . to speak with the animals."

George nodded. "And?"

Henry bowed his head. "I heard a rumbling sound from far away. And then the sound of an animal in distress. I knew it was a horse. I could not ignore it, so I followed the sound north, where the woods narrowed and there was a bridge spanning a great chasm with a stream at the bottom.

"I could see that the bridge had broken and that a horse had fallen into the ravine below. A horse and also a child. That boy." Henry pointed to the child who had accused him of animal magic, and though there was no malice in his manner, the boy turned away and cried out in fear as though the look alone could kill him.

Henry went on. "I had to climb down toward the ravine slowly, step by step, because of the fall of rocks, which had also caused the bridge to break and had carried away the child and the horse with it. If I had caused more sliding of the rocks, it could have been the end of the boy, and the horse too."

But he did not say a word of his own danger. Did anyone else hear that? George looked through the crowd. He saw one man who was listening very intently, with furrowed brow and a look of interest rather than fear or anger. He glanced back, and there was Marit too, a step behind George, tears standing in her eyes.

"I called out, and the boy answered me. I could not see all of him, amid the rocks, only his blood-smeared leg just beyond the horse. I was afraid that the leg was broken, or worse, that it would have to be cut off entirely, after the weight of the horse had destroyed it."

Could anyone doubt that Henry had cared at least as much for the boy as for the horse?

"I told him I was coming and shouted to him not to move. He begged me to come quickly and waved an arm. Then the horse, agitated by this new movement, began to adjust its position, trying to find its head. I had to use my animal magic then." Henry looked to George for pity because he did not expect it from any other source. "I do not use it often, for it is feared so much. But in this case I thought surely no one could argue against me. It was to save a boy's life."

Perhaps Henry had also hoped, George thought, that people would not believe the rantings of a small boy

351

who had been in such a terrible accident. They would think it was simply a fantasy his pained mind had created, and it would have been true if only it had been about anything but animal magic. There was no rationality where animal magic was concerned, not in Kendel.

"I called to the horse in the language of horses, to lie down." Henry continued. "But he did not hear me, or he would not listen. And so the rockfall started again. I watched as it pulled the boy down farther."

"He called the rocks down!" one of the crowd shouted. "He meant for the boy to die!"

George stared out until silence reigned once more. Ridiculous. He had experienced the full extent of his animal magic now, and it was great. But that did not mean he could call down a rockslide from a mountain. Might as well say he could change the boundaries of his kingdom at will, and the faces of all those in it. Changing their hearts would be more convenient but, alas, equally impossible.

"I was sure that I would die with them then, but it stopped after just a moment. I was closer to the boy and the horse then, and I inched forward bit by bit, searching for stable footing." Henry was sweating as he thought of it. George could imagine how frantic he had been.

So much about Henry made sense now. He had left his home and the woman he loved and refused to name.

Why? To hide himself. To keep any suspicion from falling on those he loved. And to make himself forget, if he could, those things that could never be his. A normal life. Friends. Family. Love and respect.

"I spoke to the horse and promised I would get it out. I put my hand out and calmed it. I spoke to it of the stable and the warm hay that would be waiting, if only it did as I said. Just a few more minutes, just keep still, I told it. And it did."

This was where the crowd should have broken out into a cheer, but it did not. The only open mouths were twisted with hatred. George cheered silently for Henry's courage. Henry, he thought, was more of a prince than George had ever been.

But that would have to change. Today it would change.

"I moved to the back of the horse and by touch found the boy's buried leg. It was not broken, only badly cut and bruised. His head was facedown in the rocks, and he struggled when he felt me touch him. I helped him first get his head clear so he could breathe. Then he looked at me. I think he knew that I had the animal magic then."

Still, the boy had not screamed or told Henry to go away. He had been willing to be helped by the animal magic.

"When he was ready, I told him I would get him out of the rocks, but that he must not cry out in pain. If he did, I was afraid of what the horse would do. I could not control them both at once," said Henry.

"I pulled him where I could and dug around the rocks where I had to. Then he was in my arms, and I promised him that he would be safe. I told him to put his arms around my neck. And I began to walk out of the ravine with him.

"I had to touch the horse first, so that it would not buck or shake the rocks while we were gone. I promised it I would be back, but I had to get the boy out first. The horse understood that, despite all the danger.

"When I had the boy settled on a high ridge, he began to spit at me and call me names. But he could not move because of his leg, so I left him and went to tend the horse."

"The horse first and the boy had to get out by himself! That's the true story!" shouted the boy's father. "Tell it true or not at all!"

But George believed Henry. And the boy's leg seemed too badly injured for him to have gotten himself out.

"By some miracle, the horse was nearly untouched, so I helped it to the top. Before I had a chance to get to the boy once more, he had climbed on his horse and ridden away."

Now Henry lifted his hands, palms up. "I did not know how to go after him. I could have followed the horse, but I would have come so much later I did not see how it would matter. I thought that he would be safe once he was home."

And so he had been.

So what now? Somehow George had to find a way to be fair to both sides. Here was that first terrible judgment day of his, come again.

"Your Highness, I am sorry to bring this shame here. I did not mean—of course I will accept any punishment you deem proper. To protect you and yours." Henry knelt. He knew what he was offering: his own life for George's safety, his animal magic so that George's could remain hidden.

Before he could speak, George felt Marit's hand on his back. He turned. Her face was white as a winter owl.

"What is it? What is wrong?"

"I am afraid for you," whispered Marit. Her eyes shone with the knowledge of the danger that George faced. And of the fact that he could turn away from it.

But she could not be asking him to do that, surely?

"I have lost her already. How will I survive if I lose you as well?" she asked, lips quivering.

"If I do not do this, then I will have lost myself," said George. He stared at her to see if she understood what he meant.

At last, she nodded. And let go of him.

How strange that he had to have more to lose in order to find the courage to proclaim himself.

"Do you agree to abide by my judgment on this animal magic?" George asked, his face turned to the father and the boy. This was important. For so long the people of Kendel had taken to judging animal magic on their own. They must agree that George had the authority.

"Yes, Your Highness." The father licked his lips. He could tell that there was something unexpected here, but he did not know what it was or what it meant.

"And the rest of you make no objections to my right to judge here?" George looked out over the crowd.

He heard no response and took that as assent.

Now to reverse what had happened on his first judgment day, when King Davit had allowed one man with animal magic to exempt all of his kind from the king's power.

"And you, guard?" George asked. "You put yourself in my hands the day you came here and took service at the castle. You will not try to save yourself with your animal magic at the last moment, will you?"

"No," said Henry. He had steeled himself against every emotion, George thought.

George did not know how to convey to him a bit of hope. "You will accept my judgment whatever it is?" he asked.

Henry blanched but nodded stiffly.

"Good. Listen to me now. I will give my judgment here upon you all." George raised his voice just loud enough that it could be heard by every person in the crowd, as long as he was listening with absolute stillness.

"The boy and his father: You are to receive compensation for whatever damage your horse received, including the choice of the king's own stables if you wish it. And your son will have the best physician in the kingdom tend to him. Do you have complaint with that?"

The father chewed at his lip. "No, Your Highness. Of course not. That is very generous. I did not think — that is, it was only for his sake that we came." He nodded to Henry.

George ignored this. He turned to the crowd. "You will disperse. You have no purpose here. It is my judgment that matters now. And as soon as I speak it, you must be gone. Are there any objections to this?"

If there were, they were not spoken aloud. George turned at last to Henry.

Marit was so close he could hear her shallow and uneven breathing. Losing the kingdom somehow seemed a paltry thing now in comparison to losing her. What kind of fool was he?

"You admit that you have the animal magic?" he asked Henry.

Henry nodded.

"You admit that you used it to save this boy's life and the life of his horse, at the risk of your own?" George spoke as solemnly as before. Nonetheless, there were a few heads in the crowd that lifted at this, eyes shifting this way and that, uncertainty gleaming.

"Yes," said Henry.

"You admit that you have served me for three years and that you have kept this secret from me? From everyone who has ever known you?"

Henry's lips moved, but no words came out. He was sweating heavily.

George held himself back. "You must give acknowledgment," he said.

"Yes," said Henry at last. "I did not mean to harm you, Prince George."

"And all this because of your fear of what I would say or do when I discovered the truth of your animal magic?"

"Yes," said Henry again. This time it came automatically.

"And have you ever told anyone that you discovered that I also have the animal magic?" George asked quietly.

Suddenly Henry's head came up. He stared at the crowd about them. "Your Highness, what do you mean? I don't know what you're talking about! You have no animal magic!" He lied bravely.

"Ah, but I do," said George. "I have had it since I was a child. It was a legacy from my mother, the queen." He looked out to the crowd. "Did no one ever suspect her? She was known to love animals. She died because of her animal magic and because of the way she was forced to hide it. And all these years my father has been afraid to let the truth be known."

The silence from the crowd lasted one more moment,

then broke out into shouts of angry denial, and worse.

George stared out over all of them, refusing to retreat, to show any sign of fear. His guards were behind him rather than in front. But in some battles that was the way it must be.

A glob of spittle came at George and landed on his face. He let it dribble off without deigning to wipe at it with his finger.

"How can I punish you, then, my guard Henry, without punishing myself?"

Henry shook with emotion. "Your—your—"

"I cannot, of course. So this is the punishment I mete out. You and I are to use our magic in the service of humans and animals wherever we can. And we are no longer to keep it a secret but proclaim it and allow all others to do the same, with the same impunity."

George took a breath and thought of Dr. Gharn. He must not forget that man's power or how he had used it. He continued. "Those who are truly harmed by animal magic, however, have only to come before me, and they will find I will punish this as swiftly as any other crime. For it is not the animal magic that is evil, any more than it is an arrow or a knife in a man's back, but those who wield such weapons. Good or evil, we all are to be judged by our actions, not by our capabilities."

"Thank you, Your Highness," said Henry at last, and fell to his knees and made obeisance more proper to a king than a prince.

George raised him, then looked out at the crowd. The people were quiet, but he did not think they were satisfied. Had he thought that they would be? Of course not. That was why he had put this off so long.

Yet it could have been worse. Far worse.

George thought back to a long-ago bonfire.

This was not the end, he knew. This was the beginning.

Finally he said, "That is my judgment. You have agreed to accept it. Now go your way." He waved out away from the castle.

Slowly a few men at the back of the crowd turned away. Then a few more.

The boy and his father went next, confusion as much as anger in their eyes. As if they were not sure that they believed George truly had the animal magic. Perhaps he should have done some proof of it for them all. But he was too tired, today of all days. He could not.

There would be other times for that, he was sure. Let them wait, and they would see it.

Chapter Forty-two

ONCE THE BOY AND his father had gone, there was no more bone to the rest of them. They wavered this way and that, but in less than an hour the ground was clear.

George put a hand on Henry's shoulder and led him back inside, then told him to return to the guardroom. Henry's ordeal was over, but George still had to face his guards and all of those who thought they had known him but discovered they had not. How many of them would still be willing to serve him at the end of the day? Would he find the palace entirely deserted?

Well, let them go.

"I'll take you to your chamber," George said to Marit.

"You will not," she said stiffly.

George was startled.

"Where then?" he asked.

She folded her fingers together, a gesture he had never seen Beatrice use, though he recalled it from the shared dreams with Marit.

"I am to leave in two weeks' time, but I have never spoken to your father," she said.

"He is ill," he said. "I do not know if he will be up to talking."

"Then I shall see him, at least."

George nodded at this. There were other things he had to do, after what had happened with the crowd. Important, urgent things. But even those could wait for a few more minutes.

The closer they got to the stairs that led to his father's bedchamber, the more concerned George became. It was so quiet, with no hint of servants coming or going. As if death had already been here and taken everything away.

Not even four-fingered Jack was at the top of the stairs.

But the door was open. George pushed his way in, Marit behind him, and saw Jack kneeling at his father's bedside. Dr. Gharn was by the window.

"How is he?" George asked quietly.

Jack leaped up at the sound of George's voice and moved back toward his post. "I should not have left my position, Your Highness," he said.

Marit stared at Dr. Gharn and would not move closer.

"If you would rather I left?" the physician said.

"Does he need you?" asked Marit in a cold voice that was very much like the one George had become used to in Beatrice.

"I can do little for him now, and that I have done already for this day."

Marit looked at George.

"Go then," he said.

Marit breathed only when Dr. Gharn was gone, and her color was now coming back to normal.

George touched her, to offer comfort, and she flinched from him, her hands high.

He stepped away. One step forward, two steps back, it seemed they were going.

"Is he awake?" Marit asked.

George moved toward his father, and King Davit's eyes opened. He was weak, it was clear, but in other ways he seemed much better. He was not shaking or wheezing with every breath, and his vision seemed clear again.

"George."

"Father, I brought the princess to see you." He motioned to Marit.

She approached, inclining her head slightly. "King Davit." And then she said no more.

Why had she wanted to see him then?

"Do you love him?" King Davit asked abruptly.

George saw a twitch in Marit's face, but otherwise

she held herself as hard as a sword. That was the difference between her and Beatrice, George thought. Marit only pretended to be a sword. Beatrice was one.

"I will know the answer. He is my only son, and he deserves to be loved."

Marit took so long to speak that George was sure she was getting ready to walk out of the chamber. Then, at last, she said, "I think I could come to love him. But he deserves more than that. You are right." Her shoulders slumped.

"Ah," said King Davit. "Good. I am glad that you see that. It shows me that you love him more than you know. I always believed that I could not love my wife as she deserved, to the day she died. Then I found out I was wrong. May you never find out the truth as I did."

He turned to George. "And you?"

George felt as though he were speaking to the lord general, being asked to account for his actions.

"What do you want to know?" he asked. He was only postponing the inevitable, and he knew it.

"Do you love her?"

It was the last thing George wanted to answer at the moment. Yet he could not lie to his father, not now. He closed his eyes, though, as if hoping for some magic, after all. "Yes, I do."

His father breathed out heavily. "I did not know if you could ever love," he said.

"I loved Mother. And you, Father," said George, suddenly affronted.

"Yes. You loved her. But after she was gone, you loved where duty led you," said King Davit. "And no further. But she—she is my hope for your future. Where I have damaged, she can repair. And perhaps you can do the same for her."

George hoped so too. If Marit would let him. But if Beatrice had been obsidian, then Marit was slate. So easy to chip off and wound. So close to the weeping girl underneath.

But wasn't that what he loved about her? Because in that they were alike.

"I had hoped to live much longer." King Davit closed his eyes again and sagged back into his blankets.

"Father! I'll call Dr. Gharn!" George said immediately.

King Davit raised a hand. "Why? What could he possibly do for me now?"

"He nearly killed you," George said bitterly.

"He did kill me. Only slowly enough that I could see all of my life before my eyes and watch it drift away from me until only what was most valuable to me was left. Some might call that a theft, George." His eyes strayed to the door, and George knew he was thinking of four-fingered Jack. "Others might call it a blessing."

"But—" said George.

"I had hoped to see my grandchildren someday, but I can let go of that now. So long as I know you are happy, and see this woman's face. I can imagine my grandchildren without having to hear them cry once."

He grinned at this, a boyish grin unlike any George had seen on his father's face before.

"A redheaded girl. She will be beautiful, I think. And with the animal magic."

"Spare her that," George muttered.

"No. Don't spare her," said King Davit. "Or she will not grow as I have seen you grow, George."

There was a long silence.

"George, I should not ask this."

"Ask," said George.

"I always hoped that you would name her for your mother."

"Yes." George did not hesitate.

Then Marit's mild voice was heard. "What is your mother's name?" she asked.

George was flustered. Of course he should not have agreed without Marit's permission.

"Lara," said King Davit.

"Lara. A good, strong name."

"Thank you," said King Davit. "I always thought it suited my wife well. She was a strong woman, in features as well as in heart. As you are strong. And as I hope that my granddaughter will be strong."

That was the end to the conversation. George left the chamber feeling oddly comforted. It was not that he had agreed to name his daughter after his mother. It was that he and Marit had agreed that they would have a daughter together. That was something to build on, surely. And she had said she could love him, even if she did not yet fully.

In ten minutes his father had done more than George imagined possible.

When they arrived somehow back at her door, Marit said, "I will not have that man at my wedding."

"My father?" asked George, baffled.

"Dr. Gharn."

"Oh." *Of course,* thought George.

"I cannot forgive him as your father has. That is not one of my gifts, whatever they are." She spoke as though there were stones in her mouth and she could not move her lips or tongue. Her back was very straight.

Did she expect him to deny her this one request?

"He will not be there," George said. "And you need not see him more than now and again so long as . . ." George did not say the rest, that Dr. Gharn needed be in the castle only so long as his father remained alive. But she understood it.

"Then I will go back to Sarrey at the end of the week as planned until the wedding."

George nodded, feeling cold at the thought of being parted from her for so long. Would she lose all feeling for him? Would she fall in love with another now that she was changed?

But George could hardly hold her prisoner here for fear of that. Now he had changed her, he did not own her. She must make her own choices.

"And," said Marit, a bit of the old softness in her face. Then she put a hand to George's shoulder, and he remembered how he had felt whenever she had circled him as a hound. At peace. Always at peace.

"We can write letters to each other, get to know each other truly," she added.

"Letters?" George tried to content himself with that. The wedding was to be in the winter. He would have to trust in Marit. And himself.

He thought suddenly of the woods in the winter, and of the bear, and Beatrice.

"Will they come, do you think?" he asked. Marit needed no reminder which "they" he meant.

"Will you call them?"

George thought about it. There was no other way for them to know the exact day, and it was unfair of him to wish them to come if he did not tell them. "I could call all the animals in the kingdom," he suggested. "And it would be like a tale a minstrel would tell."

"Like King Richon and the wild man," said Marit, smiling shyly.

"Would you like that?" George asked, ready to give her anything she asked for. So long as she asked for it and let him get it for her—that was more the difficulty.

"It would be foolish, a child's fairy dream," said Marit. But she did not deny it.

"I will do it then," said George. "And the bear and Beatrice before them all."

She laughed, a small sound constrained by a hand at her mouth. George had never heard her laugh before. It was a pleasant sound. If only she were more free with it. How many times could he get her to laugh before she left?

And what letters could he write to her that would make her laugh when she was gone?

"I love you," he said, pressing his face next to hers.

She did not move away, but neither did she move forward.

He bent his lips to hers and kissed her lightly. Then she kissed him back—for a moment, only a moment.

"I—" She started to speak.

George held up his hand and put it to her lips. "Don't say it. Not yet. When you are ready."

She nodded, then kissed him again, lightly, like a little girl, and ran into her chamber.

George did not know whether to laugh or cry. He thought he did both as he moved back down to see Sir Stephen. There was much still to be done before the wedding. And things that had nothing to do with the wedding as well.

CHAPTER FORTY-THREE

"*Y*our Highness?" said Sir Stephen when he saw that it was George. "How can I serve you?"

"I want to make a proclamation," said George, coming to the point quickly.

"A proclamation?" Sir Stephen's surprise gave away the fact that he, at least, had not heard what had happened outside the castle that morning. "But the king—"

"The King will not object to this," George said. He hoped he was right. His father had never done this himself, but it had always been out of concern for George. George did not want that protection anymore.

Besides, his father knew that he was dying. Whether it was a month or a year from now, George would be king very soon. It was time for the people to see him in that role.

"But it is not his proclamation?" Sir Stephen looked anxious.

George wondered if it would come down to a power struggle between them after all. As a child he had some-times seen Sir Stephen as the man who kept him from the things that he wanted. Sir Stephen was his father's man. Would he stand in George's way now?

"No," said George, watching Sir Stephen very closely.

The man paused for a long moment, his face giving no hint of his thoughts. Then he said, "I trust you, George. What is the proclamation? I assume I shall make it an official proclamation for the entire kingdom."

"Yes," said George. He took a breath and went straight ahead, not allowing himself to think of the con-sequences or dangers of his action. If he thought of that, he might become like his father and put it off until next year or the year after that, again and again, until it never happened.

Sometimes there were dangers that had to be faced, no matter the cost. Though those with animal magic had always been a minority, they must not be sacrificed any-more to the rest of the kingdom's fear. It was just possi-ble that the animal magic was not as isolated as George had always assumed it was. Once it was spoken of openly, without taint, there might be more and more who found they could use it. Not a minority after all.

"I want you to announce that I have the animal magic and that henceforth animal magic is not to be considered an offense. In fact, write that anyone with animal magic is free to come to the castle for defense or to come to the king's judgment to ask for redress against any wrongs. And write that those who hurt or murder others who have made no offense against them save for having the animal magic will face the king's utmost punishment." He said it all in one breath and then found himself gasping.

Sir Stephen did not speak for a long moment. "Are you sure, Your Highness?" he asked.

"Yes," said George.

Sir Stephen nodded and said no more, waiting for George to speak, because this was George's proclamation.

"Add that if animal magic is used wrongly, those hurt by it must also come to the castle to ask for judgment, and it will be fairly given. As with any power, it is both the intent of the user and the consequences that will be seen as evidence. Those with animal magic are not to consider themselves free from any justification of themselves, nor are they to be seen as above other men. Rather, they have a gift and as such should be seen as having a greater responsibility than any others to use it wisely and cautiously, for the benefit of all."

George said this in bits and pieces, for he had not thought to compose it in his mind beforehand. He did not know if it sounded kingly at all; he hoped that Sir Stephen would give him advice on how to correct it if it needed correction.

Sir Stephen wrote it all down with a pen, then looked it over with a slight frown on his face.

"What is it? Is there something wrong?" asked George anxiously.

"It is only—" said Sir Stephen. "I wonder if you might add something about the origin of the magic and its history in our kingdom."

George looked up blankly. "But I know almost nothing of that, only a few stories, and I do not know if there is any truth in them at all." Or how to tell the truth from the fiction.

"Ah," said Sir Stephen. He did not need to speak the next part aloud. It was as if George could hear him in his mind. Sir Stephen had not been his tutor all those years for nothing.

"Say, then, that I wish for any men or women who have studied animal magic, either those with it themselves or those without, to come to the castle and teach me about it. For though I have had it myself all these years, I have been forced to hide it, to keep it secret, as have so many others. And so we have not spoken together or shared the varieties of magic that are possible.

"Nor do we know what the past mistakes or glories of our magic are, save for a few tales like that of King Richon and the wild man. Ask for those who know more stories to write them down or bring them to the castle. They will be rewarded for their effort." George felt warmed at the thought of collecting the stories himself, becoming a scholar of the animal magic like the man Dr. Gharn had met, but here in Kendel.

George thought for a moment, then burst out in excitement. "A school, Sir Stephen. That is what we need. A school for all those who have the animal magic or those who wish to get it or to learn of it. Can you imagine it? Teachers who can speak about it openly, giving lessons in the language of animals, and . . . all else that there might be. Students learning, talking to one another, practicing together."

"Where?" Sir Stephen asked.

"Here, in the castle," said George, as if nothing could be more obvious.

"But, Your Highness, there is no space for a school such as you describe here. We have only enough bedchambers for a few visitors, and there are already the servants. Unless you are imagining the dungeon—"

"No, not the dungeon," said George with a shudder. He forced himself to stop and leaned against the wall. The light streamed in from the window and made the whole room seem as vast and bright as the future George saw ahead.

"We shall build a school then. Near the castle," said George. "Small at first, but able to be added to when needed."

"Yes, Your Highness," said Sir Stephen.

"Can that be done?"

"If you proclaim it must be so, then it will be so."

"The money for it?"

"I shall find it somewhere," Sir Stephen replied.

"Well, then. Is that too much for a single proclamation?" George asked.

"It is ambitious," said Sir Stephen, "but all the parts hang together."

George did not want to be talked into moderation. "Then have it sent out, to be read in every town, every village, every noble's house and holdings. Wherever it must be sent."

"At your command," said Sir Stephen.

George dismissed him, then suddenly felt much lighter. He had not known how his secret had weighed him down. Even when he admitted the truth to the crowd and saved Henry, it had not been the same as this.

For a moment George sat down to collect himself. A minute later he had to stand again. And walk. And then move around the castle. He itched to know what people were thinking, feeling, talking about.

He went to the kitchen first, not the least because he was starving. He thought simply to observe, but as soon as Cook Elin caught sight of him, she was throwing herself toward him, kissing his face and laughing and then begging pardon and pulling herself away.

She bubbled at him something about her cousin and the animal magic and her young niece and how it would all come out right and that she had always known that George was a good boy and would do great things for the kingdom. He ended by having a good many of Cook Elin's pastries pushed at him as he left.

He was not received as generously everywhere else. When he went to the stables, he found the lord general staring at him with a look of disgust.

"Is anything wrong?"

The lord general spat on the ground, then spoke to the stablemaster. "I cannot work here one moment longer. I will not be around men who are corrupted by animal magic. If you would be so kind as to send word of my resignation to the king?"

The stablemaster looked to George, who nodded, then turned back to the lord general. "As you say, sir."

The lord general stared at George for another long moment, then stalked away.

George wondered whom he would get to replace the lord general. The man had not been well liked, it was true, but he had been a tradition of a sort, and George had always believed it when he heard the old soldiers say that the lord general might have a hard heart, but he could get his men to work twice as hard as anyone else.

Nor was the lord general the only man to leave the castle with hardly a word. George heard of at least nine others who had gone, servants most of them, but one of them Lord Rochester, his father's chamberlain and the only man who could make any sense of the castle accounts. Sir Stephen sighed and shook his head, saying that he doubted there would be any sense to be got from the records for many years to come.

George went to Henry when it was dark, partly to make sure he had suffered no bad effects personally as a result of what had happened. Henry was in the barracks, quietly packing his things into a single satchel. The barracks had been deserted, as if to give him his privacy. George was glad to be able to speak with him alone and hoped it was a good sign from his fellow soldiers and that they did not all think as the lord general did.

But if they did, well, George would have to find new men. To go with the new lord general.

"Where are you going?" George asked.

"Home," said Henry.

"But you can stay now."

"Yes, and I have you to thank for that. But there is someone I left behind, someone I would very much like to speak to."

"May I ask her name?" George said quietly.

Henry first took a breath, then nodded. "Lisette."

"Does she love you? Enough?"

"I think so," said Henry. "But I never felt it was right of me to ask her before now."

"If she is worthy of you, I can see no difficulty," George said with full confidence.

But Henry was guarded. "It is not that," he said. "She loves her family and would do nothing to hurt them."

"What about hurting you?" asked George.

Henry shrugged. "I have been hurt before, and I will

doubtless be hurt again. I will live with it."

"Will you come back?"

"Oh. Yes!" He looked at George, as if in surprise. "Of course. How could I go away now? You need loyal men around you, and especially those who are . . . like you."

"Say it. Say those who have the animal magic," said George.

Henry did it, stiffly. Then he did it again, half laughing, with vigor. "I did not mean for you to think I was deserting. I have a week's leave owed me. And I thought if I went to her quickly and came back, I would be here in time for the greatest problems. After the news has spread, you see."

"I see." Henry had proved himself many things. Not just a loyal friend, though that might be the most important to George personally, who had had so few friends in his life. But Henry was also farseeing and closemouthed. He was a man who knew other men and could make sacrifices. In short, he was the perfect replacement for the lord general.

"I have a job for you when you come back," George said. "If you will take it."

"What job is that? Master of the animals?" asked Henry.

George told him.

Henry was silent for a long time. But he did not refuse it. "It is not a reward, is it?" he asked. "A job like that—it is enormous."

"You are wise to see that already. But you may find others who do not look as clearly at the truth."

"Idiots," said Henry.

"Idiots you will have to command. If you can."

"I will do it," said Henry.

"Even if she does not come back with you?" asked George.

"Even so."

George stayed long enough to see Henry off with his satchel, hurrying away despite the impending dark. When he returned to the castle, he went back to his father's bedchamber and there saw four-fingered Jack.

For some reason, he had not thought to ask Jack's opinion before. Had he heard about it then? Certainly he looked at George differently now, appraising him, cautiously. As if George were a person Jack had never seen before and did not trust near his king.

"I am still Prince George," said George in defense.

"Are you?" asked Jack.

George thought over it carefully and realized that it was not so easy a question as it might seem. "I am who I was before, and more," he said at last.

"And still your father's son?"

"Still that, above all," said George.

Jack nodded, satisfied. And George went in to say good night to his father and was relieved to find him breathing still.

CHAPTER FORTY-FOUR

ORE THAN A WEEK later, to George's astonishment, he found King Davit out of his bed, sitting in the chair by the window.

"Father?" asked George.

The king turned. His face was gray.

"Father, should you be sitting there?" George hurried to his side, ready to help him.

"Dr. Gharn says that a little sitting up will not damage me, though it may fatigue me. You do not need to fuss over me like a mother hen."

George moved back. "I thought — that is, I was used to —"

"Yes, I know. I have been neither king nor father, truly, for these last months. But I am not dead yet."

George flushed. "I did not mean — I know you are not —"

"George, what did you come to say to me? Surely you are not here because you heard that I was sitting up out of bed."

"No," George said. "I came to tell you that I intend to go out into Wilbey today and into the villages within riding distance of the castle. I want to let them see me, to know I am no coward, and to hear their complaints about the proclamation."

Spoken aloud, it sounded so bold. Would his father forbid it? There were dangers, certainly, but George had to be allowed to face them.

"I see," said King Davit. "And do you go alone?"

"Do you mean that I should take some guards with me? I had thought I would bring two. Enough to prove who I am, but not so many that they could not be overwhelmed."

"You wish to be overwhelmed?"

"I wish to show that I am not afraid of being hurt," said George, "and that I do not depend on my guards to protect me from my people."

"Because you can call the animals to come to your aid?"

George was flustered. Was that what the people would think? But he could not see how to stop those who would think ill of him. He must not do everything for their sake. "They must come to trust me," he said at last, "and this is the best way I can see to do it."

Would his father offer another way? Would it be

381

better? Then George would have to accept it and do as he was bid. But he desperately wanted to be allowed to do as he had planned. Even if it was not the perfect plan.

"You will take this Henry of yours as one of the guards?"

George nodded. Of course he would take Henry, now that he had come back. All had gone well with his beloved, and they were soon to be married. Sooner than George and Marit. George felt a bit of envy at that, but also pride, that he had helped make this union a happy one. And Henry was certainly happy.

"I plan to make him the lord general," he added. Then he realized he did not have the power to do that. Not yet.

But his father only nodded. He had already heard of his old friend's defection from Sir Stephen.

"What of the princess?" he asked next.

"I shall ask her to come with me," said George. "The people should see her at my side."

In fact George must go quickly to Marit if he was to persuade her to come with him before she had to return to Sarrey. They would need most of the day to get to Wilbey and the villages beyond, and George did not want to leave the impression that he believed his villages unworthy of his presence.

His father had one last thing to say. "George, you will make a fine king. I only wish I could be here to see the whole of it." A small smile fluttered across his face.

George went to Henry and told him what he intended to do. The guard seemed several inches taller now that he no longer had to hide half of himself in fear of reprisals against animal magic. He would do very well as lord general. Very well indeed.

"Do you have a recommendation for the second guard?" George asked.

"Of course," said Henry. "His name is Trey, Your Highness."

That phrase had always rankled George. And yet he could not escape from it, any more than he could escape from his animal magic. He had to accept both of them now.

"Tell me about this Trey," George said.

So Henry said simply that he was the most close-mouthed of the group.

"Does he have the animal magic himself?" asked George.

"He says that the animal magic is no more or less a skill than playing the flute. And as he himself is tone-deaf to music, he does not care the one way or the other about it."

"Ah," said George. Good. He needed to get both sides to trust him now, and he would rather not be seen as favoring those who had animal magic so that he would have no others close to him at court.

Now George hurried to Marit's bedchamber.

She agreed to come with him readily enough, but

once they were out riding, she seemed to grow silent and unsure. George reached for her hand as they approached the central road that led into the town of Wilbey. She was cold and trembling nearly as much as his father had been.

He motioned for Henry and Trey to stop just ahead of him.

"What is it?" he asked Marit.

"I do not know if I am ready for this," she said. "I hear a voice in my head, telling me I am worthless, that I can do nothing of value. How, then, can I be your queen?"

"It is your father's voice?" George asked.

Marit nodded unhappily. "For the years she was with me, my hound, Beatrice, replaced his voice with her love. But now she is gone, and—"

And George was not enough. Well, though that put an arrow through his heart, he had known her for only a few weeks' time. Perhaps in several more years she would hear his voice instead.

"Would you rather go back to the castle then?" George asked. He could do without her if he had to.

"No." Marit's lips twisted in a defiance that seemed familiar. He had seen it on the same face, but when it had been inhabited by a different soul. Or had the hound stolen Marit's original expression? Had it been hers all along?

"I shall go with you. And before you think me coura-geous, realize this: When I leave you, I must face my father. And I can think of nothing your townspeople can show me that is more terrifying than the thought of him."

"Are you sure?" George asked one more time.

"I am sure I should do it," said Marit. "But whether I will run away—that I cannot tell you."

George did not believe it for a moment. But there was nonetheless a terrible courage in this honesty of hers, to show herself so vulnerable, so certain of failure in one way or another.

"Marit—that is . . . should I call you Beatrice or Marit now?" George had not asked her outright before but had come to his own decision. Would she be unhappy with it? He had gotten used to it, but he could go back if he had to.

"You think of me as Marit still?" she asked, her eyes shining with tears.

"Yes," said George guiltily. "It is how I first met you. But if it pains you, I will—"

"No, no. You do not understand. I am glad that you still see me as I was. That I am not simply enveloped by one body or another. You came to know me as the hound, as Marit. I am the same now to you, am I not?"

"Of course you are." What other answer could there be to that? "Who would think differently?" he asked.

It did not take a moment for Marit to name him. "My father," she said.

Her father. It always came back to King Helm for

her. "Ah. He never knew that you were changed. Do you plan to tell him even now?"

"Never," she said with certainty.

"So you will go back to being the Beatrice he has always assumed you were?" George could not suppress a shudder. This seemed worse than death, never to be allowed to grow or change.

"I do not know . . . how to be anyone else," said Marit. "With him." She thought on it longer, then added, "Yet I cannot let him treat me as he has always treated me before this."

But George could see that Marit must try harder.

"You could play the game of kings with him," said George. "That would be a beginning."

"But would he play with me?" asked Marit.

George stared at her. "You must insist on it," he said. "And that will be the first of the changes."

"That is one way of doing it," said Marit. But she did not seem to think it would be her choice.

"You can hardly challenge him to a duel in the court-yard," said George.

"Can I not?" asked Marit.

George's face fell. He had not meant her to take it seriously. He had faced her father himself, and it was not something to be taken lightly. And he was a man her father respected and had no intention of killing. If King Helm were truly angry, what might he do? "He would simply refuse," said George suddenly, with certainty.

Marit did not argue with him. "If I came to him dressed as a woman, yes, he would. But if I were in disguise—"

"In disguise? He would not take any precautions. He would dare to truly battle with you!" said George. It was only when he saw Marit's face turn to him that he realized what he had said. He did not think she could win against her father. He, of all people, still thought of her as a woman first.

"I lost to him badly," George muttered. And he was not a woman.

"You do not know him as I do. You have not watched him on the battlefield time after time, facing opponent after opponent. You do not know his every weakness, his every strength. I know his style, his pleasures, even the count of his breaths."

"Yes, but—" He could not stop himself from objecting again.

"If I beat him, he will see me differently. Truly."

"But if he kills you . . ." said George.

Marit blinked at him. "Then I will be dead." She said it as coldly as if it were Beatrice speaking, a hound that had lost all her family and did not care to live any longer.

"And you will not think of me and what your death will do to our kingdoms?"

Marit's face was splotched red and white, but she did not look away. "If I think of you so much that I forget myself, then my father will be right. I will be only a woman. Not Marit. Still Princess Beatrice, now and always."

George opened his mouth to tell her she was wrong, that it did not have to be that way, but only a low croak came out. It was exactly the way he had felt about declaring his animal magic. She had to be herself. Even if she did very well and was wounded. Even if she did badly and was killed. Her father would think of her differently ever afterward.

"He had best beware then," said George softly.

Marit reached out and embraced George, over their horses. Then she gave him a shy little kiss on his cheek.

"You don't offer to send animals in with me to protect me?" she asked.

George knew what to say then. "I had better send them to his aid, I think."

And she sparkled with that. He had done the right thing for her soul, he was sure. He wished he could be as certain it was the right thing for her life.

But no, he should not doubt. He would not doubt.

∞∞∞

CHAPTER FORTY-FIVE

*N*EAR THE TOWN square of Wilbey they slowed, then stopped and dismounted. Hand on Marit's shoulder, George moved her forward and looked out over the gathered people. In a loud voice, he said, "This is Princess Marit of Sarrey, my betrothed."

The murmurs began then, as the townspeople stared at her from one side or the other, trying to decide if this was the same woman they had learned to call Princess Beatrice or if this was her sister, perhaps, and very like her.

George did not wait for a consensus. He went on. "I have come to settle any complaints to be made regarding the recent proclamation on animal magic. And to answer any questions."

A roar of voices answered him, and it was only when he pointed to a man holding a knife in his hand that the noise died down, though Henry and Trey gave each other nervous glances.

The man waved the knife at George. George motioned for Henry and Trey to step back. After all, he had brought them more for show than for real assistance. If a mob meant to kill their prince, they could do it.

"What is your concern?" George asked.

"You think there is no evil in animal magic?" the man demanded.

"Not inherently," said George carefully. "Of course there is evil everywhere, and those with animal magic are not above it any more than anyone else." Was that the right answer? Well, it was the only one George could give.

"Then you will not mind taking my son from me," said the man. He nodded to a man behind him who held a boy tightly roped with his arms behind his back.

The boy was pushed forward and nearly fell on his head. When he got to his feet, he snarled both at his father and at George. Then he burst into the language of the bear, so that George could have no doubt that he truly had the animal magic.

Was the boy mad? Had the animal magic done that to him?

"He eats my food and does nothing else all day but snarl and bite and sleep. He is a beast, I tell you. And if you think he is more than that, then you take him. I will have no more to do with him."

George moved closer to the boy, tried to speak to him gently. "Friend, I am a friend. No danger here."

But as soon as he was close enough, the boy bit George's hand.

His father laughed harshly. "I told you. He is a beast." And he spat on his son, then kicked him down so that he was in the dirt once more. Without another word, he strode away.

And George was left to find some solution from this. Wasn't this what he wanted? To have the chance to improve the lives of others who had animal magic? To meet them, to know who they were and what their challenges meant to them?

But now he was in the middle of a swelling town square, all eyes on him, his people waiting to see what he did, in justice and mercy.

How had the boy been treated as a child? How long had his father known that he had animal magic and despised him for it, even as he tried to conceal it?

George closed his eyes for a moment and imagined himself as the boy. What would he have been like if his father had been this boy's father?

The wound on his hand throbbed. George felt his heart beating fast in his chest.

And he put out his hand again. This time he spoke in the language of the bears. "Friend," he said simply. "Friend."

The boy stared at him, quiet.

George put out his hand and touched the boy's head, gently moving down to his back. Then he moved close enough to touch the ropes that bound him. He tugged at them, to no avail. They had been pulled too tight, for too long. To judge from the sores on the boy's wrists, he had been tied this way for months on end.

"Henry, a knife," George said.

The gathering crowd gasped when Henry flashed the steel and brought it to George. Did they think that he would kill the boy, slit his throat and leave him for dead? Or abuse him and threaten him as his father had?

The boy flinched as George brought the knife closer.

Again, as a bear speaking to another, George said, "Just a moment, and you will be free."

The boy braced himself, and George flicked the knife at the ropes. They fell away, and the boy was still for a moment, his hands held to his back as if they knew no other place to go.

The crowd was silent.

Then suddenly the boy jumped up, hissed at George, and clawed at his face.

The crowd gasped.

And the boy turned on them, raking and clawing at those who were nearest.

Should George have killed him while he had the chance?

Henry and Trey raced through the crowd to pull the boy away.

Still, George thought he could see the outrage on the faces of those he looked at. They were willing to accept difference only so far, and no further. Prince George having animal magic was one thing, but this boy was another.

"What shall we do with him, Your Highness?" asked Henry.

George raised his knife to the boy's face.

Suddenly the boy was quiet again. It was as if he were begging for death. A madman does not beg for an end to his madness, does he?

George gave the knife to Henry instead.

"Let him go," he whispered.

"Your Highness!" Henry protested.

"Let him go!" George commanded, so there could be no mistake.

And Henry stepped back.

George spoke to the boy in the language of the rabbits then. He remembered how he had loved rabbits when he was a boy, first learning the rudiments of animal language.

"I shall give you food," he said, "if you come with me. Quietly, quietly."

The boy hesitated. "Food?" he asked, his voice hoarse, but the one human word clear.

George nodded.

The boy sagged to the side, and George held him by the shoulder.

"Go with this man. He will take you to the food," George said.

The boy sniffed at Henry, but he did not attack. Perhaps Henry smelled of animals as well.

"Can you talk to him?" George asked Henry.

Henry shrugged. "I suppose," he said. "If I must. But that does not mean he will understand me or do what I ask."

"I think he will," said George. "Help him onto your horse, and take him back to the castle. Make sure he is well fed and then given a warm bed to sleep in."

"I should not leave you, Your Highness," Henry protested.

"I am not alone." George pointed to Trey. "And I swear I will not be long."

"What if this—boy harms someone?" asked Henry.

"He will not," George said. He was sure of it. He had to be. He trusted his people, so that they would trust him.

The boy followed Henry with a nudge from George.

With Marit at his side and Trey at his back, George asked who was next. After a moment a woman came forward. She told her story, that she had once had the animal magic but had suppressed it so long she did not know if she could get it back. She hoped to, though, and wanted to know if George had any advice to give her on the matter.

"Did you get the headaches?" he asked.

She nodded.

"And you ignored them? But you did not die?"

"I came close to it, with the fever. But I survived."

Perhaps the animal magic was burned out of her then, George thought. But he could not be sure. "You must come to the school, to tell what you know of the animal magic and what happens when it is ignored. And perhaps there will be those there who can help you as well."

"But you yourself know nothing of it?" the woman asked.

George cleared his throat and admitted the truth, that he did not.

The woman nodded sadly and went on her way.

And so it went the rest of the day. Trey reminded George to break away some three hours after noon, to get to the villages he had hoped to. This was just a beginning. There was more excitement than George had guessed at, but there was fear too, and violence.

Not many of those in the crowd closest to him had been violent, but he had heard them beyond, and when he and Marit rode away, there had been a few moments when he wondered if they would live another hour.

In the villages things were quieter. People there were in awe just to see the prince and princess who would rule them one day. They asked less than those in town had and offered him the best of their food. After a long day George realized that he would have to come back to them later, allow them questions when they were not afraid what to say.

At last he and Marit rode off as the sun was beginning to set. Trey followed at a discreet distance.

But Marit was quiet, and George found himself thinking about his proclamation. He had thought it so all-encompassing when he had first made it, but now he could see so many holes in it, mistakes even, and places he had not begun to touch.

"If I had a hound still, what would your people think of me?" asked Marit.

George did not know what to say. "Do you wish to have another hound?" he asked, and tried to suppress the sudden feeling of jealousy that rose in his heart. She had already said that she had heard her hound's voice louder than her father's. If she got another one, then what about George's voice? Would it be drowned out altogether?

But did he have any right to insist that she hear him inside her mind and heart? They were only to be married, and that did not mean they had to live inside each other that way as well.

"I might . . . someday," said Marit. "I do not know if I will ever be completely comfortable inside stone walls. I am like my father in that way, and always will be."

"You must do what is right for you," George said at last.

"Do you think you would have loved me if there had not been the two of us, the hound and I?" asked Marit next.

George puzzled over this for a moment. "I knew from the moment I saw you together that I need never worry about your knowing the truth of my animal magic. But I believe I would have come to love you regardless. It might have taken me longer to find you, however. Underneath that hard skin of yours—and I do not mean the skin of the hound that covered you."

Marit smiled at this. "I believe you," she said. "You are not blind as my father is. It is good to know that others in the kingdom will be judged by those same clear eyes."

George found himself speechless at this unexpected compliment.

"I do love you, George," said Marit.

The horses had stopped, as if George had asked them to, in the language of the horses. But no, they could also hear another language, the language of love.

"I love you, Marit," said George. And he had never been so sure of anything in his life.

*M*ARIT LEFT TO RETURN to Sarrey until the wedding ceremony. George promised to write her letters whenever he could and begged her to write and tell him what happened with her father. He waited in increasing distress for six days until he received her first letter.

It read:

He says he never liked the name Beatrice anyway. It was my mother's choice, and when she died at my birth, he had no heart to take that away from her as well. He says Marit is a stronger name but wonders if I would like to choose something less houndlike. He suggests Rover or Pointer. He is joking. I think.

As for the battle, it went for four hours without stopping, and then I stepped away from him to take a breath, and he fell very slowly to the ground, all the way proclaiming that he was not giving up, that this was not surrender, that I would not leave the battlefield if I valued my life.

When I saw that the physician was truly afraid for his life, I took off my mask and revealed myself to him tearfully. He said terrible things to me then, and I smiled through it all because he would never have thought it appropriate to swear at me before.

When he was better, he asked me what it had been about, if I expected that he would make me general over his armies, if you were a man I could not bear to marry. I told him I only wanted him to see me as I was. He looked me up and down and said that he did. I believe him. I think.

Yours,
Marit

George missed the dreams he had shared with her more than he had known possible. His nights seemed so empty, and the letters were only words. Marit's words, but still. He wanted to see through her eyes and breathe through her mouth.

But he was able to see the bear and the hound when he wished it. He tried not to look often, but he saw a bit of the hound as she fell asleep inside a dark cave. She seemed content, more so than she had ever been when George had known her as human. The bear too seemed happy.

Though the letters from Marit came every week without fail, they felt increasingly stilted, and George began to wonder what would happen when they met again. Or if they ever would. But leaves fell from trees, and the world turned cold. And soon it was but a few days before Marit was to arrive again, in preparation for the wedding itself.

During this time George watched his father closely but saw no sign of his growing weaker. He came out of his bed now and again, to sit at judgment, but it cost him dearly. George thought that someone should tell him to rest more, but no one else dared to, and when George brought up the subject, his father made remarks about George's wishing to become king before his time. George could not bear those, so he let his father do as he wished.

George's visits to the woods were frequent and therefore far less urgent than they had been before. He enjoyed speaking to the animals in their own languages and wondered many times who might know the full secrets of the animal magic. The school for animal magic was being built, and already some of its students were gathering in an abandoned farmhouse nearby.

George stopped in now and again to see what they were learning, but no one seemed to know much more than he did. They told tales, and now and again there was one George had not heard before. He paid great attention to them, especially to the story of a woman who had been able to marry a wolf and have children with it. Each child came out of her body as a different kind of animal. None of them was either human or wolf, but badger, otter, and even once an ox.

He wondered if he should tell it to Beatrice if he saw her again in the woods. Or Marit, for that matter.

There was a bonfire lit in the early autumn, and George could hear animals being thrown into it, mostly tame, but a few wild ones. He rode to the rescue, but by the time he and Henry and a dozen of his guards arrived, there were only flames. Whoever they were who remained hostile to George and his animal magic, they were not willing to come out in the open. Not yet. But when George became king, it might be different. And they might not use the bonfires to burn only animals.

George woke up, throat dry and eyes wet, many nights, haunted by the thought of what he had done. Bringing those with animal magic into the open, shining the spotlight on them, was not necessarily a kindness. And yet he would not take it back. There would be bad times to get through, but he was determined not to go backward.

The nobility was largely on George's side. But two of them close to the southern border in Thurat sent messengers to King Azal to ask for protection if they chose to sever their ties with their own king. He not only refused but sent the messages on to George himself. He said he was tired of animal magic's being so vilified and

401

would be an ally to George in that one thing. All silently, of course. He would deny it all if George mentioned such a thing aloud.

Sir Peter Lessing was one of the men who had sent to King Azal. George was not surprised. It was strange how all the battles of childhood, left unresolved, had returned for him to fight again. Bigger now than ever before.

George dealt more severely with those who were inclined to gossip about Marit. He did not intend to bring her home to a court that was in any way like her father's. George heard one noblewoman laughing about a woman who looked like a hound, and he had her arrested and sent to the dungeon. She remained only one day and then came before George at judgment day, when he let her go with a warning.

The woman's father was white with outrage and promised revenge. George told him that if he heard of any attempt at it, the man himself would be hanged summarily, no second judgment day necessary. He went off cowed, but George was not sure how long it would last. Perhaps the man would die before he got his courage back. George was surprised to find himself so ruthless, but he did not regret it.

More often George dealt with those who came to the castle, eager to have favors bestowed upon them when they oozed their acceptance of George's animal magic. He received many gifts of animal talismans, full-size marble and wood statues of animals presumed to be his favorites, from bears to wolves to the humble fish. He accepted them graciously and had a chamber in the dungeon set aside to hold them all.

He set Sir Stephen the task of dealing with the requests for lower taxes from those of the nobility who assumed they'd flattered George sufficiently. Sir Stephen handled it well, despite his recent interest in an older woman of good breeding whose husband of many years had died and left her destitute. She had come to the castle originally to ask for the king's mercy—and been granted two purses of coin. She had remained at Sir Stephen's request.

George was pleased to see the man who had been so stubbornly alone all those years smile again at the touch of another's hand on his face. He did not know if Sir Stephen would remain in the castle after his father died or if he would find a way to ask politely to retire to the woman's small estate in the countryside.

George would miss him severely, but if anyone deserved a rest and some small happiness, it was Sir Stephen. And George was glad that he was staying for the wedding at least. He could not have borne the preparations for that alone.

"You would make a mess of it," Sir Stephen told him.

George admitted he would. He wanted it over and done with, as soon as possible, with no pomp and circumstance. He knew that Marit agreed with him.

But there were kingdoms to consider here.

So the planning went on and on, down to the tiniest detail. At times George was tempted to call ants in to eat everything in Cook Elin's kitchen, so that he had no more decisions to make. But he withheld. He was learning patience with his magic as well.

Finally, the first day of cold, hard autumn rain hit just as Sir Stephen was directing the final outdoor preparations for the wedding. Streamers were ruined, and Sir Stephen came back to the castle rather less pleased than when he had left.

But the next day he went out once more, and it was a fine day. Three more days were all that remained until Marit's arrival. The kitchens were frantic and hot with cooking pastries and meats, and George kept away from them for fear of being drafted into fetching and carrying for Elin, as everyone else seemed to be. She did not look at a face but saw only a body that she could use and put it to work.

Dr. Gharn saw to King Davit daily, but George did not see that he did much for him. The physician offered suggestions of herbal teas that might allow the king to stay awake longer and be more alert, but not much more than that. George asked his father if he wished to consult another physician on the matter of his health, but the king would not hear of it, and George did not bring the subject up again.

Two days before the wedding, Dr. Gharn disappeared once more. His bedchamber was cold with morning dew, the window left open. Sir Stephen had spoken to Dr. Gharn many times about letting the dove go, to no avail. Yet now George thought he saw in the distance a bird, a dove perhaps, flapping its wings. But he could not be sure. It might have been his own fancy, and it was just as likely the physician had decided to walk away from the castle. After all, Dr. Gharn had been certain that his animal magic was gone from him.

George did not send anyone after the physician this time. He had made up what he could for his mistakes, and if death was what he wished, or forgetfulness in a new life, or simply the end of all memory of this human one, who was George to say that he was wrong?

The morning Marit was to arrive with her father, George made sure to get to the gate an hour early, to be sure that nothing went wrong. But when he came closer to the guard, he saw that her carriage was already there, and she was being helped out by Henry.

George hurried to her side and watched as her father came out. He was astonished at the change in King Helm. The man was thinner around the stomach, making him look more fit, but a shock of white hair had come in around his left temple, a scar at the base of the white streak, and George could not help staring at it.

King Helm touched it. "Cut there with a practice sword," he said simply, then nodded to Marit.

"You?" asked George, though he knew the answer already.

Marit smiled and tucked her arm into George's. She

seemed at ease both with him and with herself as never before. But still, they had been apart for three months.

George wondered if there would ever be a time when he felt secure in her love.

At dinner King Helm spoke jovially, and Marit was quiet at George's side. But there was no reason to insist upon a change there. King Davit did not come down to eat; and when George offered to take King Helm to see his father in his bedchamber, King Helm refused, saying he would rather see his old enemy at his best on the morrow, for the wedding.

George walked with Marit to her bedchamber that night, his thoughts in a jumble as he stood by her door. Should he merely wish her good night? Should he kiss her? Should he tell her he loved her once more?

It was Marit who acted first, turning directly at the top of the stair and putting her lips on George's. It was a quick kiss, but enough to set George's heart racing.

"That was for the letters," she said.

Then she kissed him again, more lingeringly.

"And that?" George asked hoarsely. "What was that for?"

"For the look in your eyes," said Marit.

George let her laugh at him then. When she was quiet, he took her hand and held it close to his heart, feeling her breath next to his cheek. "Dr. Gharn is gone," he said at last. "I do not think he will be back."

"Oh," she said. "Do you think he will ever see his daughter again? In human form?"

George thought of Dr. Gharn's travels to find information about animal magic. It was possible he had found all there was to know. But it was also possible that the school, with its openness, might discover more.

"I don't know," said George. "But perhaps he has found his own solution." And he explained about the flash of wings he had seen in the sky two mornings ago. Perhaps not a fancy after all.

"I shall not sleep tonight," said Marit as she pulled herself away from his arms at last. She rubbed at her arms as if she were cold.

"Nor I," said George.

"Good. I shall think of you while I am awake and miserable."

"And I you."

George took his leave of her and went to his bedchamber, only to be summoned a moment later by a page with a message that King Helm demanded to see him at once in the dining hall but privately.

Did he mean to kill George at last? That would be one way to get revenge for all that had happened, and King Helm might see it as George's fault.

He made his way down the stairs, stifling a yawn, and opened the doors of the dining hall.

King Helm was there holding a new sword, steel this time and with no decoration at all. It had a simple twisted handle and hilt, but that did not make it less than beautiful.

"A wedding gift," King Helm said, and offered it,

lying flat in his palms, to George.

George held his hands out and took it. Then he brought it up to the firelight in the hearth, staring at the gleam of light on the blade and feeling the balance in his hand.

"My thanks," he said formally, with a bow to King Helm. "And my kingdom's thanks." Though he wondered why this gift could not have waited for after the wedding in the morning.

"That is the sword I had made many years ago to fit the hand of the son I was sure I would have," said King Helm. "I never felt it right for my nephew to have it, for all he will rule the kingdom after me."

It was as if the sword had suddenly grown much heavier. George did not feel as if he could ever be worthy of the gift now. Was he the right one for it?

"You will not give it to Marit?" he asked, daring the king's anger.

King Helm's eyes flashed a moment. Then he sighed and bowed his head. "She has not changed me that much," he said. "But if you allow her to use it from time to time, that is your choice, not mine."

"Ah," said George.

"Do you understand me?"

"I understand you very well. And I am sure that whoever wears it will wear it with honor."

"Yes, I expect so. Even if it is never used for anything other than to cut through thorns in the forest."

George nodded gravely. "I thank you," he said, on his own behalf, and Marit's.

"And I thank you," said King Helm.

He and George stared at each other a moment longer. Then King Helm yawned. "Time for bed now."

George took the sword back to his own bedchamber and waited impatiently for morning. He had not forgotten what was to occur at his wedding, and he wanted to be sure he was ready for it.

Yet when he closed his eyes and tried to search once more for the dark vision of the animal world that he had seen on only one other occasion, it would not come to him. He rested and tried again, with the same result. He left his bedchamber and wandered through the castle and even out to the moat, then tried there, in the outdoors, where he could smell the animals in the air.

But he could not see their shapes in his mind or call to them in that way. Until the dawn came, and the first rays of sun hit him, crouched stiffly over the ground where he had so often buried the small creatures of his childhood. Then, suddenly, he could see again in that other way and speak silently, and with power.

He called to all the animals everywhere he could see. To deer and foxes, to mice and birds, to owls, to moles, to voles, to rabbits, squirrels, possums, wolves, hounds, and bears. And to exotic animals he had no names for, with stripes and large, drooping ears, and necks as tall as any tower George had seen made.

They answered him with raises of their heads and acknowledgments. And they began to come, streaming toward the castle at their own pace. The humans in the villages nearby were coming too, to see the celebration of a prince and princess married. But they were as nothing in numbers, compared with the animals.

George tracked one couple very closely, a bear and a hound, as they came ever closer, for what might be the last time.

"You are not even dressed." George heard a voice from behind him.

He turned and saw Marit.

"Unless you plan to set a new style for princes to be married in their nightclothes," she said, pulling at his hem.

George blushed. "I shall go now and be back in an hour's time." Sir Stephen would have a fit if he heard of this breach of propriety, for a princess to see her husband in this way before they were married.

"And when you return, shall we both find ourselves becoming the stuff of legend?" asked Marit. She stared deeply at the horizon, her eyes catching on the very place where her hound was.

"The stuff of legend? No. We are merely the end of it, that is all," said George.

eXTRAS

The Princess and the Hound

A Q&A with Mette Ivie Harrison

A look at the first meeting between
Beatrice and George, through the Princess's eyes

A sneak peek at the upcoming sequel,
The Princess and the Bear

A Q&A with Mette Ivie Harrison

What kind of romance do you like best?
I used to read a lot of series romance novels, but I find now that I tend to prefer books where the romance is a surprise, something that happens along the way with the rest of an exciting adventure. I think this is the way it is with real romance. The more you look for it, the more it eludes. Then, when you're not looking for it anymore, determined you will never have it and don't need it—it strikes. Maybe because, by no longer focusing on yourself and your own needs, you have finally become a person that someone else would be able to love. Robin Hobb, Lois McMaster Bujold, Megan Whalen Turner, and Kate Elliott are masters at this.

Why did you choose to retell the story of Beauty and the Beast this way?
I didn't. I was at first doing a retelling of "The Princess and the Pea," but the princess who showed up at the castle drawbridge had this dog with her, and I had to figure out the mystery of the dog. The "Beauty and the Beast" part of the story came into it accidentally. I only saw it when it was finished, but I think that's because it's a timeless story that in some sense shows up in every romance. I usually think of *The Princess and the Hound* as an original fairy tale. I hope that it feels like a retelling of a fairy tale that you never read as a child, but are sure that you would find somewhere in one of Lang's collections, if you looked hard enough.

Where is Kendel?
While writing *The Princess and the Hound*, I wanted to

EXTRAS

give the feel of a traditional fairy tale, but I did not want to set it in a specific place. Fairy tales are always in a medieval-ish world, but could be anywhere in Europe. I lived in southern Germany as a teenager, and so for me, *The Princess and the Hound* is meant to give the flavor of that place: the dark forests; the rich, fertile land; the small villages and ancient buildings; the streams everywhere flowing to rivers, and then to the Mediterranean.

What made you decide to write a sequel?
I was reading the galleys for *The Princess and the Hound* and realized that I hadn't finished the story of the bear and the hound. There wasn't room in the first novel for it, so I had to write another one, but I didn't set out at the beginning for there to be more than one book.

How long did it take you to write this story?
I wrote the first version of *The Princess and the Hound* in 1998. It was accepted for publication seven years later, in 2005. Over the course of that time period, it changed dramatically. Beatrice and Marit were always there, but in the beginning, Prince George didn't have any magic of his own. He was just trying to figure out what was going on between the princess and her hound.

But I realized eventually (about five years into the process), that if I was going to write from George's point of view, he needed to have a story that was just as or even more compelling than theirs. He needed to change and develop, and he had to have the key to the story. Since magic was essential for Marit and Beatrice to be helped, I delved into George's early life and first gave him a mother with magic. After that, I set up the whole kingdom where magic was forbidden, so that he would have a reason to become a very strong, self-contained person, as Beatrice and Marit were—and the bear, for that matter. All of them are isolated because of their various hurts and differences, but in the end, it is that isolation which makes them strong. And only all four of them together can make the miraculous climax to the book that I was still tweaking up to the very last month before publication.

This seems like the wrong way to go about writing a novel, but I find that the more I try to plan things in advance, the less real they feel to the characters. The whole process is very organic, and I feel as though I am discovering the novel for the first time each time I revise it.

How do you choose names for your characters?
Well, Prince George is named after Mr. George Knightley from Jane Austen's *Emma*. King Davit is named after one of my best friends in the world, with a slight name twist (though the rest of the character isn't based on him at all). King Helm comes from the German name "Wilhelm," which I always wanted to use to name my first son. I love the character of Wilhelm Meister from Goethe's novels (I wrote my dissertation on him). But my husband for some reason thought that it would be strange to name our children after characters in German novels, so I saved the name for another day. And "Helm" also hints at how hardheaded the king can be.

Who do you write for?
I think every writer writes on some level for him or herself. But it's also true that I write for the teenager I used to be, who

EXTRAS

wanted desperately to find a good book to get lost in, but was also drawn to sophisticated books that were on the adult shelves. I wanted to have the candy of an adventure with romance, and the meat of a story that had something to say and did it in an elegant way.

When did you know that you wanted to be an author?
When I was in kindergarten. It took me a long time to get up the courage to actually throw myself into it, no holds barred. It is one thing to have a great dream, another thing to really pursue it. Because if you pursue it, then there's a chance of failure, and that is a hard thing to look in the face.

How much reading do I need to do in order to be a good author?
Spend about ten years reading before you start writing. Then spend at least half of your time reading after that. It keeps your ear good, like listening to music that's in tune will keep you aware of when you're not in tune.

Plus, it's fun. One of the perks of writing for me is having an excuse to read all the best books written today, hot off the presses.

What did you read when you were a teen?
I read some Robin McKinley, but other than that one exception, I never read any children's books. I went straight from Louisa May Alcott and Edward Eager and C. S. Lewis to Sherlock Holmes, Perry Mason, Isaac Asimov, and Shakespeare. My mother used to ask me why I wanted to read all of the Perry Mason books straight through without a break. I just did. I had intense interests, satisfied them, and went on to something else.

I used to walk around school with my nose in a sophisticated book, in part to escape the whole social scene which I was painfully bad at, in part to show off how smart I was, and in part because it was really what I preferred most to do. I loved books and language even then. I was fascinated by the texture of the language of Robin Hood stories and I wrote many pastiches.

I didn't read any fantasy until I was in graduate school and needed a break from long German Bildungsromane. Then I read Stephen R. Donaldson and Orson Scott Card and Elizabeth Moon and Marion Zimmer Bradley and Jennifer Roberson and Kate Elliott. That was when I also started to read the best of young adult literature. Cynthia Voigt was then, and remains, one of my favorites. I also discovered Lloyd Alexander and Susan Cooper (in a box of books my mother had given me for Christmas one year but I had never read, because I figured if my mother liked them, they had to be bad!).

How does your background in German affect your writing?
Studying German for so many years has given me an acute sensitivity to language, due to my years spent reading German. I remember in high school German I finally understood English grammar. I think the same thing is true of language. You don't love English as a lyrical creation until you really know another language to compare it to.

What is the best part of a romance for you?
I love the part of a romance that I call the "revelation." In *Pride and Prejudice*, it's Darcy's proposal, where he lays himself on the line and makes himself utterly vulnerable to rejection—

EXTRAS

even if he doesn't realize himself that is what he is doing.

I also love the reconciliation at the end. And to be honest, I wish that more romances would go on after the marriage ceremony because I think a lot of the best romance scenes fit there. Look at Megan Whalen Turner's *The King of Attolia* or Lois McMaster Bujold's *Barrayar*. Best married romances ever.

Who is the first reader of your books?
I have two daughters who love to read, but they have different styles. One likes deeper, darker books. The other loves the fun stuff. So I have them read different things, and they like to feel like they have the first look at, and the first chance to shape, my books.

Do your kids think it is cool that you are a writer?
No. They think writing is an utterly boring profession, since I sit in a windowless office all day and stare at a computer. They all have plans to be much more interesting than I am. Some part of me secretly wonders if it will work out that way. Maybe genetics and environment together are stronger than they think.

What household chore do you hate the most?
All of them.

When I was a teenager, my mother was forever bothering me about making my bed. I could never understand why I should do this, since I would just get in it again and mess it up that night. And besides, I kept my door closed.

Now that I am a parent, I still do not make my bed except once a week. That's what I require my kids to do, too. Once a week, and the rest of the time, keep the door closed.

First Meeting

I OFTEN SET a kind of formal challenge for myself when I begin writing a novel. For The Princess and the Hound, I wanted to write a romantic fairy tale from an authentically male point of view. As I got further into the story, though, it turned out there were reasons I couldn't tell it from the princess's point of view without revealing too much too soon to the reader. In the following passage, I rewrote the first meeting between Beatrice and George from the viewpoint of the princess.

In the woods was the one place where Beatrice did not feel as if she were trapped inside herself. The loping run of a hound here was so much like what she had always imagined herself to be doing even when she had had only two human legs to propel her forward. The glorious feel of the darkness under the thick branches of trees tightly pressed together was what she had often longed for when dressed in an itchy gown and propped up to be stared at by her father's noblemen. They looked at her with canine teeth and drooling lips. But in the forest she was the hunter.

It could never last long enough, though Marit would never be the one to call her back. She had known Beatrice's constrictions before now, but she had not felt them cut off her own breath. She loved the freedom of being out of the castle as much as Beatrice did, and more so, for she lost all consciousness of what waited for them beyond the woods, and Beatrice, even still, could not do the same.

But if they were not back soon, her father would send a

EXTRAS

party of his soldiers out to search for his daughter. He would begin to call out threats against the neighboring kingdoms, even against Kendel and its prince, who had no reason to harm her. The farther it went, the angrier all would be when they found her wandering alone as no princess had any reason to do. Her father would make her promise not to go back in the woods without a guard again, and she would be forced to either lie to him, which she hated, or to refuse him, which was worse.

Or in this case, it would be Marit who would say the words for her. Marit would have no compunction telling her father the truth as loudly as Beatrice never had. Marit did not care enough about him to lie. But it was Beatrice who would be hurt by her father's blustering response. She told herself there was no hope of making him love her, but it did not matter. She hoped for it even so.

Suddenly Marit made a sound and stiffened her back—almost as a hound would. Beatrice stopped as well and looked where Marit's face was turned. There was a man there. One of her father's men?

No. He was not nearly muscular enough, and there was something in the way that he stood that made her see a frightened bird in the lines of his shoulders.

He was not taller than she was, and he wore well-made clothing, but nothing that would have set him apart. He had the tanned skin of a man who spent frequent time out of doors, but his face was very young, the cheeks soft on his angular jawbone.

It only occurred to her after a long moment that he wore on his shoulder a braid in green and black that denoted the kingdom of Kendel. And in her head she heard her father's dismissive voice, "Prince George, the crown puppy of Kendel."

A puppy? One close to being grown, with enthusiasm still in him, but waiting to let it out because he had been nipped too many times by the older hounds around him.

She was thinking like a hound now. Well, why should she not? It was not as if she believed that she would ever be a woman again.

Marit began to walk toward him and Beatrice realized that her father's words had been spoken to Marit. She, too, recognized the prince, and saw no reason not to face him openly.

Would it be a greeting?

Of a kind, Beatrice supposed. She wondered if the prince would notice that he was being sniffed out, and not only by the one who appeared a hound.

"Prince George," said Marit coldly.

"Princess Beatrice," he said with a nod.

Marit might have walked right past him then, ignoring his words entirely. She had done it before, but Beatrice found herself holding her breath, hoping she would not. Because Marit's opinion of people was inevitably accurate, and Beatrice would rather be married to someone who was not an utter lout.

Though in some sense, it would be Marit who was married to him.

How her head ached at the jumble of identities that surrounded her now.

"Yes, I am Princess Beatrice."

He looked her up and down. Did he think her ugly? Beatrice had never spent much time trying to make herself

11

EXTRAS

beautiful, even before. It had never been any use. People who saw her always saw her father's daughter, and no more.

But not this man.

"You are not what I expected," said Beatrice after she had looked him up and down in turn.

Did he think it impertinent that a woman should take the same liberty with him as he had taken with her?

Beatrice moved forward and the smell of the man was so inviting that she circled his leg. She would never have dared to be so close to him, except that she was a hound and could do as she wished. It was another freedom of this body. Dr. Rhuul had intended her no kindness, but it amused Beatrice to find ways in which she was glad of what he had done to her.

She would kill him if ever she saw him again, however. For what he had done to Marit, if for nothing else. And for the pure evil of him, in taking such power upon himself.

The prince bent down and offered his hand.

Marit licked at it, and tasted the salt of his sleepless night. She wondered what he had to be sleepless over.

And now, suddenly, Marit found the prince's eyes lingering on her, as no man had ever bothered to look at her before. She was only the princess's hound. Yet he looked at her with every bit as much attention as he had shown the princess. As if she were a woman of equal interest—and power.

He winced after a moment and turned away.

There was no knowing if the sight of her had brought him pain or if it was something else entirely, but she wished she could help him nonetheless.

"Shall I walk you back to the palace?" asked the prince when he had smoothed out the wrinkle on his brow.

"If you wish it," said Marit, taking the arm he offered.

But he had offered it first to me, thought Beatrice. To the hound.

"Do you take walks often outside the castle?"

Beatrice did not step in between them, but walked on the prince's other side, so that he was flanked.

"Every day. It is good exercise," said Marit, as if daring him to contradict her.

He did not. He also did not ask the question that others would have, and Beatrice tried to decide if she liked him for this reticence or not. On the one hand, it showed respect for her. On the other, it showed weakness—or at least her father would have said so. Any man who showed respect for a woman was weak in his opinion.

"Is that why you came out as well?" asked Marit.

"Yes, yes, of course." He stumbled over the words, then looked back at Beatrice, as though it was easier for him to converse with a hound than a woman.

"Will you tell me your hound's name? She is a wonderful creature," he said.

Flattery? Beatrice was instantly on guard. There had been another man who had tried to gain Marit's attention by flattering her hound. It was some months ago, but the thought of him brought a bitter taste to Beatrice's mouth. She had nipped him on his backside. Twice. But it was only when her father told him he was a fool to try to coax a woman to do something that she ought better to be commanded in.

"Her name is Marit," said Marit.

Did he notice the small hesitation in her voice, the slight

13

accent of someone speaking a language only recently learned?

"Marit. And how long have you had her?" he asked.

It made Marit stiffen again, and Beatrice knew, if the prince did not, that he had lost his chance to make a good first impression—at least on her.

"Had her? We met five years ago, in the woods. We have been together ever since."

Marit walked stiffly away from the prince, and Beatrice did not look back to him, much as she would have liked to have seen what he did next. Go back to the castle? Or to the woods, where he had been headed in the first place?

A puppy of a prince perhaps. But she liked him.

Don't miss *The Princess and the Bear,*
the enchanting sequel to
The Princess and the Hound, out soon!

———⟨∞∞⟩———

*S*he pulled up her magic once more. This time
she did not use it as a defense, but pressed it
into the cat-man. She thought as she did so of
all the moments in her life that had been unforgettable.

Her first hunt.

The first sight of the princess.

The smell of the bear in the cave.

Fighting with the bear.

The wild man's gap in time.

Her new body.

Her own magic.

And now this.

Even the pain was life. She savored it, and pressed
that feeling against the cat-man.

This was her magic, and she poured it into him far
beyond his capacity to receive it. It had been so long
since he felt true magic, and even then it had not been
magic like this.

15